LOST IN

Emily stepped deeper into the trees. Rain hammered the maze and branches scratched her back as she tried to decide which trail would lead her home.

"Nigel?" she whispered, feeling miserable. "Where are you, boy?"

The sound of treading earth met her ears. Her heart banged against her chest.

"Lady Emily." Before she could do more than turn around, she found herself gazing into a pair of cool, amber eyes.

"What the devil are you doing here by yourself?" Jared asked harshly.

She blinked. What was *she* doing here?

He whipped off his dark cloak and placed it about her shoulders, not waiting for an answer. She shivered at his touch, pressing her lips together in both anger and relief. He towered over her like some Viking king. Breeches clung to his muscular thighs, and his tanned hands rested on tapered hips. She swallowed.

He leaned over, his hand innocently brushing her cheek as he fastened the clip. His warm breath whispered along her neck, and Emily wanted to fall into his safe embrace, seeking the comfort she remembered so vivdly. She wanted to ask him why he had left her, why he had broken her heart, but the iciness in his voice brought her back.

"Traipsing into this maze was a stupid thing to do, madam."

She refused to let him make her feel like a fool again.

"Your dog Nigel was the one who led me here," she countered.

"My dog, madam, is the one who found you." The culprit gave a sudden bark and appeared around the corner, as if daring Emily to dismiss his heroism.

The Rejected Suitor

Teresa McCarthy

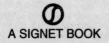

A SIGNET BOOK

SIGNET
Published by New American Library, a division of
Penguin Group (USA) Inc., 375 Hudson Street,
New York, New York 10014, U.S.A.
Penguin Books Ltd, 80 Strand,
London WC2R 0RL, England
Penguin Books Australia Ltd, 250 Camberwell Road,
Camberwell, Victoria 3124, Australia
Penguin Books Canada Ltd, 10 Alcorn Avenue,
Toronto, Ontario, Canada M4V 3B2
Penguin Books (N.Z.) Ltd, Cnr Rosedale and Airborne Roads,
Albany, Auckland 1310, New Zealand

Penguin Books Ltd, Registered Offices:
80 Strand, London WC2R 0RL, England

First published by Signet, an imprint of New American Library,
a division of Penguin Group (USA) Inc.

First Printing, April 2004
10 9 8 7 6 5 4 3 2 1

 REGISTERED TRADEMARK—MARCA REGISTRADA

Printed in the United States of America

PUBLISHER'S NOTE
This is a work of fiction. Names, characters, places, and incidents either are
the product of the author's imagination or are used fictitiously, and any resem-
blance to actual persons, living or dead, business establishments, events, or
locales is entirely coincidental.

To Chris, Brendan, Tim, Mary, and Christopher
And to all the believers
You know who you are . . .

Chapter One

How dare they do this! If they thought to dictate whom she would marry without a word from her, as if she were a mere child toddling about their knees, then they had better think again. This was intolerable!

Seated at the lavish dining table of Elbourne Hall, Lady Emily Clearbrook clenched the folds of her gown and leveled a withering gaze toward her four older brothers. "Did it ever occur to you, gentlemen, that I should have been consulted about this monumental decision?"

Without a word, her eldest brother, Roderick, the twenty-seven-year-old Duke of Elbourne, finally looked her way, blinked lazily, and lifted his wineglass to his lips.

Emily bristled. Guardian, indeed! That indolent look said it all. Roderick would not be moved. Advancement was impossible. Yet retreat was unthinkable. His guardianship of her was maddening. Moreover, Clayton, Marcus, and Stephen were following his lead as if they always went along with his dictates, a ludicrous assumption to say the least. As for Roderick including all her brothers in this decision, it was a cunning move worthy of Wellington himself. They were acting as if she had four guardians now instead of one.

She softened her gaze, trying to conceal her turbulent

emotions. "This entire arrangement is quite intolerable. If any of you had consulted me first—"

"Consulted you?" Roderick said abruptly, raising his right brow in censure. "And pray, why the devil would we be consulting you? *You* are our baby sister. There is no consulting to be done. The four of us will take care of the matter entirely. We are merely informing you of our decision."

"But Father would have let me choose," she said, impatiently.

Roderick's lips thinned. "Father died three years ago, leaving your future in our hands. Count yourself fortunate that all your brothers have returned home from the war intact."

Oh, she loved her brothers. Indeed, she did. But Roderick seemed to be using her vulnerability to his advantage, and she would not have it. "I am well aware that we have been blessed with a healthy homecoming, and I realize that you are doing what you think proper, but believe me, I am clearly able to look after myself and my future."

All four brothers stared back at her with open mouths as if she had just pronounced her loyalty to Napoleon.

Inwardly she fumed. Though her siblings were all powerfully built men, and challenging them was a feat in itself, she would fight for her freedom. Never again would she be at the mercy of a man.

"I am merely seeking a compromise on this," she added impulsively.

"Compromise?" Roderick's dark eyes turned menacing. "There is no compromising to be done. We have made a decision. You must leave all the details to us. In fact, you should be happy that we are to partake in your choice in a husband." His tone suddenly became gentle. "It is for your protection and comfort, Em. We think only of you."

Emily knew her brothers loved her, but at that moment, all she wanted to do was box their ears, especially Roderick's. She would have laughed out loud if the situation had not been so vexing. But she did not need their help in setting on the path to disaster—certainly not since she had been there already.

"Let me understand, then. You believe that the four of you should partake in the choice of husband for me?" she asked calmly, her gaze sweeping over Clayton, Marcus, and Stephen as well. "Is this not correct?"

Four relieved smiles shot her way.

She clasped her hands tightly together. They had no idea that she could take care of herself. She had been on her own for three years. The scar beside her shoulder blade was proof of that. But without a doubt, informing them about a pistol ball ripping through her back while she had secretly worked for Whitehall would not only propel her brothers into a more frenzied state, but would also do nothing to further her cause.

"Daresay, Em, you understand perfectly." Marcus toasted his glass her way. "Knew you were not the kind of female to take offense."

At this point Emily's anger outweighed any patience she had left. "I will tell you this, *dear brothers*, that there is no choice to be made . . . by any of you."

Marcus clanked his glass against his plate. Roderick let out a low growl. Clayton stared back in confusion, and Stephen pursed his lips as if waiting for the final cannon shot.

Emily did not disappoint him. "You must be insane. I am twenty! I believe that is old enough to know my own mind. So why in the name of King George should I be happy about you four simpletons choosing a husband for me?"

"Simpletons?" the brothers replied in unison, four dark heads snapping to attention.

"We are not simpletons," Clayton finally replied with a sigh, leaning forward as he helped himself to another slice of beef. "We are the most devoted of brothers concerned only for your welfare. Come now, Em, do not jest with us. This is an important matter."

So they seemed to think she was teasing them, did they? She doubted they had even heard her announce her age. Did they believe her just out of the schoolroom? The ninnies. Perhaps they had not come back from the war intact at all. Well, they would be shocked to know that she could play their game, too.

Girding her resolve, she gave them a halfhearted smile. "Believe me, I understand your concern and am deeply touched. Though I have missed all of you since you took your stand against the Little Corsican, I cannot sit by and let you make this important decision for me. I am a full-grown woman, capable of making choices according to my own needs and wants, and I believe that it would be best for all concerned that you leave this most important choice to me."

"This is not a punishment, Em," Marcus said gently, "but a rite of passage so to speak. Important decisions should not be left to the weaker sex. You must leave these type of decisions to us wiser men."

Emily almost choked. Save her from the male mind. With a sense of the inevitable, she tilted her head toward Stephen. Her youngest brother had let out a muffled laugh at Marcus's pompous words. Though Stephen had avoided her gaze before, she knew that he would be her last hope. He had always given her the benefit of the doubt, but at the sight of his brown eyes growing wide with guilt, her chest tightened with dread.

"Peagoose," she muttered, narrowing her eyes on him.

Roderick leaned back in his chair and dabbed a white napkin to the corner of his mouth, setting the cloth down in neat, decisive folds beside his plate. "I will refrain from comment on your last retort, Em, because peagoose is debatable here."

Stephen's brows snapped together at Roderick's comment. "Peagoose? If you think—"

Roderick palmed his hand in the air, aborting Stephen's rebuttal. "See here, Em," the duke went on, "we are not simpletons. We are your brothers and will only choose a suitable gentleman. You must see that."

Emily wanted to roll her eyes. Roderick's words were said in kindness, but they were also etched in stone as if he were some pharaoh making a momentous decree. But the problem was, in most circles in London, his proclamations wielded as much power as an Egyptian god. The mere thought of him choosing a husband for her sent a ripple of uneasiness down her spine.

"Indeed, we are not peageese or simpletons, Em," Stephen put in hotly, staring at Roderick, then back at Emily as if waiting for a reply.

Emily sat silently, her heart pounding. "Forgive me. The use of the word *simpletons* may have been the wrong choice."

Four sets of well-formed shoulders visibly relaxed. But she would not let them decide for her. No. She would think of something. She would never again be at the mercy of a man and have her heart dangling like a target for hunting season. She had learned her lesson all too well.

"Indeed, simpletons was a poor choice to describe such thoughtful brothers."

Curling her fingers around the seat of her chair, she was determined to set them straight. She paused, waiting to see that she had their attention. Oh, they were a handsome lot, with their hair colors ranging from blue-black to rich brown. They had been blessed with twinkling eyes of sky blue or chestnut brown as well. Healthy male specimens, they could send the most callous of women drooling like hungry puppies at their feet.

They also had no inkling that their baby sister had information about many of their escapades in Town, and they would turn quite pink with embarrassment if they knew she had knowledge of the London ladies who ran circles around them at the Assemblies and routs—among other places. Inwardly she smiled. Indeed, they had yet to realize that she was not one of those silly women to be led on a leash.

"So we are not simpletons in your opinion?" The question came from Stephen, whose lips quirked upward. He seemed to think himself cleared from the field of fire—and *him*, a commissioned officer, Emily thought wide-eyed. No wonder Napoleon made such a comeback.

"No, no." Emily raised a delicate brow, her eyes

gleaming. "Not simpletons exactly . . . I believe fools and half-wits would be more appropriate."

Roderick glared at her, Clayton frowned, Marcus choked on his wine, and Stephen blinked, clearly at a loss for words.

Emily pushed back from her chair and stood. "Mayhap now I finally have your attention."

With a muttered oath, Roderick shot from his seat, his eyes darkening with anger. "Indeed, you have our attention, madam. However, nothing you say changes the fact that, since Boney's no threat to us and Waterloo's behind us, an entire army of unfit suitors will be marching this way in hopes of an expedient marriage with you, and I won't have it!"

A throng of brotherly grunts rippled in the air.

"By Jove, disgusting thought," Clayton answered with a shake of his head.

"Mass of cork-brained suitors," Marcus replied, bringing his wineglass to his lips.

Stephen cracked his knuckles. "An entire army. Don't like that. Had enough of that in the Peninsula. No indeed."

"No indeed," Roderick said coolly, taking his seat as if everything were resolved. "Not a pretty sight. You will marry the man we choose, and that is final."

Emily's fingers curled into two fists. "Then I won't marry at all."

Roderick leapt from his chair, knocking over his wine. "By Jove, you will obey us!"

Emily faltered slightly at her brother's outburst. Never before had he been so adamant or insistent on matters concerning her. As a child, he had always indulged her slightest whim. But she was no longer a child, and his temper had run away with him. Roderick would never lay a hand on her, but now that he was home, as her guardian, he had control over her life whether she wanted it or not. It seemed he fought against the notion of her falling under the spell of a rake—not knowing, of course, that Emily knew all her brothers were categorized as such by the ladies of the *ton*.

No matter, their foolish idea of choosing a husband for her was one that had been gaining momentum ever since Roderick had seen her speaking to a couple of his gambling companions two weeks ago in Hyde Park. The very next day she had been sent home to Elbourne Hall.

But whether they believed it or not, she would not marry a man of their choosing. A marriage of convenience could be possible if her future husband agreed to her independence. But *she* would be the one to choose, not her addlepated brothers.

"I will choose the man I will marry, that is, if I ever marry in the first place," she replied firmly.

To her shock, Stephen gave her an acknowledging wink. What was his game? She was certain no one else had seen the mischief in his eyes. The noose around her neck began to loosen and her hope soared.

"Enough of this nonsense," Roderick said, throwing an agitated hand to the back of his neck and massaging it as he sat down. "See here, Em. The only choice you will have is the lace on your wedding dress. Now, take a seat and finish your meal."

Emily refused to sit down. Hovering over her brothers seemed to give her the edge she desperately needed. "I beg to differ. You cannot force me to marry a man I do not love or want. If there is a choice to be made, I will choose. Can you not understand?"

"Want? Love?" Roderick said with a cringe. "Hell's teeth, your womanly instincts are the very reason we will do the choosing. Have I not made myself perfectly clear?"

Stephen surveyed Emily, his eyes turning tender with concern. "Jupiter, Em, you cannot wish to marry that Fennington fellow? Man's a scoundrel. Odious dandy if I ever saw one."

Before Emily could answer, Clayton laughed. "Catch sight of that quizzing glass the man had? As large as a door knocker. Man's right eye looked three sizes bigger than the left."

Emily frowned. Mr. Fennington had been one of her latest suitors, and according to her brothers, the man had obviously chosen the wrong woman to woo. She held no interest in any particular man, but nothing she could say was going to change her brothers' wretched plan to find her a husband.

However, the more she thought about it, the more she realized Mr. Fennington had the qualities of a husband who would grant her the freedom she needed. He was a simpleton, as her father would say, a man a woman could wrap her ringlets about in one turn of the room.

"You smash that idiotic piece of rubbish or was that Roderick's doing?" Stephen turned his beguiling smile up a notch as he spoke to Clayton.

"Smash the piece?" Roderick chuckled, his demeanor obviously lightening with talk of a man who dared to run past the blockade of the Elbourne brothers. "We did no such thing. Chap would have no notion how to walk straight without the blasted piece hanging from his eye."

"Besides," Clayton added, "the fool needed the fanciful piece to see his way back to Town."

All four brothers roared with laughter.

Emily grasped the back of her chair in outrage. "Mr. Fennington was quite agreeable, and you four popinjays have no business jabbing your noses into my life."

The laughing stopped abruptly. Yet it was Roderick's smoking glare that made Emily flinch. She dropped her hands, wondering if she had gone too far.

"Agreeable?" Roderick snapped, his gaze narrowing in rage as he deliberately rose and strode toward her.

"For all it's worth," she said, backing toward the door, trying to ignore Roderick's approach along with the hardened glares of all her brothers now weighing heavily in her direction, "I t-told the gentleman that he should not have come to visit me here."

Roderick slapped his hand against his thigh. "Here or any other place! Confound it! James Theodore Fennington is a drunk and a cad. I will not have you wed the man, and that is final."

Emily lifted her head in outrage. "For your information, Papa said that I may choose."

"Papa is dead," Clayton snapped out. "He left you in our care, as your protectors in a way. We are of one mind on this, Em. You may not marry without our consent."

"Truly, this idea of yours is absurd," she went on, wringing her hands on her gown. "You cannot do this."

Roderick shook his head and walked back to his chair. "We can and we will." His tone was calm, but firm. "We have a say in this whether you like it or not. Fennington wants to wed you for your dowry, and we won't have it."

Pausing, he cleared his throat and gently pointed his finger toward her seat. "Come now, Em. I daresay, if you had been there, you would have heartily agreed that it was rather comical the way Fennington gaped at me, eyes bugging out of his sockets like a pig ready for slaughter, especially after I told him that if any of us found him within earshot of you, I would call him out. The insolence of the man to think he could come a half day's ride from London and court you without our consent."

"Call him out?" Emily was horrified. Roderick's threat was absurd. He was a crack shot, and anyone who tangled with the Duke of Elbourne would be dreadfully stupid, or dreadfully maimed for life.

Stephen tipped back on his chair, popping an olive into his mouth. "Good riddance, I say. Man's an odious creature, not to be wed to any damsel I should think. Way I see it, we should all take to Town. Yes, that's the way of it. We find this mysterious suitor for Em before any more adventurers try to seek her out and be done with the whole matter before Christmas."

Emily turned toward Stephen, her eyes locking with his. Her strongest ally's betrayal squeezed her heart. One moment he seemed to be on her side, the next moment not. "I cannot believe that you would abandon me."

Stephen dropped his gaze to the table, fiddling with his fork. "Christmas is less than nine months away, Em. A long time to look over the prospects."

Her breath left her. So this was the meaning of that sly wink. He would find her a suitable husband. The traitor! "And what will you do if I do not comply with your wishes? Send me to Bedlam? I should sooner live in Paris as a milliner with my own little shop than marry a man you have chosen for me!"

Marcus flew from his seat. "You will obey us," he countered. "There is no question of noncompliance. Dare you take one foot outside England and I will take you over my knee."

Emily flinched when all brothers instantly stood, as if agreeing that Marcus's plan had a bit of sense to it. The deafening silence that followed sent her heart racing. Never in her life had she opposed all siblings at once. Well, not like this, and she usually won any kind of argument regardless.

Drat and double drat! Now all could be lost. She should have used her brains instead of her anger.

Ever since that day Roderick caught her merely conversing with his cronies in Hyde Park, all her brothers seemed to have acknowledged that she was no longer the innocent child they remembered and treated her accordingly.

As if realizing the full force of his angry outburst, Marcus moved around the table and gently tipped Emily's chin with his finger. "Come now, dearest, we have no wish to attack you, but do not believe us addlepated nincompoops. Any man would do anything for the coin attached to you and your name."

Emily was about to open her mouth when her mother, the Duchess of Elbourne, sashayed into the room. She was draped in a gown of blue silk and lace, holding her snow-white cat, Egypt, close to her breast as she peered over her spectacles. "Forgive me children, so very sorry to be late. Cannot believe I read through dinner. My new Radcliffe novel, you know."

With a frown, the lady floated across the rug toward Marcus, tapping him on the shoulder. "But indeed, my absence does not suggest you may use that nincompoop language at the dinner table, young man."

"Mother," Clayton said, hiding his smile. "Em has one of the richest dowries in the country and is a beauty besides. Her good looks have caught the attention of every rake we know."

Emily burned with rage. So that was it. Their friends were vying for her hand. "That is ridiculous. I can handle any rakes that come my way. You cannot—"

"Em, please do not interrupt. Not ladylike at all." Clayton sent her a warning glance and continued to speak to his mother. "See here, if we dare let Em choose her own husband, Elbourne Hall will be infested with every pest known to mankind. By the by, get a good look at that Fennington fellow? Looked worse than Stephen here."

Stephen snorted in response. "I say!"

Ignoring the sibling rivalry, Emily paced beside the table. "I am not a stupid girl, making stupid decisions. I am a woman of sound mind and body with every intention of leading my own life. I know you want the best for me, but I ask everyone of you to trust me in this." One man had destroyed her girlhood dreams, and no man ever again would determine her destiny.

The duchess frowned as she stroked her cat. "Though Emily is beautiful, it takes no great talent to realize her dowry alone will fetch a grand husband. And he must be grand. I won't have my grandchildren running around like little peasants."

At the mention of grandchildren, Emily froze. "Mama."

Stephen came around the table, patting Emily's hand. "Now, now. We can work all of this out to everyone's satisfaction." He set his gaze on Roderick and grimaced. "Why be so hard on the poor girl. It's not as if she has fleas. Even females have the right to make some decisions."

"Fleas?" The duchess narrowed her eyes on her son.

"I don't mean she has fleas, Mother," Stephen said.

"You have no inkling to what I want," Emily said, tears clogging her throat. She was no longer able to fight the four of them, five along with her mother. "I beg you to excuse me," she said tartly. "My head is beginning to pound." She departed from the room before anyone could say another word.

"Whatever is the matter with the child?" the duchess asked, concerned.

"By Jove," Clayton replied as Emily's slippers slapped up the stairs. "Do we dare believe that our sweet little Em had some affection for that Fennington fellow?"

Roderick frowned, clasping a fist about his napkin. "The devil. We need to find a suitable husband for her as soon as possible. If Fennington were the least bit decent, I would consider him, but the man's a scoundrel. Women, drinking, and gambling are the only things in life he knows."

The duchess pressed her lips together and stared at Emily's full plate of food. "Should we call the doctor?"

Roderick glanced toward the open door. "No."

The duchess rested her purring cat across her shoulder, imparting a regal glare upon her sons. "Then I implore you to look for the minimum of an earl. This talk of marriage gives me a wretched headache. Your father would have known what to do. Daniel always had a way with Emily.

"Then again, Daniel doted on Emily as if she were his only child. He would have granted her anything her heart desired, including that despicable Fennington. Oh, this entire matter vexes me to no end. I cannot eat a thing now. I must have a cloth put to my head." Frowning, the duchess swished past the door in a flourish of blue and white, her sons staring helplessly at one another and sinking back into their seats.

Stephen combed a hand through his unruly dark hair. "Roderick's correct. We must make our lists for a reasonable match as soon as possible. This entire situation is maddening."

"Maddening is the way Em has been acting." Roderick stared at his sister's empty chair. "We need a reasonable man. Someone who will not travel the world at a moment's notice. A man with our political views, a man who sees that she stays away from those daft female notions of independence."

"Speaking of reasonable," Stephen added speculatively, "believe Jared returned from India. Now, there's a decent chap."

"Brother died in that carriage accident a while ago," Clayton added, frowning.

Roderick shook his head. "Not Jared. Man's too much like us. Not even his late wife could make him stay in one place."

"Blasted shame about his brother," Stephen added. "Saw Edmond last year at Brighton." He shook his head. "But I have heard gentlemen do settle down a bit after having a wife. Might work, you know. Maybe Jared and Em—"

"Never," Roderick said, interrupting with a steely edge to his voice. "Jared Ashton is not on the list. We need to find Em an agreeable fellow, not shackle her with a man like us."

Stephen made a fist. "Hell's bells, Roderick. Why not Jared? He may be a bit like the rest of us, but what man worth his weight in salt does not have a bit of a rake in him? Jared could be the answer to our prayers. Did Emily not meet him years ago? Believe she fancied him then. Could be perfect."

"Father was not impressed," Clayton cut in. "Em liked any gentleman who paid her attention. But Father wanted a title for Em, and nothing short of that would do, especially not Mr. Jared Ashton, the second son of an earl. Took the wind right of out of Em's sails. Good thing Jared had no interest in her then."

"Yes, but some of those men in Town did have an interest," Marcus added thoughtfully. "The girl almost had me fighting in her corner with that Queen of Sheba act, not to mention those ebony locks and violet eyes. Strong willed, she is. Needs a firm hand. Sooner we find her a husband, the better."

The sound of pensive sighs filled the room.

"Needs to be sent away," Roderick said. "Agatha

Appleby's is a good place for her until we decide on a suitor."

Clayton pursed his lips. "But ain't Agatha Jared's aunt?"

Roderick nodded. "If we keep Em here, no telling what type of guttersnipes will be waiting for her in the bushes, ready to drag her off to Gretna Green. And with her independent streak, I don't want to leave that possibility open. More I think about it, the more I believe Agatha's the best place for her. In fact, Jared owes me a favor. He's staying there now. I'll see to it that the man keeps an eye on our sister and shoos off any would-be suitors. Won't like it above half, but he'll do it."

Clayton frowned, rubbing a finger thoughtfully against his chin. "Hear tell, man's searching for a wife. Won't like settling with an old maid and Em for the Season. As the new Earl of Stonebridge he has estates to tend, tenants to visit . . ."

"Estates?" Marcus put in. "Man has a steward for that. Besides, last I heard he was on White's books, and odds are favored toward a Miss Susan Wimble for a wife. Engagement almost carved in *stone*." Marcus snickered over his wineglass. "No pun intended. Also hear he is without funds."

Roderick drummed the table with his fingers. "Ah, Miss Susan Wimble. From personal experience she is not the sort—" He stammered, cutting himself off. The brothers stared back in awe, as if indeed this was a new revelation.

Roderick shook his head. "Never mind. Yet I must say that Jared's wealth is not in question at all. But enough about him. We have Em to worry about and must make our way to London. Each of you can bring your list of suitors to me, and I will make the final choice. In the meantime, I will contact Jared about watching Em. Never fear, he will keep scoundrels like Fennington at bay." A small laugh escaped him. "Of course, one of you could stay and watch her if you object."

All faces turned pale at the thought of guard dog duty over their stubborn sister.

"Quite so," Roderick said with an amused snort. "Not an agreeable post for a sibling. Besides, we will need everyone's effort to search for a husband before the Season is out."

"What about Em's say in this?" Stephen asked.

Roderick rose. "In the end, she will be thankful. We must find her a husband before some rapscallion marries her for her money and ruins her life."

Stephen crossed his arms over his chest. "Tell me, your mighty dukeness, how do we know our guarding earl will not go after her for himself? I, for one, would not trust any man between the age of fifteen and seventy-five."

"Believe me," Roderick said, "Jared may be a rake, but he will have no interest in Em. She is by far too independent for his taste. The man favors submissiveness in a woman. His late wife was evidence of that. Heard she bowed to his every whim."

Stephen frowned. "The devil, Roderick! Tastes change. I daresay, one look at our Emily can turn the tables on any man."

Clayton grimaced. "For once, Stephen has a point here."

"Don't like to agree with baby brother," Marcus said in a disturbed voice, "but can't be too careful. Can you believe Wendly and Fisk have been asking about Em? Good cardplayers, but blast, don't want them coming anywhere near our sister."

Roderick stiffened at the mention of the two well-known rogues. "If those peabrains come within a foot of Em—"

Marcus laughed. "Told 'em so myself. But back to our devoted earl who owes you a favor. His wife may not have been as meek as you say. Mayhap she was just like Em."

"No need to worry," Roderick said, smiling. "Jared and I have a similar understanding of women. Though I love Em with all my heart, independence is not a quality either of us would wish for in a wife. Believe me, the man would never consider to look upon Emily as anything more than a sister."

"And pray, why is that?" Stephen asked skeptically.

"Because, gentlemen," Roderick grabbed the port on the nearby sideboard, tilted a good amount of the liquid into his glass, and gave his brothers a swift salute, "I would kill him."

Chapter Two

Would he never have any peace?

Jared James William Ashton, the sixth Earl of Stonebridge, sat in the small library of Hemmingly Hall, perusing the missive he had been sent by the Duke of Elbourne only two days hence. Jared's vow to distance himself from Lady Emily had died a quick, agonizing death the minute he had broken through the duke's wax seal.

Muttering an oath, Jared reached for his glass perched upon the massive desk holding stacks of papers pertaining to his recently inherited estates. It was but ten o'clock in the morning, and the aged bottle of brandy that he had confiscated the previous evening from his aunt's cellars was three-quarters gone. The best his employer had, good French brandy, Agatha's new butler Filmore had proclaimed as the elderly man escorted Jared to the cellar.

Jared took a sip of the amber liquid and held the drink up to the dusty light streaming through the fourteen-foot-high windowpanes. Zeus. It was excellent French brandy, most likely smuggled in from Dover. How the devil his aunt had obtained an entire box of the sacred liquor was beyond him.

He leaned his head back against the cushions of his chair and closed his eyes, his lips hinting at a smile as he thought about smuggled goods and Aunt Agatha. Ridiculous thought. The lady had no secrets from him, even after all these years. Though he adored her, she was a woman with a glib tongue, a fact he never forgot, and smuggling at Hemmingly was the type of information he would have eventually intercepted with his clandestine activities on the Continent the past few years.

A crisp spring wind howled past the windows of the mansion, pulling Jared back to the problem at hand. He dropped a narrow gaze to his desk, his fingers curling tightly about the duke's letter. With a feeling of foreboding, he threw the cream-colored paper into the glowing fire behind him and sighed.

There was no question about acquiescing to Roderick's wretched request, even though the duke had no idea of Jared's past with his lovely sister. But Jared owed the man his life, and honor demanded that he assist the duke in this infernal plan to find Emily a suitor.

It seemed absurd really. Jared knew he would be the last man in England the lady would ever want to see again. Moreover, the blasted request had come at the worst time. He had his daughter Gabrielle to think about now, not to mention his ward, Miss Jane Greenwell, his very reason for returning to Hemmingly. But to make matters worse, no one in England knew he had a daughter, and until Jared's life was deemed safe from a certain Bonaparte agent, no one would discover his secret about Gabrielle until his affairs were in order.

A muffled grunt sounded from the corner of the hearth, turning Jared's head.

"What the devil are you whining about now, Nigel?"

Jared's massive dog and companion of the past two years lifted its huge brown eyes and let out a dismal howl as it peered at the duke's now ashen-edged paper curling into flames.

"Sorry, old boy, seems we are to be sent on another mission, and this one may be the hardest one yet."

Nigel lifted up onto his mammoth paws and gazed at the brandy bottle resting on the desk. Another bark.

Jared's lips curved into a sardonic smile. "Ain't no

use for it, boy. Your brandy days are over. Don't need you sick on me like you were in France. Later we'll sneak into the kitchen and confiscate one of the beefsteaks Cook was saving for dinner. What say you to that?"

Nigel hung out his large pink tongue and wagged his tail.

Jared laughed and raised his glass to his dog. "Here's to your beefsteak with all the trimmings . . . and to a suitable husband for Lady Emily." Another bark.

Jared swallowed the remainder of his brandy and turned a grim countenance toward the hearth. Memories of the old duke's rejection still burned in his brain as if it were yesterday.

Do not say one word to her, my boy. Dare to push this any further and I will see Emily married to Lord Whitefield faster than Prinny can spend ten thousand pounds.

Jared tightened his hold on his glass. Whitefield had been at least seventy if a day.

Although the duke's threat had never been carried out, another one had taken its place, that of blackmailing Jared into another marriage and sending him away, so he could never have Emily. Ever. She had never known the truth.

At the time of Jared's proposal, the duke's motive for revenge bordered on the ridiculous. But to Daniel Clearbrook, the Duke of Elbourne, the reasons were nothing to laugh about. It seemed that long before Jared had been born, Daniel's heart had been broken when his offer for a certain woman had been adamantly rejected by her father.

Jared set his glass on the desk, his lips thinning in anger as he turned his gaze toward the ashes of Roderick's letter. How ironic that the lady in question had been Jared's mother, Miss Elizabeth Garland.

The late duke had told Jared the facts without blinking. The refusal had been based on a feud that had begun years ago when Daniel's father, then the Duke of Elbourne, and Elizabeth's father, George Garland, had fought a duel over a card game. Jared's grandfather had lost a finger in the scuffle, which had hurt his pride more than his flesh.

Unaware of the duel, Daniel Clearbrook, a marquess at the time, and from what Jared could deduce, a man that was proud of his station in life, assumed the Garlands would welcome his marriage proposal with open arms. It seemed to Jared that Daniel had loved Elizabeth from afar and sought her hand the day after he had danced with her twice at Almack's. The refusal from Jared's grandfather was a blow to Daniel's pride. He would be a duke someday, and no one refused a duke.

Jared realized that Daniel had never forgotten the deep humiliation he'd felt that day, and when he became the Duke of Elbourne, he had used his power to the fullest.

Nigel barked and Jared looked up, his lips slipping into a bitter smile. He had realized too late that his naïve offer for Emily's hand had twisted the knife deeper into the duke's heart, reminding the man of his past, of his loss, of his broken pride.

Indeed, Daniel had sought his revenge well.

But Jared was no longer the stupid boy who had fallen in love with the duke's only daughter. It had been a foolish dream. A mistake he would never make again. Love like he thought he had with Emily was an illusion. A folly of the younger set.

He was a score and six now, a seasoned man of the world. A man with a duty toward his title, his daughter, his ward, and his country. In the past three years, he had seen more than most had seen in a lifetime. Lady Emily was only another duty to fulfill, and he must remember that no matter what the price.

Outside the Elbourne mansion, heavy rain soon slowed to a mere drizzle, while inside a lone candle flickered beside Emily's bed as she thrust her fist against her pillow in frustration. What did she do to ever deserve this?

The last two days she had suffered such a string of

annoying speeches from her well-meaning but ninnyhammer brothers, concerning her duty to honor their choice of a husband, she thought she was going mad.

Jupiter and thunderation! Did they think she had wool for a brain? Did they think for one solitary minute that she would let a man dictate to her what her life should be? Did they truly think she would allow them to choose a husband for her? How foolish did they think she was?

She gave the pillow another punch. She would travel to her great aunt's in Yorkshire before she let the unthinkable happen. If she must marry, she, and no one else, would choose her husband.

Husband. The very word made her throat tighten with pain.

Turning onto her back, she picked up the book of Wordsworth poems that lay on her nightstand and opened to the first page. "To the woman closest to my heart," she read softly, vividly recalling Mr. Jared Ashton and his deceitful lies.

A painful twinge stabbed at her heart. He was an earl now, Lord Stonebridge. A title that made no difference to her in India or in England. Though, when she had heard of his wife's death, she had instantly felt a pang of sympathy for the man. Except he did not need her pity, not after the way he had played her the fool.

Stop it, Emily. Jared never loved you. Never. You were a fool. A fool. A fool.

The words repeated in her brain like a horrid chant, never ending. With a snap, she closed the book, furious at herself because she was not able to forget the handsome cad or his chaste kisses, even after three long years.

"Emily, dearest?"

Emily started at the scratch on the door and quickly pushed the book beneath her pillow. "Come in, Mama."

The comely dowager scurried into the room. Her red velvet robe swished about her slender ankles while Egypt relaxed in the lady's still youthful arms, purring like a newborn babe. Frowning at her daughter's supine position, the duchess stroked the cat's milky fur and leaned forward. "Are you ill, child? Or is it this wretched storm that bothers you so?"

"Nothing but a headache, Mama." And a house full of obstinate, opinionated brothers.

Her mother rested a cool hand on Emily's forehead. "Not crying over what your brothers said to you at dinner tonight? I daresay, they have been rather forceful the past few evenings, but you must realize they are only concerned about your future."

Forceful? They were tyrants! Emily scooted off her bed, fighting back the rage that consumed her. "I know they are concerned, Mama. But I beg of them to leave well enough alone. I am a grown woman, and they seem to think me a mere child."

The duchess chuckled. "Oh, they are males, my dear. A bit overprotective, I fear. And I do admit I would like them to find a suitable husband for you, but I will not force you to marry. However, I believe it is the female mind that causes your brothers genuine discomfort." Her eyes twinkled. "You know it is our secrets that scare them silly."

Secrets? For a moment Emily thought her mother was speaking of her past with Jared. "Mama, I may have some secrets, but I am twenty years old." And no longer a fool.

"Well, dearest, believe it or not, they have an odd notion that you might elope with Mr. Fennington. The man is a drunk as Roderick said, and that quizzing glass vexes me to no end."

Dumbfounded, Emily threw a hand to her breast. "Fennington and me?" The notion of the idiotic man posing as a possible husband to give her independence had crossed her mind, but she certainly would not elope with him.

Emily struggled to hold in her fit of giggles. "Oh, Mama. I am not eloping to Gretna Green with the man."

"I believe you. But your brothers have their notions, you know. They are thinking of sending you on a little trip. I think it might be good for you, Emily."

Emily's bubble burst. "Oh, no, Mama. Please. I won't

run off." And it was a fact. She could never elope. She was not one of those heroine's in a Mrs. Radcliffe novel. She was the daughter of a duke and must act appropriately—in public that was. In private she had her own secrets. Her work with the war effort had been the only thing that had kept her sane the past few years. Only a few people knew about her liaison with Whitehall, and she intended to keep it that way.

"I know you have no wish to leave, dearest," her mother went on, "but your brothers are adamant. They mentioned something about Miss Agatha Appleby's. I could fight them on this, but I think it might be best for you." The duchess stroked Egypt's back. "I do believe this time of the year Agatha is staying at Hemmingly. You have enjoyed staying with her in the past, have you not?"

Emily's heart leapt. Of course. Why had she not thought of it sooner? Agatha would help her make sense of her future. The planning was perfect, brilliant in fact. "I adore Agatha."

Her mother swallowed. "Yes, well, perhaps during your stay, your brothers will find you a suitable husband. You might even come to love the man they choose, you know. But remember, dearest, love is more than a feeling. I should know. Sometimes people do not love you back, but it still can be love."

Tears came to her mother's eyes, and Emily instantly felt a prickle of guilt. Her father had always been kind to her mama, but as the years progressed, Emily noticed it was not a marriage based on love or even mutual trust, but a marriage of convenience, nothing more, at least from her father's side.

"Well then, that's settled. Your abigail will pack your bags, and you will be leaving Elbourne Hall as soon as we can make arrangements." She kissed Emily's cheek and sighed. "Never fear, I have told your brothers to look for an earl and no less, unless he is that elusive Black Wolf, then, of course," she gave a giggle, "I would make an exception."

When the duchess took her leave, clicking the door

closed behind her, Emily fell onto her bed in a fit of laughter. The very idea of Fennington and her off to Gretna Green was absurd.

And the Black Wolf? Mama must have been reading the latest gossip in the *Times*. Heavens, most women in England dreamed about eloping with the Wolf. The English revered the man as much as Wellington himself. No one knew the identity of the man that had crossed French lines serving as a secret agent for the British during the war. Rumor had even declared that the Black Wolf had made it into Napoleon's bedchambers to steal a missive and had barely escaped with his life.

Emily sank back into her pillows and smiled at the thought of her mama and the Black Wolf meeting at a masquerade ball. Goodness, the man would probably be old, fat, and bald. Would not her mama be surprised?

Emily sat up, her face instantly sobering at the disturbing thought. Old. Fat. Bald. Three more reasons why *she* would be the one to choose her husband. There was no telling what kind of man her brothers would choose for her.

Egypt pounced onto her bed, and she jumped in surprise. "Ah, did Mama leave you to guard over me?"

Emily stroked the cat's snow-white cloak, fingering the scar she had stitched up a year ago when Egypt had fallen onto a fireplace poker. Before the accident, the fluffy feline had hissed whenever Emily came into the room, but now Egypt was her best friend, that was, besides Agatha and Jane Greenwell.

Jane, only a year younger than Emily's twenty years, had resided at Hemmingly since the girl's parents died about five years ago. Emily smiled when she thought about how her friend would react when told about the plans to find Emily a *suitable* husband. Needless to say, she would be furious.

Emily turned suddenly when Egypt began to hiss and arch her spine. "What is it, sweeting?"

A slight tap on the window drew Emily's attention where a soft breeze sent the curtains rippling against the frame.

"Why, 'tis only the wind, Egypt."

"Lady Emily," a voice called softly. "I say, Lady Emily, are you awake?"

Egypt hissed again, and Emily slipped her wary gaze back to the window. That low, raspy voice belonged to only one man. "Mr. F-Fennington?" Disbelief hung on the end of his name.

"I say, Lady Emily, can you hear me?"

Emily shot from her bed, crossing the floor to peer over her sill. "Good gracious! Whatever are you doing?"

The large figure of Mr. James Theodore Fennington clung precariously to the trellis outside her window. The dark cloaked body looked more like a swinging pendulum than a man on a mission, especially with that wretched quizzing glass winking in the glow of a lantern he held in his hand. How daft could the man be? Her brothers would shoot him on sight! To think she thought of marriage to this idiotic male was enough to send her into another fit of giggles.

"Mr. Fennington, do have a care."

"Help," the man croaked, grasping for leverage on the ledge as he miraculously clipped the lantern onto the vine.

The light gave Emily a clear picture of the situation below, and her expression stiffened at the sound of an inebriated belch. Shock quickly turned to annoyance at his stupid feat.

"Mr. Fennington, you are foxed to the gills! You must leave here at once! The way you came, if you please."

"I fear, dear lady, I cannot. Indeed, I may die in the next few moments if I am not carried into safety. But I would die for just one touch of your delicate hand."

"Doing it bit too brown, Mr. Fennington, even for a man in your state." But Emily knew if she did not think of something quick, the idiot would fall to his death. With a murmur of disbelief, she bent over the sill, grabbed the swaying man, and with his help, dragged him into her chambers.

"Good evening, Lady Emily. Your servant, madam."

He bowed, his tall frame swaying before her, mimicking the uneven cadence of the curtains rapping against her window.

Emily stared in openmouthed wonder. A drunkard was standing in the middle of her bedchambers, acting as if he were meeting her at Prinny's Christmas ball.

"Mr. Fennington, I daresay, this is the most incredulous thing I have ever been witness to."

He simply smiled back . . . swaying.

Emily reacted with an icy stare that would even set Roderick faltering back a few feet. Thunder and Zeus, the man was mad. "Mr. Fennington, if you think for one minute that I would take kindly to your visit, you had better think twice."

To her surprise, the man took hold of her hand and squeezed. "Knew you were a shy one, my dear. Precisely why I climbed through the window without a word to you beforehand. Time is of the essence here, and I beg you to allow me to handle all the details while we slip away into the night sight unseen."

"Oh, for the love of the king," Emily uttered, stomping her foot and trying to pull her hand away from his grip, amazed at the impertinence of the man. "If you do not believe me, I daresay, my brothers will not take kindly to your visit either."

"The devil with your domineering brothers." With one quick move, the man jerked her into his arms and pressed his wet lips to her neck. "Dearest, lady. I love you. Love you."

"Mr. Fennington, I beg you!"

"Ah, my little cabbage, we will be together soon and you will never have to beg me for anything."

Little cabbage? Beg him? Why the insufferable pig! Emily flattened her hands against his broad chest and pushed, but she was no deterrent to the insistent man and his roving mouth. "Have a care, sir. My brothers will boil you in oil if they discover you here. You must take your leave, I implore you!"

"Oil? Ha!" His strong hands gripped her waist in a

tightening embrace, and at that moment, she wished she had let him fall to the ground.

"Unhand me, sir . . . before I do something rash!"

"Come away with me, *ma petite*."

"Are you mad?" She grabbed his waistcoat for balance, accidentally grabbing hold of that stupid quizzing glass. She gave him a swift kick in the shin and was instantly released.

Curled on the bed, Egypt hissed loudly. Fennington fell back, stunned, but before he could say a word, his eyes widened in what Emily could only perceive as sheer black terror.

Her heart all but stopped as she slowly turned around.

"Roderick," she said, quickly drawing away from her intruder. "Th-this is not what it seems."

Roderick stalked across the threshold of her bedchambers, his eyes darkening with fury. Like a general, he stood feet apart, his voice as hard and cold as the pistol pointed toward Fennington's belly. "Do believe we can do better than oil, do you not think so, *gentlemen*?" he replied, glancing over his shoulder.

Fennington stood like a prisoner awaiting his execution as three more pairs of shiny Hessians thudded across the floor.

"Oil might be too good for the man," Clayton replied, circling the now pale-faced intruder. Marcus's broad shoulders blocked the doorway. Stephen, looking as if he had been interrupted from his bath, stood clad only in a pair of fawn-colored breeches, crossing his bare arms over a well-muscled torso, daring Fennington to make a move.

Emily took in the overwhelming sight and swallowed hard.

Fennington staggered back. "G-gentlemen, I am unarmed."

"That," Roderick ground out, "is the only thing that saves me from pulling the trigger, you conniving dolt."

Emily watched in horror as Roderick drew the pistol higher. "Roderick, please!"

Roderick's steely gaze turned on her. "Stay out of this."

She stiffened. She had no wish to further Mr. Fennington's design on her, but her amorous intruder had turned a ghastly white and his knees were knocking like billiard balls. This was dreadful. She opened her mouth, intending to save the fool when to her surprise, the strapping man fainted dead at her feet.

Roderick shot her a disgusting look. "What have you to say for yourself, Emily Anne?"

Emily's head shot up from Fennington's limp form only to meet four pairs of hard, glaring eyes, but for some insane reason, she almost let out an hysterical giggle. What could she say? It was as if she were at Drury Lane watching a comedy of manners. The entire evening was absurd.

However, Roderick's next words sent her into a pure panic. "You think this amusing? Perhaps we should send you to the wilds up north to live with Great Uncle Cathaven."

Emily's eyes rounded in shock. "You would not dare?"

Uncle Cathaven was an old, eccentric man who lived like a hermit in a worn-down castle in the most desolate part of Scotland. He refused to talk to anyone but his housekeeper and butler and only when he deemed it absolutely necessary—like once a year when it was time for his bath. She shivered at the thought. Not even Stephen could abide the man. But she must proceed to Hemmingly. It was her only chance of freedom.

Avoiding the hardened glares sent her way, she dropped her gaze, catching sight of Mr. Fennington's blue eyes squinting up at her. Why, the bamboozler was acting! Well, if he could do it, so could she.

"Did you hear me, Emily Anne?" Roderick growled.

Emily looked up. Oh, she heard every incredulous word. Her brothers were going to marry her to some suitable fop by year's end. Over her dead body! She gave Roderick one last look and threw her hand to her head, swaying like the girls she had seen in a squeeze at one of Lady Cherwood's balls. She added a groan for emphasis. Men hated that. Especially the males standing before her, their eyes turning wide with fear. What a ninny she had been. She should have tried this days ago.

"Em?" Frowning, Roderick moved toward her, stuffing his pistol into Clayton's hands. "Em? I meant only . . . Em?"

Inwardly smiling, Emily gave a light gasp, sending the males encircling her like four mothers to a cub. With another angelic groan, she snapped her eyes closed, and for the first time in her life, faked a swoon, dropping both her body and Fennington's monstrous quizzing glass into Roderick's open hands.

Chapter Three

An early morning walk on the grounds of Hemmingly Hall was exactly what Emily needed to calm her mind from her brothers' bothersome plans. She raised her face to the puffs of clouds overhead and allowed herself a much-needed sigh, taking in the cool, crisp air. Here she could think clearly without her overbearing siblings vexing her at every turn.

It was good to be back at Hemmingly. She felt as if a great weight had been taken off her shoulders when she arrived the previous evening and spied the familiar redbrick mansion with its neatly trimmed evergreens lining the graveled drive. Exhausted, she had retired to her bedchambers and no sooner had slipped into bed than Agatha had entered with a tray of hot chocolate and biscuits. Eventually Emily poured out her problems to the older woman.

Smiling as she made her way into the hall, Emily recalled Agatha's vehemence on her behalf and felt a growing confidence in her bosom. Agatha would let her stay as long as she wished.

Feeling better than she had in weeks, Emily headed toward Hemmingly's library to search for a new novel from the Minerva Press that Jane mentioned had been added to Agatha's extensive book collection. Emily, an unconscious grin still tipping the corners of her lips, opened her Wordsworth book that she had taken on her morning stroll and was so engrossed in one of the poems that when she turned the corner, she failed to notice the man withdrawing from the library.

She slammed into the tall figure with the elegance of an intoxicated dandy. With a horrified gasp, she bounced backward and fell onto the marble floor with a thud. Behind her a salmon-colored porcelain vase crashed to the floor, shattering into infinite pieces. Heat engulfed her.

She blinked and caught sight of a pair of shiny Hessian boots a foot away. How utterly humiliating. With a groan, she pushed her raised skirts back over her ankles and lifted her gaze slowly, knowing instantly that this was no ordinary guest. It was strange that Agatha had not mentioned any other person staying at Hemmingly. Unless—

Her eyes immediately clung to a pair of athletic-looking legs encased in buckskin breeches. She vaguely heard a male voice, but her ears were roaring with the inevitable. Shock thickened her tongue as she raised her gaze higher only to meet with a waistcoat of burgundy followed by a neat white cravat and a pair of wide shoulders wrapped up in a perfectly fitted brown coat. Dark brown hair tilted toward her, but it was when a pair of familiar amber eyes stared back at her that her blood froze.

"Do beg your pardon, Lady Emily. Are you hurt?"

The sound of her name on Mr. Jared Ashton's lips cut into her heart like a guillotine. No, he was Lord Stonebridge now. She stared numbly at the tanned hand reaching out to her and stiffened.

His voice was deeper than she recalled, more controlled, and much to her dismay, it sounded as if the man were truly concerned about her welfare. He appeared larger than she remembered. This man was no longer the long-legged boy that had stolen her heart. No indeed.

Before she could rise, a steely grip took hold of her elbows, whisking her to a standing position, as if she were a mere feather.

"Pray, forgive my clumsiness. I have not hurt you, have I?"

Her blood tingled from his touch. "I'm f-fine."

But she was not fine at all. Shock had paralyzed her. He was supposed to be in India. Agatha had mentioned that very fact in a letter posted only two months ago. Why was he here? Now of all times?

The scent of soap from his morning bath filled her senses, reminding her of the last time she saw him, the last time she rested her head against that broad chest when he had promised to come to Elbourne Hall and claim her as his own. But he had not come. He had broken her heart, and now she felt as if a thousand pins were pressing into it.

"I cannot say the pleasure is mine, Lord Stonebridge," she said stiffly, lifting her gaze to meet his.

He seemed to ignore her jibe and continued his lame apology. "I missed you coming around the corner. You startled me." He watched her intently, as if waiting for her to answer.

He finally broke through the unbearable silence, ripping her composure in two. "How long has it been, Lady Emily?"

How long? The man must be mad? Did he not hear her rebuff? "How long?" she asked tartly, inwardly shaking with fury. *How long does it take a heart to heal?* Did he believe for one minute she had forgotten? Did he believe she had pined for him all these years?

"Let me see . . ." She tapped a stiff finger against her chin. "How long since you broke your promise? Tricked a naïve young girl into dreams of a future? Made her see the true meaning of cad? Hmmm, how long ago was that, pray tell?"

"I had obligations," he said harshly, his eyes turning swiftly to anger. "You were . . . young."

"Young?" she snapped, ignoring the thin layer of ice

wrapping around her heart. "You were a coward. Could you not have written once? Or were you too afraid to tell me the truth? Perhaps it was my father you were afraid of?"

A muscle jumped in his jaw. "One, I am not a coward. Two, I wrote. And three, fear is not a quality I have ever admired." He paused. "Situations occurred that altered my plans."

Emily stared, dumbfounded. Oh, why had not Agatha told her that *he* was staying at Hemmingly? She would have rather remained with Uncle Cathaven up north than have had to endure this torture. Of course, dear Agatha had no inkling of her attachment to Jared, so why should the older lady even care to offer the information that her long-departed nephew was making an unexpected trip to Hemmingly?

"You're bleeding," he said, grabbing her hand.

She jerked away from his touch. His closeness was like a magnet, pulling her to him, but she needed to keep her distance, needed to think. Needed to keep away.

"I have no designs on you, my lady." His mocking smile only angered her further. "Only look at your finger. I daresay, it is bleeding."

She dropped her gaze to her hand. A bead of blood fell from her pinky finger to the floor. At that precise moment something in her chest tightened painfully. Seeing this man again crumbled the armor she had erected so carefully around herself for the past three years. It galled her that one look, one word, from Lord Stonebridge tumbled her back into a blithering fool of emotions.

"Don't ever touch me again." Her words were a bare whisper, but he immediately dropped his hand to his side. Head held high, she gave him one last glare and spun on her heels to leave. But a viselike grip wrapped around her arm, holding her in place.

"Emily, stop this nonsense. We are adults now, not a pair of cow-eyed youths. We need to put the past behind us."

She whirled around to glare at him. Cow-eyed youths? Was that what he thought of their relationship? "I asked you not to touch me, my lord," she countered icily.

"You've changed, little one." His short bark of laughter held no amusement as he released his hold on her.

Of course she had changed. She was no longer an innocent girl who believed in love at first sight, and he was no longer her knight in shining armor. The thought brought a lump to her throat, making her all the more determined to choose her own future. She fought her swirling emotions trying to calm herself. "As I see it, Agatha and Jane have no reason to believe we have had any past history except being mere acquaintances. I, for one, would like to keep it that way."

His dark eyes sharpened like the points on the end of a quill. "I, too, have no wish to dredge up the past, *Emily*."

Her gaze met his in a battle of wills, and she fought the need to ask him why he had done this to her. Why had he made such a fool of her? Why had he made her fall in love with him and then vanish with another woman, without a word? He had never written to her. Never.

"So we are agreed, then?" she asked.

He nodded silently, his expression tight.

"Very good," she continued, her heart thudding. "When we meet upon further occasion, which I know we will since you are Agatha's nephew and I am to be staying here indefinitely . . ."

"Indefinitely?" He raised an inquisitive brow as if he could only hope her stay was of short duration.

She boldly met his gaze. "Yes, indefinitely, and as such, I will remind you that I have not given you leave to use my Christian name. I am Lady Emily to you, and I always will be."

The corner of his lip twisted upward. "Direct hit, my dear. I daresay, we might have won the war quicker if we had you firing the cannons at Waterloo."

Emily felt her cheeks warm. The insolence of that man. How dare he!

Feeling there was nothing more to say, she pivoted on her heels and started down the hall, her slippers thwacking the marble hallway with every angry step. She would have made a dignified exit if her feet had not met the water spill trailing along the hall from the cracked vase, but the next thing she knew, her legs lifted out from under her and she hit the floor with an undignified plop.

She was more embarrassed than hurt since it was the second time she fell that day. However, when the sound of clamoring footsteps closed in behind her, she flinched at the thought of the man touching her again and raised her hand in warning. "I will be quite all right. Just stay away."

The clack of heels stopped abruptly, and she could feel Jared's withering glare burning into her back. His presence had shaken her more than she wanted to admit. Heavy footsteps retreated down the hallway, followed by a curse. Tears of frustration filled her eyes. He meant nothing to her now. Nothing at all.

She took a deep, consoling breath and started to rise only to be startled by a loud bark. Heart thumping, she raised her blurry gaze and immediately locked eyes on a colossal brown ball of fur racing toward her as if she were a piece of raw meat for the taking.

The scream died in her throat. She whipped her hands to her face, curling into a ball, and waited for the bite. She waited for the end of it all when something slimy pressed against her face. Letting out a squeak of protest, she stiffened while the hot, pungent breath of the massive dog almost made her swoon.

"Nigel!"

The shouted command came from behind, and the creature gave one last lick to her face, whimpered in her ear, and pulled away. With a shaking breath, Emily dared to look up, realizing that it was Jared who had given the firm order for the dog to retreat. As for the enemy, *Nigel* had moved away from her, taking a grand seat in the small alcove of the hallway where a knee-high statue of some Greek goddess watched the scene with glaring eyes.

Except for the earl's command, she had never heard the man approach. "Nigel is *your* dog?" she asked, looking up.

To her dread, the corner of those beautiful golden eyes crinkled with amusement, and he nodded. "Brilliant creature. However, Nigel can be a bit overbearing sometimes, and even a bit playful with the ladies when I'm not around to supervise."

"Playful? Your dog came at me as if I were a huge bone!" She loved dogs, but that beast was a menace.

The earl's mouth twitched upward as his gaze roved slowly over her person. "Must be that scent you're wearing. Nigel rather enjoys the smell of rose water and lavender." The smile in his eyes grew. "Adores the ladies who wear it, too."

She avoided his steadfast gaze, but there was almost an inexplicable note of tenderness in his voice that unnerved her, and she slapped a hand to her skirt. "Well, I daresay, as long as *Nigel* roams the halls of Hemmingly, I will make a point of wearing nothing at all then."

Too late, she realized her mistake.

Jared's deep laugh rumbled down the hall. "I do not believe that would be a deterrent for anyone, *Lady Emily*. You might receive more than dogs licking at your face."

His meaning was quite clear, and she clamped her mouth shut. There was nothing she could say that would save her dignity, so she said nothing at all. Needing to separate herself from this disagreeable man as soon as possible, she pushed to stand, but before she could protest, he reached beneath her arms and gently pulled her upward . . . again.

Except this time she stumbled into his chest, and his warm breath pressed upon her cheek, doing silly things to her stomach. The heat of his firm fingers lingered on her skin, and her heart skidded to a halt. Horrified at her body's treacherous behavior, she stepped back, her slipper crunching against the broken vase. "You sh-should teach that dog of yours some manners."

"Nigel would never hurt you."

She said nothing as he stared at her, his lips parting as if he wanted to say something more. A hollow silence swept through the hall like the echo of a cold arctic wind.

"Jane is expecting me in the drawing room," she finally blurted out, and without waiting for his reply, grabbed hold of her skirt and turned blindly down the hall, walking with as much dignity as she could gather.

Why did he have to come back into her life? She was a silly twit. Every fiber of her being had wanted to cling to him, and it had taken every bit of resolve to pull away. He was dangerous. Dangerous to her heart and to her future. What had happened to the independent, confident woman she had become?

For the first time since her brothers returned home, she wished they were there beside her, spouting their little speeches and watching her every move. But most of all she wished they were protecting her from the world and all the disagreeable baggage that went along with it, including a certain earl that could do more damage to her heart in five minutes than an entire army of suitors could do to her in one day.

Jared purposely missed Emily's arrival the previous evening at Hemmingly, but he was not ready for the bitterness that radiated from those violet eyes when he literally ran into her this morning. She was no longer the slim, dark-haired girl he remembered. She had grown into an independent beauty who challenged his resolve to stay away. Dash Roderick and his plans! If the duke had not rescued him from a French prison, Jared would not be put in this position in the first place.

Honor, of course, demanded that Jared do as his friend asked and watch over Emily until her brothers found a suitable husband for her. Yet as Jared strode back toward the library, he realized he could make a list a mile long of the very reasons he should leave Hemmingly . . . and Lady Emily. Reasons that would set the duke and his brothers onto him like hounds to a fox.

Naturally, Jared would never run from them if he had his mind set on their sister, but Lady Emily was no longer part of his plans.

His thoughts turned to his daughter and his reunion with her as he stalked past the maid brushing up the shattered vase in the hallway. By chance, he dropped his gaze to a small black book resting at the foot of the Greek statue. It looked oddly familiar.

"Wordsworth," he said, picking up the book and opening to the first page. *To the woman closest to my heart.* He cringed.

The written words had come back to haunt him like a ghost from the past. So the little spitfire had kept the book he had slipped to her in Hyde Park the last afternoon they had been together. Did she still love him? No, impossible. What the devil was he thinking? Their love had been but a fleeting emotion of youth.

Slapping the book closed, he strode into the library and slammed the door. Whether she carried the book in her heart or in her hands, it mattered not. He had no right to her now. No right at all.

Hours later Jared raised his cool gaze over a cup of tea and greeted his aunt as she joined him for an impromptu nuncheon, a spread consisting of hot croissants, rolls, ham, cheese, grapes, and biscuits. Breakfast had been missed by all for one reason or another, and Agatha had asked Cook to set a small meal for her and her nephew. It seemed Jane and Lady Emily were preoccupied with an invitation at the local vicarage.

Jared thought the trip to the village an innocent excursion, but in the event the legitimate outing turned into something havey-cavey, he secretly conveyed to James, one of Agatha's new footmen and Jared's former aide, that should any eager gentlemen present themselves to the ladies for want of closer acquaintance, James was to hasten the ladies back to Hemmingly as soon as possible. Using James as an extra pair of eyes had made guarding Lady Emily much easier, Jared decided. He put down the tea and gave the newspaper he was reading a determined snap. Much easier indeed.

"It appears Lady Emily is quite good friends with Jane," he said, making small talk.

Agatha leaned her plump body forward, setting her trusty parasol, a handy weapon she carried everywhere, beside her chair, and deliberately folded her chubby hands onto the lap of her green morning gown.

Jared's brain instantly registered the militant expression. Two salt-and-pepper brows arched above steel gray. Blast. He was going to have another setting down by his aunt. These little talks were becoming most intolerable.

"If you would have deemed to come home for a while instead of spending your time in India, you would have known that Lady Emily has been a frequent guest here the past three years."

Jared swallowed his ham. "I had obligations to my wife and my country, madam. I was a major, if you do remember, and was stationed in India."

One plump hand flitted in the air. "Major, Smajor. Do not deem to tell me that you could not have visited the last few years. But nevermind about an old aunt like me, it is Jane that I am concerned about. She has missed you terribly." Agatha's accusing glare reached out to him like a noose chafing about his neck. "Or did you forget that you happen to be the girl's guardian?"

Jared had never forgotten that indeed he was Jane's guardian. Harry Greenwell, the girl's father and Jared's cousin, had died in the war. The man's death had been followed immediately by his wife's suspicious drowning in the Thames. Jane was a sweet girl having lived with Agatha for the past five years, and he never doubted that his ward would not be in the very best of hands.

"I daresay, Jared, that I simply cannot fathom your reasoning forbidding me to meet your wife." Agatha gathered a croissant off the platter in front of her and lapped on some butter. "Surely you could have brought Felicia to Town before you made your hasty departure. At least have introduced her to me."

Were those tears in his aunt's eyes?

Jared hastily shook some salt on his eggs. The devil! His stay at Hemmingly was bound to drive him mad, but he refused to divulge his past about Felicia or Emily. The late duke's vehement rejection of Jared's suit to marry his daughter was not a fact for discussion. However, there was no denying the fact that when he set his eyes on Emily this morning, the painful memories of the duke's revenge surfaced as if it were yesterday.

It had been almost three years ago at Lady Rosalind's ball when Jared had been sent a letter telling him to meet Emily beyond the French doors, down the garden trail, at the birdbath near the rosebushes. However, it was not Emily he encountered, but a swooning Felicia Fairlow, ill from too many glasses of champagne given to her by her scheming, indebted father, whom Jared later realized had been paid a good sum by the duke for his role in his daughter's downfall.

Moving quickly, Jared caught the tiny lady in his arms. It was only seconds later when Felicia's father, along with the Duke of Elbourne, came upon Jared holding the limp female across his lap. With the duke as witness to the scandalous scene, Felicia's father demanded satisfaction. Deciding his honor was at stake and Felicia's as well, Jared found himself coerced into a marriage he never wanted.

"Felicia barely made the trip to India," he said calmly, avoiding his aunt's comment about meeting Felicia when he had first married. He set his fork down, watching his aunt's eyes narrow. "She was a delicate creature. I assure you another trip back home would have killed her." The words were out of his mouth before he thought twice. He had never admitted Felicia's frail health to anyone, not even Roderick.

Jared and his new wife had settled in India, where he had purchased a commission. He had hastened away to another part of the world, away from Emily, away from scandal, away from his foolish dreams.

A year after leaving England, Felicia had died of typhus three weeks after giving birth to their daughter,

Gabrielle, now a two-year-old whom Agatha knew nothing about. Immediately after his wife's death, Jared began to work for Wellington as a special agent to the War Department, working in both England and France, leaving his daughter to be raised by friends in India until he returned. Though he had sold out months ago, some of his work with the Foreign Office in Whitehall was still ongoing.

"Well, goodness. I had no idea," Agatha went on. "Forgive me, my boy. I had no wish to pry into your life. But one does wonder when one's favorite nephew does not even deem to post a single letter." The accusation hung in the air like fireworks at Vauxhall.

Jared pursed his lips at his aunt's attempt of diplomacy. He loved Agatha, but for Felicia's sake; no one but a small contingency of people had known that his marriage had been a forced union. Any communications he sent were either letters posted to Lady Emily at Elbourne Hall, all of them never received, or letters of business through his solicitor in London, hence his way of informing Agatha and Jane of his nuptials and consequent departure to India.

If he had made any contact with his aunt concerning his forced marriage, he knew without a doubt, the older lady would have crossed the ocean to ease his burden, not to mention along with sweet Jane, who would never have left Agatha to make the journey alone.

At first, Jared had been too distraught to write Agatha, and after the birth of Gabrielle, he had been too protective. Agatha and Jane had no need to know about his covert actions in the war after his wife had died, and his enemy had no need to know the soft spots in his armor either.

Of course, with Napoleon finally interred at St. Helena, Jared had decided his covert missions must eventually come to an end. His decision seemed to coincide with his brother's demise, a fact that had shattered Jared's happiness like a French cannon ball to his heart. Jared had loved Edmond and regretted having to return to England to carry on the earldom his brother had lost.

Jared had learned one too many times that love must be kept at a distance or avoided altogether.

Hearing his aunt clear her throat, he looked up. What in the world had she been chattering about now?

"You have not upset Lady Emily, have you?"

Jared's fork halted halfway to his mouth. Had Agatha knowledge about his past with Lady Emily and the old duke's wretched scheme? "Upset her? What do you take me for?"

Agatha's burning gaze drilled into him as if she were Wellington himself.

He clenched his jaw. "What?"

Agatha picked up her trusty parasol and thumped it twice on the rug. "You are concealing something from me. Your eyes have fallen halfway open like a cat that ate his favorite mouse. For your information, when Emily departed for the vicarage, her face was as pale as Lord Beelhaven's ghost."

"Dash it all, Agatha. Lord Beelhaven has no ghost. And I have done nothing to upset the lady." *Liar.* "However, if I had done such a thing, I would not be the one to confess it to you."

"Oh ho, there is a ghost. I have seen it." His aunt tore off a piece of her bun and raised her head with a cool glare in his direction. "For depend upon it, you are an incorrigible liar, *Lord Stonebridge.*" She skewered his title with a heavy dose of sarcasm that hit its mark quite accurately.

"Incorrigible now, is it? Last time I was here I was lovable."

"Hmmmph. Lovable liar. What's the difference? And pray, remember the last time you were here was three years ago, after which you bought into the army and sailed off to India with your new wife." She paused, looking at him suspiciously. "And now you have no one."

No one but his little girl whom he would see soon. Yet because of his direct involvement in stealing missives from Napoleon himself, Jared had no wish to involve his daughter in any type of confrontation with one of Boney's loyalists, namely Monsieur Devereaux, who vowed revenge and could still be alive, though most thought the contrary.

As to Agatha and Jane, Jared knew the chances of revenge against them were slim. Yet as a precaution, he had installed more secret aides from Whitehall to act as servants at Hemmingly to watch the ladies as well.

All this extra security seemed to amuse the duke, since Roderick was one of the persons who knew of Jared's covert actions. In fact, the duke, himself, had been involved in similar activities. Roderick assured Jared that the French agent, Monsieur Devereaux, was dead. Roderick proclaimed he had shot the man while rescuing Jared from prison.

No matter, Jared thought. He knew he was being obsessive about the situation, but he still needed to make certain of the man's death and consequently awaited a confirming letter from Whitehall.

Avoiding his aunt's penetrating gaze, Jared turned his head and whistled for Nigel. The dog immediately pounced from behind the curtains, coming to sit at his feet. He gave the dog some scraps from the table and glanced across the silver teapot resting on the table in front of his aunt. Heaven save him from interfering females. Agatha's determined gray eyes were fixed on his face as if he were a prize to be raffled.

"From the look of you, I believe that you have someone in mind for me to marry?" he said with a scowl. "Well, forget it."

Devil take it. He had no wish to discuss his past or the bonds of matrimony. He had his own plans for a future wife in a marriage of convenience, and he was quite determined that Agatha would not be involved.

"Ha! So you read minds now, do you?"

Understanding finally dawned on Jared. "By Jove, you cannot be thinking of marrying me to Lady Emily?"

Agatha gave him another withering stare. "I can assure you that Lady Emily is not looking to marry your money or your agreeable personality, my dear boy."

Jared lifted a sarcastic brow. "Agreeable now, am I?"

Agatha inclined her head over the teapot and lowered her voice. "I assure you, this is not about Lady Emily. I have had no reason to speak of this before, but . . ." She stopped talking to swallow a bite of buttered bread, then to Jared's surprise she stood, shooing the servants away with that cursed parasol. The door inevitably snapped closed, and Jared groaned.

His eating instantly halted as soon as the ugly parasol winged his way. Nigel, the fiend, had hightailed it to the opposite side of the room. "Man's best friend," Jared muttered to his dog. "Whoever coined that phrase certainly had no aunts with black parasols."

"I heard that!"

Jared's lips thinned as Agatha plopped her parasol beside the table and sank back into her chair. "Another one of these private talks, Aunt Agatha." He raised his cup of tea to his lips. "Have you forgotten I am a man now and not a little boy who has raided Cook's cupboard?"

She shot him a cool glare. "I will say nothing of that beefsteak that disappeared days ago." Nigel barked. "But upon my word, you are an insolent pup. It would behoove you to take care of your ward. Since her parents died, Jane has been alone, save for you and me."

An embarrassing heat crawled up Jared's neck. He admitted he had left Agatha with much of the responsibility for Jane. But he never doubted his ward would not be safe. Agatha was like a lioness with her cub when it came to the girl's welfare.

Agatha regarded him with a keen eye and continued, "So good to know you at least have a conscience, my boy. I daresay, I forgave you for the past two years when you hopped from England to France and back again in those war games with Whitehall, but our dear, sweet Jane is—"

Jared shot from his seat, his chair crashing to the floor. "War games!" How this sweet elderly lady had possibly uncovered information about his covert actions during the war was beyond his comprehension. He glared at her, but to his amazement, she continued her speech as if she had just recited something to him as simple as the alphabet.

"As I was saying, Jared, Jane is without—"

Flabbergasted, Jared interrupted. "Pray, what war games are you speaking of?" His voice took on a chilling calm as he waited for her answer. Nigel yelped, hiding his nose beneath his paws.

Agatha dropped her gaze, pushing her buttered bun about with her fork. "I have ways, my boy." She took a small bite, tipping her round face his way. "Now, as to Jane, she does open her mouth a bit too often in front of the gentlemen, and of course, I realize that you are not aware of her capabilities as a hostess. The Season she was out did have its shortcomings, the weather and all, you know. However, never mind that. London can be so dreary sometimes. 'Course, Lady Emily had been with us for a few years off and on. Still, I believe the best thing—"

She clamped her mouth shut as Jared's purposeful strides ate up the rug between them. "Confound it! Have you been snooping about my quarters?"

The older lady put a hand to her chest as if in pain. "*Moi?* How could you conceive of such a thing? And do I detect a bit of censure in your tone, young man?"

Jared grimaced. If his aunt knew about his work with Whitehall, it was possible others knew about him as well, including a certain Monsieur Devereaux. A cold knot formed in the pit of his belly as he thought about his daughter's safety. At least Agatha hadn't mentioned Gabrielle . . . yet.

"How did you know about my work?" he asked, his mind reeling.

Agatha stiffened as Jared found himself attacked by two huge gray eyes, accusing him of an insensitivity he was well known for. "You are Jane's guardian, *Lord Stonebridge*, and you left her for three long years. You were not in India the last two, one could only assume that the Black Wolf—"

Jared drew in a sharp breath and felt as if someone stuck him with a bayonet. "The Black Wolf?" His voice held a hardness that he was certain even Agatha had never heard before.

He had kept his cover a secret from the deadliest of men, and now this lady, whom he loved like a mother, seemed to have uncovered his secret as if it were mere child's play.

"Pray, dear aunt, I can only hope that you have not spoken of this to anyone, including Jane. I have noticed that her mouth opens at the strangest of times."

Agatha blinked in surprise. "Gracious, what do you take me for, a gabster? I traveled down to Whitehall to inquire about well . . . things." She shrugged and popped another piece of bread into her mouth. "One thing led to another, and I began to deduce your role as . . ." she lowered her voice, "you know, a secret agent over the last few years."

Jared's anger turned into a white-hot fury. "You went to Headquarters?"

Agatha reached across the table, buttered another raspberry bun, and looked up. "I assure you, Jared, no one was the wiser. I am quite good friends with the Secretary. And do quit looking at me as if you were going to throw me into some witch's brew."

Jared's gaze sizzled with reproach. Agatha's explanation still did not tell him how she knew who or what he was. It was all he could do to hold in his anger at the danger his aunt had put herself in, and his daughter, and him, and Jane . . . and now Emily. Come to think of it, it was simply amazing this paragon of information who sat before him had no notion of his relationship with the duke's daughter . . . or had she?

"It would be best if you keep these small facts to yourself, Aunt, and never, never bring them into conversation again. Do I make myself perfectly clear?"

Her gray eyes lit up like a lantern in a storm. "Perfectly."

"Very good, then. We will speak of this later." He headed toward the door, looked back at his aunt, and shook his head, afraid to let another word pass his lips before he did permanent harm to their relationship. He must get word to Headquarters.

"Oh, and, Jared dear."

He threw an icy glare over his shoulder. "What, pray tell, could you have to say now?"

"You are not truly out at heels, are you? I do have some money from my mother's side that is quite a good sum. You may use that if you have need."

Out at heels indeed! "No. I am not broke! I lost badly at White's one night, and the incident has grown into an annoying rumor that I am in debt. A joke gone astray. That . . . is all."

"I see."

He reached for the door, whistling for Nigel to join him. In seconds, the dog was by his side.

"And, Jared dear?"

He leaned his head against the door and swiveled. Life in a French prison was easier than this! "Yes?"

He clenched his teeth as he watched Agatha leisurely drop three lumps of sugar into her teacup as if she were on a holiday in Bath. "I daresay," she said, not looking at him, "Miss Susan Wimble is not for the likes of you. You can do better then her if you would only cool that fiery temper of yours."

The lady then added a dollop of cream, completely oblivious to the madness engulfing him. "Do hope you are not set on the engagement."

Jared closed his eyes and counted to ten. He had no wish to say that he would rather choose his spouse now than be forced into marriage as he had been earlier. A compromising position, as with his late wife Felicia, he would not be found in again. Though he had become fond of his wife, their union had been singed from the beginning, and neither could ever forget the wrongs done to either of them.

"I asked you if you are set on the engagement," Agatha demanded.

"We are somewhat engaged, and that, dear aunt, is to be kept a secret until the end of the Season."

"A secret?" Agatha set down her cup. "And pray, is that your only one?"

The devil! What else did she know?

Jared took a deep, calming breath before he spoke. "I am obliged to ask you to keep my marriage plans a secret. The settlement between the families has not been signed, and we have yet to publicly announce the engagement because Miss Wimble has been attending to a sick cousin in the country. When we meet again in London, all things will progress in due course."

With an irritated snort, Agatha returned to her tea. "I see. A cousin now, is it? Believe I smell a rat, and I daresay, I do know how you loathe those little beasts, Jared. Ever since you were a child and caught in Mr. McHugh's barn, you know."

Determined to leave at all possible speed, Jared reached for the doorknob. He had his reasons to marry. He needed an heir. His brother and father were dead, and Miss Susan Wimble was more than decent to the eye. She would do, and besides, Gabrielle had arrived only a few weeks ago and was residing at a cottage in the country. His daughter needed him to set aside his problems as quickly as possible, but his problems seemed to be growing by the second. The matter of information leaking from Whitehall would be on his to-do list as well, along with his duties to Lady Emily.

"I was so hoping you would marry again." Agatha's voice drifted to his ears like artillery fire. "Felicia may be dead, Jared, but you are still alive and well. Do not live on your mistakes."

"Mistakes?" Jared all but shouted the word. He had grown close to Felicia, in a protective sort of way, and he felt he failed her. Failed Lady Emily and even his daughter, whom he had not seen in ages.

"Yes, mistakes." The lady gave him her sternest look. "I believe it would be quite the thing if you wed a pretty piece such as the Silver Fox."

The name slammed into Jared's brain like an anvil dropping from the ceiling. "Blast it to hell! This is an insane conversation, madam."

"Why is that?" Agatha asked calmly, peering over the rim of her teacup. "And please refrain from cursing, Jared. I am a delicate woman."

"Pray, forgive me for my language," he said hotly, "but for one thing, the Silver Fox is not a woman. And another, you should not even be mentioning the man's name. Confound it, are you going to tell me who leaked this information to you?"

Agatha lifted a cool brow. "And have them hanged for treason?"

"Th-this is maddening," Jared sputtered and began to pace about the room, locking his hands behind his back. He stopped and turned to face her. "I must insist that you curtail your visits to Whitehall at once."

"At once? By George or what are you going to do?"

He rubbed a hand across his face. "I have no idea." Though his superiors had kept Black Wolf and Silver Fox apart for reasons of safety, the danger had greatly diminished now that Napoleon had been banished. Yet, he was led to believe the existence of Silver Fox had never been disclosed to the public.

"I can see you are not going to disclose your contact," he said to his aunt as he tried desperately to curb his rage, "but I demand to know what you know about Silver Fox."

Agatha pounded her parasol against the floor. "I refuse to speak. I have obviously said too much already. Moreover, everyone in England has heard of Black Wolf, and a handful of people have heard about Silver Fox as well. So there."

A handful of people? Was she mad? "Come now, Agatha. Tell me of your information. I promise you, it will go no further than this table."

"Goodness," she laughed. "You do not truly believe that I would divulge any top-secret information, do you?"

What in the name of the king had she been doing the last few minutes? "Not divulging, Agatha, just simply passing information on to a colleague."

"A colleague now, am I?" The older lady threw down

her napkin and wobbled to a standing position. "Only a minute ago you were about to send me to the gallows."

"I was not!"

"You were," she said, shuffling her small, round body toward the door. "And another thing, you will take Jane and Lady Emily to the balls this Season, or else."

He raised a dark brow in challenge at the lady's uncompromising look. "Blackmail does not become you, Agatha."

"Well, it does now."

As the door slammed behind her, Jared collapsed into her chair and scowled. How the devil had the conversation shifted from secret agents to the London Season? Women! All he needed now was for that Fennington fellow Roderick had warned him about to come sniffing around Hemmingly. A harsh laugh suddenly escaped him. It seemed the thought of Emily riding away with one of her suitors bothered him more than the idea of Monsieur Devereaux appearing before dawn with pistols drawn. Dash it all. His mind was a jumble of confusion, all thanks to Agatha.

"If I may be so blunt as to suggest a remedy for what ails you, my lord."

Jared raised a speculative brow as the butler made his way into the room. Obviously Filmore had determined that his employer was sending her nephew to Bedlam. "What kind of remedy, Filmore?"

The butler coughed. "Of the digestible kind, my lord. In times like these, I save a bit of the Irish whiskey back in the corner pantry. The O'Keefe brand. Straight from Ireland."

Jared smiled. "Your full Christian name, Filmore?"

The butler gave a curt bow. "Your servant, my lord. Michael Filmore Brian *O'Keefe*."

Jared laughed at the unmistakable Irish brogue in the man's voice. It seemed Agatha had more secrets at Hemmingly than Prinny had chandeliers at Brighton. What in the blue blazes had his aunt been up to the years he had been gone, traveling to Whitehall and sifting out secrets? The lady had always liked adventure. But there was no doubt something havey-cavey was up involving that French brandy and now Filmore.

Jared's brows snapped together, and he suddenly wondered if either Jane or Emily had any inkling to Agatha's secrets. The maddening notion scared the hell out of him.

"Come here, Nigel. Give the pretty black book back to Lady Emily." Emily took a hesitant step forward and grimaced. She had been chasing the dratted dog in the back gardens of Hemmingly for over an hour. Drat and double drat!

Her stomach growled. The biscuits and tea at the vicarage had been barely a meal. But she would starve before she would leave the gardens without that book.

Gritting her teeth, she took another step closer when Nigel suddenly dropped the book onto the wet ground and let out a loud bark. If Emily had not known better, she would have thought the odious dog was playing with her as if the entire affair were a peekaboo game.

Exasperated and shivering from the cold, she sat back on her heels and sighed. She hated to admit it, but the dog had been outwitting her at every turn. "Nigel, dear." She took off her gloves, reaching out her hand. "Give Emily the book."

The dog lifted its wet nose and gave a disagreeable howl. Before Emily could stand, the book was clamped between a large set of teeth, and Nigel quickly disappeared around an old oak.

"Odious beast!"

She threw her hands to her hips, stared up at the sky, and frowned. The warmth of the afternoon sun seemed to come and go, as if it had devised a similar plan with Nigel, taunting her with promises of comfort, then turning on her, changing from hot to cold in mere seconds.

Another chill snaked through her as she dropped her gaze to her wet gown. She fisted her hands in rage. She had bested some of the smartest men in France, and no mere dog was going to make a cake of her. Short of shooting the creature or calling his master for help, she realized that following the abominable canine was her only recourse. But the wretched beast was becoming more annoying than all her brothers put together.

"Dash it, Nigel. I won't hurt you. All I wish is my book." To Emily's surprise, the dog dropped the book and wagged its tail, as if consenting to her plea. Triumph at last. She leaned forward, her slim fingers grazing the cover of the book with the ease of a Captain Sharp at his best game of whist. But before she knew it, a huge ball of brown fur tumbled toward her, shoving her onto her back. The damp ground reached up to meet her. Next thing she knew, the dog swiped the book into his mouth and ran. "Nigel, you come back here this instant!"

Emily jerked upright and stomped her foot as the beast turned the corner of the garden and bounded into the fields. Her eyes narrowed on her enemy. This was no longer a game, this was war. She picked up the pace, striding across the grassy pastures where Nigel had fled. Glancing over her shoulders, she dismissed the overcast sky. Hemmingly Hall, its cozy façade of evergreens stretched at least a quarter mile behind her.

"Nigel, you wretched creature! Give me that book!"

The dog stopped and turned to stare at her. There seemed to be a faint glimmer of humor exuding from those two brown eyes that set Emily's nerves on edge. "Enough of these games, you odious dog. I know what you're up to, and it won't work."

With the book still in its mouth, Nigel gave a whine and made his way toward Hemmingly's overgrown maze ten yards away.

Emily gasped in outrage. "Don't you dare go in there, you beast." The dog defiantly backed up into the maze.

However, Emily refused to be goaded. The maze was said to be the place of Agatha's first kiss with her one and only true love. But since the man's death at the Battle of Trafalgar, no care had been taken to keep up the grounds. Jane had made a point of telling Emily more than once never to enter the overgrown web of vines and trees lest she become lost.

Emily glared at Nigel's mischievous expression. Though many a day curiosity had begged her to investigate the mysterious maze, now was certainly not the time to do so.

"Nigel, I forbid you to go in there with my book!"

Her warning seemed to fall on deaf ears. For as soon as she took another step, the dog spun around and padded into the maze with the bravado of a young bullfighter.

"Nigel!" She hurried forward and ducked her head beyond the tunneled opening into a nest of gnarled vines and overgrown evergreens. Her heart thudded with unease. Nothing.

"Nigel, come here immediately."

A chilling silence filled the air as she waited for an answer. But seconds turned to minutes as the sky thundered above her, bursting forth with a bone-chilling rain. She hesitantly inched forward onto the matted path, the cold droplets falling against her back. Guilt immediately burnt any traces of anger in her veins.

"Nigel, sweeting. Can you hear me?"

A strong wind rustled eerily through the trees, and a small whimper of pain reached her ears. Emily halted. Fear for the dog soon replaced any apprehension for her book. She swallowed and moved forward, her gown snagging on the tangled vines.

"Nigel, sweeting, are you hurt?" Another whimper. "Keep calm, Nigel. Emily will save you." She bit her lip, fought back a wave of hot tears, and hastened forward. *Dear heaven, let the poor thing be safe.* If anything happened to Nigel because of her, she would never forgive herself.

Chapter Four

"I tell you, Jared, I am more than worried." Agatha sank her plump body into the sofa of Hemmingly's drawing room, letting out a troubled frown. "That sweet girl has not been seen all afternoon."

Jared threw a booted foot onto the hearth, shoving a hand into the pocket of his coat, trying to ignore the alarm that rippled through him. "When did you see her last?"

Agatha rested her parasol against her gown, wincing as a clap of thunder hit the room. "Not since she came home from the vicarage with Jane."

"Jane is with her, then?"

"No, Jane went directly to her room with a headache." Agatha sniffed and pulled out a handkerchief. "This is not like Emily, not like her at all."

Jared placed his hands across the fire and let out a deep sigh. The thought that he might have been the cause of Emily's disappearance made him ill. Still, there was the possibility that the raven-haired beauty had left the grounds of Hemmingly with one of her suitors, escaping the notice of his aides. The very idea made Jared furious.

Were his aides watching the roads in the village, or had they left their posts?

With a grimace, Jared tilted his head toward the window, watching as an eerie blanket of leaden gray rolled across the sky. He shifted his gaze back to Agatha's wary face and frowned. His mind frantically went over the places Emily could be.

"Jared? What have you done?"

His head snapped up. "Nothing." Nothing but break a poor girl's heart.

"Oh ho, do not lie to me. You look like you just poked your finger in Cook's plum pudding."

Jared avoided Agatha's intense gaze and picked up a crystal decanter on the nearby table, pouring himself a small brandy.

Could Emily have slipped through the woods? A meeting perhaps? The notion of a rendezvous with Emily and some stranger suddenly began to gain momentum in his mind like a carriage careening out of control.

Were Roderick's assumptions correct? Could that Fennington fellow have had the audacity to follow Emily to Hemmingly and whisk her away to Gretna Green under his very nose?

Jared's grip on his glass tightened. If that were the case, he would find the couple and shackle Emily to her chambers, then proceed to thrash Fennington and every one of his aides who left their post.

"Jared, are you listening to me at all?"

"Indeed. I intend to look for her, Agatha. But I am not setting out on a wild-goose chase either."

"Goodness, do you think she was abducted?"

The disturbing thought of Monsieur Devereaux came to mind, and Jared's blood froze. Devil take it, he could no longer wait for his people to report to him. He had to go search for Emily himself.

"Has Lady Emily been seeing anybody?" he asked in a sharper voice than intended. "In the years I was not here, perhaps."

Agatha's head shot up in outrage. "Gracious, how can you dare suggest such a vile thing?"

"I am not suggesting," he said in a calmer tone. "I am merely pointing out the fact that there may be other reasons she is not here."

"I tell you, this is not like Emily." Agatha's bottom lip trembled, and sweat began to bead along her brow. "And do you know, last week the groom told me a wolf has been hunting the grounds near the village?"

Worry for Agatha's health made Jared hesitate to leave. "There are no wolves in this vicinity, Agatha. I assure you."

Her eyes blinked back tears. "You have no idea if our poor Emily is lost or perhaps even trapped by some ferocious animal." Agatha paused, her face stiffening with dread. "Good heavens, you don't suppose she ventured into that wretched maze?"

Jared's mind jerked at the thought of Emily ensnared in the tangled vines and he felt a sinking dread. "The very devil, Agatha. That stupid maze should have been done with long ago."

Watery eyes stared back at him in horror. "What if that wolf . . ." Agatha's words drifted into nothingness as she blinked again, putting a hand to her ample breasts.

"There is no wolf," he repeated, even though Devereaux and Fennington instantly came to mind.

"Do you really think so? Emily has always adored her walks about Hemmingly."

Jared lifted his aunt's trembling hand and kissed it. "I will find her, never fear." He brought Agatha a glass of brandy and told her to drink it. "But you must promise me, you won't worry. Trust me on this. You of all people know who I am."

She gave him a reluctant smile. "I know I'm acting like a wretched old ninny, worrying about her." She tried to laugh. "Of course, there is always Gretna Green. She does have a large dowry, you know."

Jared hid his grimace as thunder clapped overhead. He brushed his knuckles against his aunt's cool cheek.

"I'm certain Lady Emily has taken shelter somewhere. She is not an idiot."

And for her sake, she best not have run off with that

Fennington fellow, because if she dared to do so under Jared's protection, it would be more than Roderick's wrath she would be facing, it would be his, and the lady would not be able to sit for a week.

Jared strode toward the hallway, his Hessian boots brushing briskly against the rug. He flattened his lips, sounding a shrill whistle for Nigel.

The dog immediately appeared beside him.

He shot a quick glance toward his aunt falling back against the sofa cushions. A tight knot twisted in his gut. Perhaps something had happened to Emily. Perhaps she had fled because of him. He had been the cause of her pain once before. He would never forgive himself if he were the cause of her pain again.

Emily was most truly and decidedly lost. Her slippers crunched against the muddy pathway as the boom of thunder rumbled in her ears. The eerie whistle of the wind and the spattering of rain were ceaseless.

How long had she been in this absurd maze? Two hours? Three? She had lost all track of time since she had heard Nigel's whimpers. Yet the dog was nowhere to be found. She imagined the worst, thinking Nigel hurt and bleeding, gasping for his last breath, all because she had forced him into the maze.

She shivered, crossing her arms over her chest and sought temporary shelter under a nest of gnarled evergreens. A sliver of sunlight peeked through the slits of the vine-covered roof above her. A mouse scurried across her feet, and she closed her eyes, allowing a shaky, but half-amused breath. She fought to hold herself upright, but her knees began to wobble.

She wondered if anyone knew she had left the house.

For once she could almost agree with her brothers, she needed a protector. Her impulsiveness always seemed to earn her more trouble than she bargained for. Was not the scar on her back evidence enough?

However, secretly working for Whitehall was something she never regretted. As Silver Fox, when she had gained access to a confidential missive from a double agent giving away the location of Black Wolf, she had realized how important her position in the agency had been. Though she had escaped that night with the missive hidden in her cloak, she would never be able to forget the ball burning into her flesh. The old wound was a ghastly reminder of how close she had come to death that day, and she was determined that a tiresome maze was not going to best her either.

She began to feel her feet going numb and wiggled her toes. She should have worn her boots, but she had no idea she would be chasing a monstrous dog all afternoon. Moreover, her light muslin gown did little to offer her protection against the freezing cold clawing into her bones.

"Nigel?" she called for the hundredth time. "Nigel, sweeting, please answer me." Nothing but the rustle of the trees and the shifting vines.

Fat, cool raindrops plopped onto her nose, breaking through her brief sanctuary. Her lips quivered. Surely she had been in worse scrapes before, had she not?

She stepped deeper into the trees as the rain continued to hammer against the maze. Branches scratched her back and she squirmed into another position, falling into a crouched pose, trying to decide which trail would lead her back to Hemmingly.

"Nigel?" she whispered, feeling miserable. "Where are you, boy?"

The sound of treaded earth met her ears. Her heart banged against her chest. "Nigel?"

"Lady Emily."

Jared? The baritone voice slammed into Emily's senses like a ball of ice, shocking her. Before she could do more than turn around, a powerful hand pulled her to her feet, and she found herself gazing into a pair of cool amber eyes.

"What the devil are you doing here by yourself?" he asked harshly.

She blinked. What was *she* doing there?

With a muttered oath, he whipped off his dark cloak and placed it about her shoulders, not waiting for an answer. She shivered at his touch, pressing her lips together in both anger and relief.

He towered over her like some Viking king. Biscuit-colored breeches clung to muscular thighs, and with a pair of tanned hands resting on his tapered hips, he appeared more menacing than Roderick when he found Mr. Fennington in her bedchambers.

She swallowed, tightening her hold on the cloak. "Th-thank you."

"You're cold." He leaned over, his hand innocently brushing her cheek as he fastened the clip about her throat while mumbling something about infernal gowns.

His warm breath whispered along her neck, and Emily wanted to fall into his safe embrace, seeking the comfort she remembered so vividly. She wanted to ask him why he had left her, why he had broken her heart, but the iciness in his voice brought her back to earth.

"Traipsing into this maze was a stupid thing to do, madam."

Emily knew he was right. It was stupid. But she refused to let him make her feel like a fool again. "Your dog was the one who led me here," she countered back.

His cool, assessing gaze cautioned her not to say another word. "My dog, madam, is the one who found you."

Her eyes widened in doubt. "Nigel?"

The culprit gave a sudden bark, and Emily flinched.

Nigel appeared around the corner, his chocolate brown eyes ogling her as if daring her to dismiss his heroic actions of coming to her aid. She narrowed her gaze on the traitor. The beast! He was wagging that innocent brown tail, looking as sinless as an angel from heaven. It was insufferable!

"Agatha is beside herself," Jared said abruptly. "It would behoove you to take care next time you decide to venture on a little escapade like this again. She does not need a simpering miss to cause her a bout of apoplexy."

Emily raised her chin. Agatha was about the most robust lady she knew in all of England. Apoplexy indeed. "Forgive me, my lord. How careless of me to put you out. You, of course, have much better things to do than search for such an ungrateful busybody as me."

To her astonishment, his lips curled into a beguiling smile, sending more warmth to Emily's bones than the borrowed cloak. "Independent little piece of baggage, aren't you? What happened while I was gone?"

"You happened," she said, not able to keep back the pain in her voice. His eyes darkened dangerously, but feeling like she did now, she had no patience left with either him or Nigel.

"You left me, sir. You lied to me. Ha. You must have thought me such an addlepated miss to have fallen for the oldest ploy in the world. You led an innocent young girl on a fool's errand and had a good laugh, did you not?"

His jaw clenched, his eyes narrowed, sending a shiver of excitement down her spine. Why, she had no idea.

Without warning, he grabbed hold of her shoulders and scowled. "I did not laugh."

A jolt of awareness shot straight to her heart.

"Nevertheless," she looked at his hands, then back to the hard lines bracketing his lips, her face trying to mask the tumultuous emotions swirling in her soul. "Y-you, sir, are no gentleman."

He released her then, and for an instant, his eyes studied her, and she thought for a bizarre moment that the man was going to kiss her. Impossible. The cold must have seeped into her brain, because for a moment, she wanted to kiss him back.

Without another word, he took hold of her elbow and escorted her swiftly through the maze, with the treacherous Nigel leading the way.

Chapter Five

Where was that dratted book?

The previous evening Emily had seen Nigel sniffing about the drawing room, and that was exactly where she found herself this morning. She was lifting pillows from the sofa, yanking curtains from their holdbacks, and hoisting skirts from the wing chairs.

Sleep had not come easy for her. Her back ached, and Jared's looming presence at Hemmingly unnerved her to no end. But she would die before she let him know how much that book meant to her.

For a long time she had told herself that Felicia Fairlow had coerced him into the marriage. Yet when there were no letters from him those first few weeks, she began to wonder. And when she visited Hemmingly and met Jane, only to discover that Jared had kept his guardianship of Jane a secret to her, did she begin to believe that he could be capable of deceit.

The light tap of footsteps jerked Emily from her crawling position. She abruptly rose and turned to peer out the window, acting as if nothing were wrong.

Jane strode into the room, her blond hair curling daintily around a heart-shaped face, her concerned gaze focusing on Emily. "Morning, dear. We missed you at breakfast. Are you feeling better?"

Emily smiled warmly. Jane was one of her dearest

friends. "Good morning, and yes, I am feeling much better, thank you."

They talked of their trip to the vicarage and how Emily got lost in the maze. Emily laughed and made light of the situation, purposely avoiding any comments about Jane's arrogant guardian and his odious dog. Eventually, Jane pulled out her needlepoint and took a seat by the hearth while Emily began to write a letter to her mother. After a few minutes Emily casually asked Jane if she had seen her book anywhere.

Jane looked up. "Wordsworth? You were reading it yesterday, on your morning stroll, were you not? Perhaps you left it in your bedchambers."

"Well, I did have it yesterday, but somehow I misplaced it." Emily gazed out the window, her brows furrowing into a stern "V." For there was Nigel romping about the grounds with *her book* in *his mouth*. The knave!

"What do you see?" Jane asked, rising from her place beside the hearth, starting to move toward the window.

"Oh, nothing," Emily said, waving her hand and laughing. "So silly of me. I just remembered I must have left it on my nightstand after all."

She hated to lie to Jane, but her pride was about all she had left at the moment, especially since Nigel had just disappeared from view like the thief that he was.

"Are you certain?" Jane asked, taking her seat. "Perhaps if you asked one of the servants to check for you."

"No, no, no. It must be there. I'm just a silly widgeon this morning, Jane. You know how I am when I miss my morning walk."

Jane lifted a delicate brow in Emily's direction. "Dearest, you must not exert yourself after yesterday."

"Ah, there you are girls." Agatha's voice bounced off the walls as she strode into the room, her parasol close to her side. "La, this is to be a grand day. There's a fair in the village, and we are all going to join in the festivities. What say you to that?"

Jane smiled, dropping her needlepoint. "A fair?"

"Yes, and we are all going to make a day of it. There

will be jugglers, musicians, flame throwers. Bakers and their wares. And, oh, those meat pies are simply my favorite!"

Agatha paused and turned a concerned gaze upon Emily. "If you are still feeling under the weather, my dear, I certainly would understand. Indeed, I thought you would still be abed. You missed breakfast. And just the thought of you lost in that nasty maze makes me cringe." Tears filled the older woman's eyes. "I declare, I should have done away with it years ago. Forgive me, child."

"Oh, no," Emily said. "It was an enlightening experience, Agatha. I am quite fine."

The older lady squeezed Emily's shoulders in an affectionate hug. "I am so grateful that dear Nigel was here to find you. He is the most magnificent of God's creatures, is he not?"

"Magnificent." Emily forced a smile on her lips. Magnificent fraud!

At that moment Nigel peeked into the room, then disappeared into the hall. Drat that dog!

"Emily," Jane said, twirling around. "A fair! Goodness, I have not attended one since I was ten."

Emily smiled, but her thoughts were on her book. She decided that staying home would be best.

"I heard my nephew was a bit harsh yesterday," Agatha said, "and I apologize. He was not always that way."

"But he has much to do with his tenants, Aunt Agatha," Jane said lovingly. "He is quite busy with his new earldom, you know."

Emily was saved from making a reply when Agatha answered. "And he will be busy escorting us to the fair later this afternoon as well."

Escorting them? Emily was suddenly anxious to avoid the earl at all costs. "Perhaps I should stay home. I fear yesterday did take a toll on me, and I would not want to ruin your day if I came along."

Jane frowned, her blue eyes shadowed with sympathy. "Then you must rest, dearest, if you need to, but we won't enjoy the fair knowing you will be at home."

Agatha sighed. "Indeed, we will not. No, we will stay home with you, Emily."

"Yes," Jane said. "We will stay here."

Emily cringed at the sacrifice they were making for her, and she could not let Jane miss out on something that would give her friend such happiness. "Perhaps the fresh air will do me some good after all," she said, smiling.

But she promised herself that before she departed for the village, she would retrieve that book from Nigel and put it in a safe place before it fell into Jared's hands.

Jane's blue eyes sparkled like that of a child's on Christmas morning. "Are you quite certain?"

Emily nodded, knowing that there was no way of avoiding the earl while she resided at Hemmingly, but she could make an effort to distance herself from him. It was only the carriage ride that might cause her undue embarrassment, being so close to the man, but she was determined to show him that he meant nothing to her anymore. Nothing at all.

Agatha took a seat on the sofa. "There, that is settled, and Jared will escort us to the fair."

"I will do what?"

Emily stiffened when Lord Stonebridge stepped into the room. His brown riding coat and fawn-colored breeches molded to his athletic frame, making her all too aware of his commanding presence—a presence that would not be easy to ignore.

Dark amber eyes took a swift accounting of her person, and Emily's face tingled with heat. Her vulnerability to this man vexed her to no end.

Agatha raised her parasol, obviously missing the encounter. "Jared, you are a delightfully obedient boy coming so soon after I called for you." She took in his riding boots and gloves and shook her head. "You won't have much time to ride, but do as you wish, only I believe I have changed my mind, we will be leaving for the fair in one hour. And pray, do not keep us waiting."

One wretched hour!

It was not enough time. After Emily changed her

clothes for the fair, she realized she had barely ten minutes at most to retrieve her book before *Jared* returned from riding, and she knew exactly where that book was, too. In Jared's bedchamber—with the devious Nigel. The hateful creature had padded past her only a minute ago, easing his way past Jared's open door, which had obviously been left ajar after the morning cleaning.

Taking a deep breath, Emily scurried into the hall like a thief in the night, her pale yellow gown flapping against her legs. She bit her lips and gave a swift glance up and down the corridor. The scent of fresh lemon wove through the air as she rapped her knuckles lightly against Jared's bedchamber door. Her heart thudded against her chest.

No answer. Thank heaven.

She slid into the room and carefully closed the door behind her. Pressing her back against the wall, she held her breath, her gaze traveling to the small fire that burned in the hearth. After a few wary seconds, she breathed a sigh of relief.

Now, where was that wretched beast?

Jared sat on the window seat at the far end of his bedchambers, half-hidden behind folds of the light blue curtains that draped across the panes of glass behind him. He rubbed a hand across Nigel's back while the dog curled up in a lump beside him.

With one boot raised against a footstool, Jared balanced the little black book of Wordsworth's poems Nigel had been slopping in his mouth but a minute ago. Jared intended to return the book to Emily, but found himself thumbing over the well-worn pages, recalling his blissful days in Hyde Park and his dances at Almack's with the raven-haired beauty by his side.

But that innocent girl he had loved so long ago had changed into a stubborn, independent woman that could lure any man into her web of desire with a mere flash of those violet-blue eyes. This Lady Emily who veiled herself with a will as strong as iron and a tongue as sharp as a knife was even more tempting than the one he had known before. Still, he could have wrung her slender white neck for trekking into that maze without a guide, especially in such inclement weather.

He closed his eyes and leaned his head against the cool windowpane. He wanted Emily more than he had ever wanted a woman in his life, and yet he could never have her. Now they were two totally different people with a past too painful to forget. Their love had died an agonizing death three years ago and so had their future.

"Blast it, Nigel, what the devil am I going to do?"

The next moment there was a scratch upon his door. Before Jared could respond, the door creaked open. Nigel lifted his head and wagged his tail.

Must be the maid, Jared thought, resting back against the window, wondering how long it would take Roderick to find a decent husband for Emily. The notion of another man touching her made his blood run cold. But he had no right to her now. Honor demanded he guard her, and she hated him anyway. Too much time had passed. Too much had happened. Love was not for him. There was no going back. Besides, he was close to announcing his engagement. He could not hurt Emily again.

Soft footsteps treaded lightly across the floor, and Jared flinched when Nigel jumped from the ledge, obviously curious about the maid.

"Oh, Nigel, it's you. I wondered where you had gone, you silly dog."

Jared blinked in awe. What the blazes was Emily doing in *his* bedchambers?

"Now, Nigel, dearest, you must be very quiet for Emily. Can you do that, sweeting?"

Sweeting? No one ever called his dog sweeting and lived to tell about it, and why the blazes was Nigel not barking at the intruder, though lovely she may be?

"I need to look through a few things here, Nigel. Of course, if you could possibly see to helping me, I would consider it a wondrous favor. And don't look at me like some angel from heaven, you know exactly what I'm talking about."

Jared froze, afraid to breathe. Why his dog would allow some simpering miss to rummage through his chambers like a French spy was beyond him. The very idea of Nigel turning traitor rattled his senses.

"I cannot seem to find it anywhere, Nigel. Aha. Did you put it under the bed?"

What was she about now?

Jared dared to glimpse from behind the curtain, swallowing the amusement that bubbled up in his throat when he saw two dainty slippers peeking beneath his Tudor-style bed. What was she doing under there? Even Nigel had joined the lady in the precarious position.

Jared smiled as Nigel's tail wagged against Lady Emily's gown. The rustling of yellow muslin and dog fur sent the bed frame shaking as if it were a ship sailing on the high seas.

"Oh, I beg you, Nigel, do have a care. I have but a few minutes to find it. Where is that dratted book? Come now, sweeting, show Emily where it is."

Realization finally dawned. So, the little spitfire came back for her book, did she? Smiling devilishly, Jared settled the book on the window seat and narrowed his gaze on two slender legs wiggling up and down like a scissors beneath his bed.

How long Jared sat there watching the maddening scene was anyone's guess, but what he did know was the way his blood surged through his veins. His head pounded like thunder. His hands clenched at his sides. All five senses went into alert mode. Emily was too comely by far to be caught beneath his bed. And confound the woman, he wanted her! If Roderick could pick his brain now, the duke would kill him.

Nigel snarled and padded his paws against the lady's gown.

Jared's lips parted in amusement at Emily's tenacity to continue to battle with his dog while she was still trapped beneath the bed.

"Nigel, please!"

At that moment Jared envied Nigel. Lucky chap.

Jared's eyes trailed up a well-turned calf, and a shudder passed through him. Devil take it! He needed Emily out of there before he went mad or did something he would regret.

Without another thought, he bounded off his seat, threw the book onto his bed, grabbed hold of two tiny feet, and pulled.

"Whatever could be keeping Emily and Jared?" Agatha asked, turning to Jane. "Filmore mentioned that Jared returned from his ride a half hour ago."

Jane, dressed in a smart peach gown, grabbed her matching reticule from the sofa. "Strange, and Emily is always on time. For both of them to be late . . ." Her lips puckered.

"Both of them late, indeed." The older lady pulled on her white gloves and poked her head outside the drawing room doors, glancing up the stairs.

Jane's eyes sparkled with mischief. "Mercy. Do you dare think—"

"Fustian, child!" Agatha shook her head and grabbed her parasol as she walked briskly toward the stairs. "How could you even think such a thing, my dear. And when the duchess comes to visit, you must keep thoughts like that to yourself."

"Emily's mother is coming here?"

"Yes, I received a letter from her the same day Emily arrived. She wishes to surprise the girl. I imagine she will show herself in a few days. So, mind your tongue."

Jane picked up her skirts and followed, her delicate brows raised in an impish grin. "I only thought that Emily and Cousin Jared . . . well, goodness knows, anything's possible."

"At this point, the duchess does not need to hear something like that, Jane. Put those thoughts right out of your mind. Besides, our distinguished *Lord Stonebridge* is practically engaged to a Miss Susan Wimble, and that is that."

Jane stopped in the hallway. "Gracious, not *that* woman?"

Agatha nodded sadly. "Unfortunate to be sure. I am

not happy about it either. But that is neither here nor there. The lady is your guardian's business, and I am sorry for mentioning it. You are not to say a thing. Do you hear?"

Jane's lips compressed into a grim line. "Yes, but I do not have to like it."

"No, you do not," Agatha said, continuing her march up the stairs, her parasol tapping each step.

"But drat, Agatha, how can he marry such a woman?"

"To tell you the truth, Jane, it is beyond my comprehension entirely."

Nigel's playful bark drifted down the stairs.

"Sounds like trouble." Jane's lips curved into a smile as they hastened up the steps. "Whatever do you think is going on up there?"

Agatha stopped and turned toward her niece. "Do not let your imagination get away with you, Jane. It may lead to dire consequences someday."

Jane's entire face broke into a mischievous smile. "I can honestly say, Aunt, that it is not my imagination I am worried about."

Emily let out a gasp of shock when she was jerked from beneath the bed, turned on her back like a pig on a spit, and thrown faceup, the rug brushing up beneath her.

Every muscle in her body stiffened at the sight of Jared's powerful body hovering over her. He smelled of horses and hay. His dark hair hung over one eye while his arms, clad only in a linen shirt with rolled-up sleeves, straddled each side of her head. She avoided his amber gaze and fixed her eyes on the open neck of his shirt. It was an admirable try, but it did nothing to rid her of her wayward thoughts or her body's treacherous reaction. The man was devilishly handsome.

A hot flush began working its way up her neck. She had seen her brothers run around half-dressed before, but this man was not her brother. He looked magnificent, clad only in his breeches and shirt, but it was more than that. She realized with a start that she still loved this scoundrel.

"Looking for something, *sweeting*?"

Like the jerk of a carriage coming to an abrupt stop, reality jarred her heart back into place. She lifted her chin with all the dignity she could muster in such a feeble position, glad of the shadows that hid the warmth in her cheeks. Insufferable man. It was obvious he had been watching every minute of her disgrace with his dog beneath that confounded bed.

"Indeed, I am looking for a book I lost," she said sharply.

He lifted his hand, and she flinched.

His mouth dipped into a frown. "The devil, Emily. I am not going to strike you, but heaven knows I should." He stared at her, leaning closer, his eyes intent on her lips. Tension sparked between them like lightning in a storm.

"Would you perchance be searching for this?" He pushed the book of Wordsworth in her face.

Emily snatched it from his hand.

"Your dog stole it," she said accusingly, her eyes frozen on his sinfully attractive face.

"Nigel?" He laughed, breaking the spell. "Why would my dog want a book of love poems?"

Emily felt as if he had slapped her. Had this man ever loved her? Of course not. How long would it take her to understand the signs of a rogue? Her own brothers took on the same attitude toward women as well.

"Take it, then. I don't need it either." She shoved the book into his face and squirmed from beneath his hold. When her hands pushed against his broad chest, a deep ache began to grow in her heart, pushing its way up her throat, almost stopping her from breathing. He had never loved her.

Dropping the book, Jared grabbed her by the shoulders and peered into her eyes, keeping her pinned beneath him. The tension mounted between them, making her extremely conscious of the magnetic power coiled beneath his steadfast gaze. She felt the warmth of his hands searing every nerve in her body. He opened his mouth to speak, but answered by lowering his face and crushing his lips to hers. To her surprise, the kiss immediately turned tender, his mouth breathing life back into her scarred heart.

He pulled back, his intense gaze becoming a soft caress.

Emily found herself limp in his arms, too surprised to speak. Did he still love her? The question no sooner popped into her mind than he spoke.

"Will you ever forgive me, Em?"

Emily stiffened. Forgive him? Was his kiss supposed to make everything better? What a fool she had been. An utter fool! She had almost said something stupid, almost fallen into his trap again. When would she learn?

"You want me to forgive you?" she asked with a cynical smile. "For lying to me in that book? Or are you speaking in regard to your little jest of making me look like a fool three years ago. Or is it the kiss you just stole?"

A second passed and he threw his head back and laughed, releasing her.

Dumbfounded at his reaction, Emily sat up, brushing her skirt back into place. "And what exactly do you find so hilarious, sir?"

"You, sweetheart. You."

The endearment crushed her heart. Why was he doing this to her?

He lifted her chin with his finger, the touch blazing a path straight down to her toes. "You are too beautiful and independent to be alone all your life. Too much passion to be wasted, my dear."

He frowned then, dropping his finger as if he had been burned, and in one fluid motion, he pulled her upward and stepped away. She felt as if a sheet of ice had fallen from the ceiling, separating them.

A brittle smile crossed his face. "I hope your brothers find someone worthy of you."

Emily drew back in horror. How had he knowledge of her brothers' plans unless he was involved? The situation finally became all too clear. "Pray then, you are to guard me until Roderick returns, are you not?"

He paled, looking as guilty as Fennington had standing in her bedchambers. "Guard you? What ever gave you that absurd notion?"

Nigel stood in the corner and barked as the tone of their voices intensified.

"Tell me the truth this time." Emily could not hide the tremor when she spoke. "I am your prisoner, am I not?"

In one quick stride he was beside her, slipping a strong hand in hers. "Listen, Em. It's not like that at all. Your brothers have obligations—"

"Obligations?" She jerked back. "I am up to my eyeballs with that word. Do not deceive me a second time. And you have no right to call me, Em. I am Lady Emily to you."

He grabbed her shoulders roughly. "You don't understand. I owed Roderick a favor—"

"So, now I am a favor?"

She turned quickly and tripped on the rug, stumbling backward, but not before a strong hand whipped around her waist in a steel grip, holding her to him, pressing her back intimately against his chest. She closed her eyes, conscious of his warm breath against her neck.

"Honor demanded I comply with your brother's wishes," he said in a husky whisper. "You have no understanding how difficult this is for me."

"Difficult?" Tears clogged her throat. "Y-you are the one being difficult." She struggled for him to release her, bending at her waist, feeling herself being lifted off the floor, her legs dangling in midair.

"Confound it, woman, be reasonable here."

"What is the meaning of this?" Agatha's voice hit Emily like a blow to her stomach.

"Emily," Jane screeched, standing at the door, staring at her guardian holding her friend like an opera dancer—after hours. "Are you . . . ill?"

Emily felt Jared stiffen. He cleared his throat, placing Emily's feet safely on the rug beneath them. Emily straightened out her gown, her love for Jared dying off like the bloom of a dried flower. Dead and gone. She was nothing to him but a friend's sister. Owing a favor to Roderick because of his insufferable honor!

"This can all be explained, Agatha," Jared replied with a halfsmile. "This may appear . . . well, the devil . . . this is all a silly misunderstanding."

"Yes, a misunderstanding," Emily offered helplessly, avoiding Jared's impenetrable gaze.

Agatha stood waiting at the door, her lips pressed together, one hand clenched at her side, the other hand stomping her black parasol against the floor as if it were a bayonet. "Indeed, Jared. I am waiting for an explanation."

At that precise moment Nigel decided to slink past the agitated entourage and out the door. "Traitor," Jared murmured to his dog. Emily almost repeated the same word herself.

"I am waiting," Agatha snapped.

Jared splayed his hands, palms up in the air.

"I was searching for my book," Emily broke in, "and silly me, I suddenly recalled that Lord Stonebridge had borrowed it. So, of course, I came into his chambers to search for it."

"Of course." Agatha narrowed her eyes on Emily, then slowly shifted them toward Jared. "A young lady prancing into a gentleman's bedchambers is so very reasonable, I have no notion why I should ever have asked."

Emily's eyes widened as she realized that Agatha was placing the entire blame on Jared—no Lord Stonebridge, he was no longer Jared to her.

"Agatha, this is preposterous. You must see, had I known Lord Stonebridge was in here, I never would . . . well, I mean to say, he never . . . uh, we never . . ."

"*Never mind*," the man beside her ground out. "Would you be so kind as to let me explain?"

Raw pain flickered in Emily's heart. Whatever slender thread had been between them was broken forever.

It took all of five minutes before the rest of the story

came out and Jane was sent downstairs with Emily, who had snatched her book from the floor, stuffing it between the folds of her skirt. Agatha and Jared conveyed that they would be coming shortly. The foursome would then attend the fair in the village as planned.

Jared paced the floor of his bedchambers taking in the scent of rose water and lavender that clung to his memory like the aftermath of a spring rain.

Blast it to pieces! Emily was in his blood as much as she had been three years ago. He had been fond of Felicia, but Emily had been the light of his life. Yet he knew if she were ever told the truth, she would always hate him for not confronting her father, and in essence, he had to admit he hated himself as well. Emily deserved better. She deserved a man her brothers chose for her. She deserved the best.

His mouth plunged into a deep, angry frown when he caught his aunt scowling at him. "Believe me, there was nothing to it."

Agatha sighed. "I believe you."

He blinked. "You do?"

"Of course, I do."

Agatha leaned against the window seat, resting her parasol on one of the beige pillows bunched in the corner. "Why would you want anything to do with Lady Emily? She is far too independent for any man of your caliber. Not that I do not have a great affection for the girl. I do. I do. But her independence is not an asset in a wife, is it, my boy?"

Jared remained silent. For some reason, Emily's independence was an asset he found particularly attractive.

Agatha fingered her gown. "La, you must know her brothers would never approve of you anyway."

Jared's brows snapped together. To think that Emily's family would dare turn him down again. Not that he would ask them and not that he was afraid of Roderick. No indeed.

Ignoring his aunt's jibes, he walked over to his chair where his waistcoat and jacket had been laid out. "And pray tell, why would Lady Emily's brothers never approve of me?"

"You are a gambler, my boy. A drinker." Agatha paused as if reflecting over her choice of words and lowered her voice, "A man about town."

Jared clenched his teeth, annoyed at the thought of Emily knowing about his past, and especially annoyed at the way Agatha was making him feel. He distinctly recalled Agatha's information about the Black Wolf and wondered what other secrets she knew about him, or his daughter. "Pray then, what knowledge have you about my life on the Continent the past few years, since you seem to know everything else about me?"

A shadow of irritation flickered across Agatha's face, followed instantly by an innocent blink of her eyes. "My, did I say the Continent?"

"No, however the meaning was quite clear."

Agatha tilted her gaze out the window. "You do realize if Emily's brothers ever discovered that you had been found in a compromising position with her, you would be fed on a silver platter to that Little Corsican in St. Helena. But, of course, if you loved the lady, you would not care a fig about her brothers, would you?" She turned back to him. "Any lady, as a matter of fact."

Jared gave his bottle green waistcoat a slight pull and strode across his bedchambers. He would not be coerced into one of Agatha's lengthy discussion about his love life. He fixed his neckcloth, stood by the door, then waited for her to depart. "Are you by chance avoiding my question?"

Agatha turned and lifted her head. "I hear the young duke is a crack shot on the dueling field."

Jared grimaced. Roderick was more than a crack shot. He was the most pigheaded, hot-tempered man Jared knew beside himself. And honor demanded that Jared keep his distance from Emily, attraction or not.

"Crack shot indeed, Aunt. Let us make a day of it and forget about this little incident. What say you to that?"

Forgetting would be impossible. It was hard enough

for Jared to forget the sweetness of Emily's body when she was pressed beneath him. But the kiss had been heaven. She was no longer a seventeen-year-old girl.

Agatha strode ahead of him. "I daresay, I will forget about the matter entirely. Depend upon it."

Jared let out a small smile. Ah, she had no wish to see him killed by the duke. "Put away your worries, Aunt, I won't be meeting the duke on the dueling field. You can rest your little head about that."

"Can I?" she said, glancing over her shoulder.

The question simmered in Jared's mind all the way to the fair.

A cool breeze brought the smell of cinnamon and butter to Emily's nostrils, and her stomach growled. The fair had drawn a huge crowd in the town square. Jugglers performed their entertaining feats, and jesters had the gatherers roaring with laughter. Wagons filled with hay escorted groups of excited children on a thrilling trip back and forth to the Red Knight Inn. Food vendors with their heavenly scents of meat pies, scones, buns, and other delectables, filled the jammed alcoves surrounding the square.

Emily had barely eaten anything all day, but she would be the last one to ask the earl for a turn toward the vendor's booth nearest them. Since Agatha and Jane had insisted she stay and watch the entertainment, she was determined to wait in silence until the two ladies returned with the famous meat pies Agatha so loved. But to Emily's displeasure, that particular food was located the farthest away from them, across the square.

Staring straight ahead, Emily kept her gaze focused on the juggler tossing three red balls into the air, yet all her thoughts were on the man standing stiffly beside her. It was obvious he was not pleased after their encounter in his bedchambers, and neither was she. Dwelling on the compromising position brought an embarrassing heat to her cheeks, and that unforeseen kiss made her feel all too vulnerable to his charms.

Sliding her gray cloak off her head, she let the cool

breeze caress her face, hoping Jared would remain silent. She needed to sort her emotions, because she had no intention of letting the recent incident in his bedchambers scatter her wits like the balls bouncing in front of her.

The raucous laughter of a group of young boys filled her ears, reminding her of her brothers when they had been drinking. Inwardly she smiled. Did all men turn into such ninnies when they had their spirits?

At that moment she could not help but sense Jared's gaze on her. She glanced over her shoulder. His steely glare bore into hers, and she bit back a sharp retort. She would never have ventured into his chambers if that dog of his had any manners at all. Refusing to be drawn into an argument, she turned back to the juggler and forced herself to laugh and clap her hands along with the crowd, praying that Agatha would come along soon.

Her eyes followed the shiny red ball flying high in the air, but like her heart, it came falling to the ground with a plop. If she ever heard another Wordsworth poem again, she would curl up and die. How could he have laughed at her book? *Their book?* She would prove to him that he meant nothing to her. She was immune to him. She was.

"Agatha adores the meat pies," she said, staring ahead. "I hear Mr. Gimby comes all the way from London. His brother owns the Red Knight Inn, you know."

Jared stepped closer to her, the energy between them crackling like the sparks from a blazing fire. "You should never have come into my bedchambers. Roderick would have my head." His sharp response was nothing at all what she had expected.

She refused to flinch at the accusation in his tone. "Ah, then am I to believe honor is your main concern here?"

He turned his head, his jaw stiff as his gaze followed a man swaying on a pair of stilts. "I attended school with all your brothers."

As if that would explain everything? Emily stared blankly at the juggler, her heart erecting a wall of steel.

"What exactly did Roderick do to make you promise

to watch over me?" she asked. "Save your life?" It was meant as a sarcastic remark, but what she did not expect was the shocking answer.

"Yes, as a matter of fact, he did."

She stiffened. "I see."

"No, I don't think you do see at all. Today could have been disastrous. Blast it, Emily, if anyone but Agatha or Jane had appeared at the doorway . . ." He plowed a hand through his dark hair. "If your brothers ever suspected that you and I were seeing each other, now or even before—"

The crowd started pressing in, cutting off his comments, pushing the two closer together. Jared was crushed up against her shoulder. Emily blinked back tears. He had never loved her. It was but a game to him. His touch was almost unbearable. He said something, but his voice was drowned out as the crowd boomed with applause and laughter when the juggler stood on his head, managing four balls in the air.

When the laughter subsided, Emily tried to move away from him as she spoke. "What a horrid thought, my lord. To think that you might have been forced to marry poor little me?"

He grabbed her shoulders, spun her around, his lips curling into a dangerous scowl. "Stop it, Em. I'm no longer the man you loved. We were children then."

Emily flinched, pulling away. Her heart shook at the sound of his words. He was right. This was not the boy she had loved. In the short span of three years, he had become a man with a commanding presence that could thwart even the most powerful of men like her brothers.

He had changed, but so had she.

"I believe, my lord, that you are to guard me, and that is all. Do not flatter yourself that I was once in love with you. It was but a silly game we played, nothing more."

With perfect timing, a short, pudgy man, holding a freshly baked bun, pushed between them. The sweet smell of butter made Emily recall that she had not eaten anything for hours.

"I will not be forced into a marriage again," Jared growled, lowering his head to hers, almost touching her.

"*What* are you saying?" Had he been forced to marry Felicia?

"I mean exactly that, madam." His mouth thinned.

Emily gasped in outrage, pulling her cloak over her face. How dare he think she planned being found in his chambers? She had loved him.

Tears collected in her eyes, but she refused to let him see. She sniffed, trying to focus on the juggler passing three flaming torches back and forth to his partner, a painted lady dressed in a revealing outfit of purple and pink boa feathers. The crowd began to grow, laughing and pushing, and she was pressed from all sides. But even the grand sight of the festive woman did not uplift her mood.

"We cannot marry, Em. We were never meant to be. This very minute your brothers are finding a suitable husband for you."

She felt herself drain of color. A suitable husband indeed. Jared waited for her answer. But she said nothing. She could not face him. He would see her grief, and she could not bear to let him see the hot tears spilling down her cheeks.

The crowd blurred before her.

"Emily. You must see why this is best."

The tender sound of her name on his lips squeezed her heart, but she could say nothing. Two boys pushed her aside, battling for space to view the boa feathers and the lady who wore them. A foul-smelling woman immediately followed, elbowing her way forward, separating Emily from Jared even more.

Whether Jared was about to apologize or not, Emily did not care. Not anymore. She hated him for what he had done to her. Hated him for agreeing with her brothers' plans. Hated him for making her feel again and throwing it back in her face.

"Blast," he said harshly, "this is a becoming an unruly mob. Stay close to me or you might be trampled to death."

Emily ignored his plea as the crowd began to roar

with glee when the woman dropped the boa. From the corner of her eye she saw Jared reach out for her, but she shrugged away. A rude man who smelled of manure stepped between them.

Jared cursed, pushing the man aside. She found herself jostled back and forth like a small fish in the ocean. People stepped on her toes and pulled at her cloak, shoving her aside so they could obtain a better view. Strands of hair fell across her face, and she barely heard Jared shouting as he pushed through the frenzied crowd.

But she was numb. Too numb to care anymore. There was a dreadful squeezing inside her chest, and she found it hard to breathe. He did not love her. He had never loved her.

"Emily! Confound it . . . Emily!"

She wanted to call to him, but every fiber in her being warned against it. He would see her heart exposed like that of a wounded puppy. How droll for him to be her protector until her brothers found a suitable husband. She decided to ride to London immediately, relieving herself of his presence.

"Emily," he shouted again, but she let the crowd push her farther and farther away. Her cloak was pulled to and fro, and she drifted like a boat without a sail in the sea of people.

More flaming torches seemed to be added to the juggling partners. The flames whooshed through the air with fiery streaks of red, snapping small sparks into the crowd.

"Add another torch!" someone cried.

"Light the purple boa!"

The clamor of the people hammered into Emily's ears. A hard shove sent her flying into another man. Her head snapped back, and she thought she saw Jared coming toward her. Suddenly, awakened to the danger surrounding her, she fell to the ground in pain, trying to fend off the people above her. Before she could shout for help, there was a sharp jab to her stomach.

And then it happened. The most frightening word she would ever hear in an already maddened crowd. *"Fire!"*

Chapter Six

Miss Agatha Appleby's pink-and-white-striped bonnet bobbed up and down as she took a seat on a small barrel of ale located inside one of the vendors' tents. She unbuttoned her matching cloak, grabbed the mug beside her, and bent down, siphoning a bit of the brew to replace what she had already drunk.

"I daresay, Jane"—she picked up a steaming meat pie with her free hand and took a bite—"is this not the most delightful pie you have ever had?"

Garbed in a black velvet cloak, Jane leaned against a tent pole, her lips twisting into a pleased smile. "You say those exact words about every meat pie, Aunt Agatha. I recall when my parents brought me to my last fair. I will never forget the sweet scent of hot cross buns." A forlorn look crossed her face, and she shook her head. "Speaking of food, Emily must be famished."

"Fustian, child. The girl is fine." Agatha took another bite of her meat pie. "Believe me, those two children need to work out their differences."

Jane pushed off the pole and laughed. "I would not call Cousin Jared a child."

Agatha slowly raised her head, her eyebrows lifting suggestively. "And neither is our Emily, dear."

Jane's eyes went wide. "You are not implying that Emily and my guardian are engaged?"

"Engaged, no. Smitten, yes."

"You think there was something to that incident today."

"No, no, my dear," Agatha replied, shaking her head. "*That* was totally innocent. But what is not innocent is Emily's eyes when she watches my nephew walk into the room."

Jane pursed her lips, surprised. "I was only making a jest about them before. He is—"

"He is a man first, Jane," Agatha said. "A man with a heart that needs softening."

"But Cousin Jared never seems to need anybody. Oh, I know he cares for me, but he is so much more reserved than the young man I knew when I was a child." Jane frowned as more people began to gather near the tent and the noisy display of the vendors grew louder.

Agatha pointed to the other side of the street near the stables. "Come, Jane. Over there. There will be less noise."

Jane grabbed the rest of the meat pies on the barrel and followed the older lady's lead across the graveled thoroughfare.

"We will be heading to Town for the Season soon." Agatha's black parasol crunched against the stones as she walked. Jane stood as the elder lady took her seat on a small wooden bench outside the stables.

"The duchess did say Emily could stay with us in London, did she not?" Jane asked.

"No, not precisely, my dear. It is her brother whom we will have to ask. On that point, I am not certain if Emily will be allowed to go with us at all."

Jane frowned, taking a seat beside Agatha. "And pray, why not? What reason would this brother of hers have to deny Emily the Season?"

"Her brother, *the duke*, my dear, is a very powerful man, and it seems that our Emily is the catch of the Season with her inheritance and her dowry. Her brothers have grand plans to find her a respectable husband of the *ton*, and believe it or not, while they are in the process of this grand feat, I do believe your guardian has been appointed Emily's protector without the lady the wiser."

"Her protector?" Jane shrieked, standing abruptly. "You mean to say her brothers have hired Cousin Jared to watch over Emily?" Jane suddenly laughed. "Goodness, Emily will be quite vexed when she uncovers the harebrained plot."

"Quite so, Jane. Quite so." The crowd was becoming more boisterous by the second, and Agatha frowned. "I am having the London townhouse refurbished, so we will be staying elsewhere, I fear. I will have to rent a house."

Jane folded her hands across her lap. "Emily's brothers must have many eligible friends for her to choose from, so perhaps it will be an interesting Season."

"I fear you did not comprehend my meaning, dear. Emily will not be choosing her husband. Her brothers have that honor."

"Her brothers?" Jane's face grew pale. "But they cannot do that. Emily should make the choice of her husband."

"Nevertheless, it seems her brothers have decided to protect her from a host of greedy suitors by choosing for her. That is the sole reason she was allowed to come to Hemmingly. It seems her suitors have gone so far as to hunt her down at Elbourne Hall."

Agatha looked suspiciously around. "And I tell you this, with the utmost confidence, Jane." She lowered her voice. "I have it straight from the duchess that one of Emily's suitors was found breaking into her bedchambers . . . through her window."

Jane clapped her hands together and bubbled with laughter. "How very romantic."

Agatha sighed. "Not when Emily's four brothers took the intruder by surprise and the gentleman in question fainted at the poor girl's feet."

"No?" Jane gasped in horror.

Agatha nodded. "Yes, indeed, my dear. So, I implore you not to bother that pretty mind of yours in defending poor Emily against her four brothers. They are powerful men, set and determined to find Emily a husband. Depend upon it, child, very few can undermine any plans those four gentlemen set out to do."

Jane's chin lifted in defiance. "Goodness, you of all people should know that I am not afraid of four men. We must help Emily this Season. It is our Christian duty. I will die before I let her brothers assign her to prison the rest of her life."

"Oh, Jane," Agatha sighed. "I fear it may be hopeless. You do not know the duke."

"It is not hopeless. I believe with Emily's help, we can forge a great alliance." Jane continued talking, but Agatha was not listening. She immediately stood, her wary gaze falling on a black glossy carriage parked on the outskirts of the village.

"What is it?" Jane asked, rising from her seat.

"My word, this is most untimely. Most untimely, indeed." The carriage door opened and Agatha grabbed her parasol. "Who would have thought *he* would show up today of all days? He must have stopped at Hemmingly. No doubt he accompanied the duchess, and she is settling in at Hemmingly as we speak."

Jane's eyes darted down the street, her eyes fixing on the black coach and four. "Who?"

"Goodness, Jane. That is the Duke of Elbourne's crest. I believe its owner has come to call."

Jane's eyes constricted into two slits of rage. "You mean the knave who is treating our dear Emily as if this were the Middle Ages and she were mere chattel?"

"Hold your tongue, my girl."

A tall, broad-shouldered gentleman, dressed in a well-fitted blue jacket, dark brown pantaloons, and a pair of freshly polished Hessians, strode in their direction.

"That is no ordinary gentleman, Jane. He must not be agitated on Emily's behalf. There are other ways around situations such as these."

Jane's lips thinned. "Indeed there are."

Agatha welcomed the duke and made the introductions. "Miss Greenwell, His Grace, Lord Elbourne, Emily's brother."

Jane glanced up, put out her white-gloved hand, and gave the man a smile that would melt the most unyielding of kings.

The handsome duke inclined his dark head, grinned, and took her hand, bringing it to within an inch of his lips. "Delighted to make your acquaintance, Miss Greenwell."

Jane was not a vain lady, but she knew her blue eyes and dark lashes were some of her better features, and she batted her eyelids like butterfly wings, sending the duke's eyebrows arching with interest as she pulled her hand back to her side.

"Delighted?" Jane gave him her sweetest, most innocent smile. "I fear I cannot say the same, Your Grace, since you are the odious barbarian who is to put our dear Emily into prison."

The crowd swarmed around the town square. Cheers and curses filled the air as the juggler tossed the fire back and forth to his scantily clad partner.

Jared looked at the back of Emily's head and swallowed hard, trying to manage a feeble excuse, anything to stop her from crying. He had acted in the most cowardly manner a gentleman could act. What reasoning had taken hold of his senses the past few minutes when he'd told her he had no wish to be coerced into a marriage with her? Did he believe making Emily hate him would change their past? He never deserved her, and proof of that was in the woman's tears that she so desperately tried to hide.

A sudden uneasiness swept through him when he noticed the size of the unruly crowd crushing in on them. "Emily." His plea was for naught when she took a step to her left. "Emily! Confound it!" The blasted female was avoiding him.

His heart began to pound as he shoved through the crowd, trying to keep her head in his line of sight. "Out of my way! Here now, move aside! Let me through!"

But the more he pushed, the farther she fell from view. Alarm raced through him when he thought he saw her cloak torn from her person. Devil take it, some protector he was!

"Emily!" He continued to call her name, but could no longer see her. He glanced at the circle of entertainment and grew more alarmed. Sparks flew into the crowd and struck near the haystacks at the sides of the street. Idiotic fools. Could they not see that the entire place would go up in smoke if any one of the torches were thrown the wrong way?

"Em! Answer me!" The only answer he received made his stomach knot with fear.

"Fire!" someone cried, and all hell broke loose.

Roderick raised his right brow and glared at Jane. "Why, pray tell, would I want to put my sister in prison, madam?"

Jane folded her arms across her velvet cloak and glared back. *"You, Your Grace,* are a monster."

Agatha gave Jane a nervous smile and stood between her and the grim-faced duke. "My, my, Your Grace, I had no idea you were coming to visit today. Lady Emily is taking in the jugglers over there." She pointed her parasol in the direction of the riotous crowd beyond.

Roderick shifted his interested gaze from Jane to the mob. He muttered an oath, his eyes simmering with anger. "Do not tell me that Emily is in that gathering of whooping men?"

Agatha frowned as she took in the frenzied movement of the crowd. "I assure you, it was not like that minutes ago. Jared is with her."

"She might have been better off with Fennington," he said, growling.

"Now, now," Agatha called, scurrying behind him as he strode toward the melee. "I assure you, Emily is in good hands."

Roderick stopped and turned on his heels, his jaw taut, his eyes black. *"Good hands?"*

Agatha stared at the duke. "A poor choice of words perhaps."

The mad roar of the panicking crowd stopped Roderick from saying any more. All three looked up to see the billowing smoke.

"Fire!" Jane screamed.

"Move!" Roderick grabbed both ladies by their elbows and quickly shoved them out of harm's way toward his carriage.

"But Emily's in there somewhere," Jane said in horror as Roderick dragged her across the street. Gravel and dirt kicked up in their wake.

"You have no need to worry about your sister," Agatha protested with a frown as she was lifted by the duke and placed inside his carriage. "I am certain Jared is with her. He would never leave her."

"Certain is not good enough, Agatha," Roderick growled. "She may be killed in that hellish bedlam."

"What about my carriage and my footmen?" Agatha asked, clearly shaken by the strange turn of events.

"Leave them to me," he said quickly, and spun around to deposit Jane as well.

But to his shock, Miss Jane Greenwell had disappeared. His keen gaze darted about the street, and he cursed. The harebrained female was hastily running back toward the frenzied crowd, her velvet cloak billowing like a flag to be burned.

"Get back here, woman!"

Jane glanced over her shoulder, her head lifted in haughty disdain. "Do not dictate to me, Your Grace. Pray, I will find Emily faster than you can give an order."

Roderick's shoulders strained against his jacket as he started for her. In six quick strides he grabbed her around the waist and hauled her back to his carriage. Ranting and raving, Jane let out a gasp of surprise when she was dislodged onto the floorboard of his carriage with a gigantic thud.

"I beg your pardon!" she uttered, pushing herself back up on her elbows.

Roderick glanced over her with an indolent eye. "You may beg my pardon another time, Miss Greenwell. Another time, indeed." He gave her no time to respond as he clapped the door closed and yelled to the driver, "Get a move on, man!"

Jared's heart jumped out of his chest when he found her in a crumpled heap, lying against a carriage wheel in a small alleyway.

"Emily," he murmured, sweeping her limp body into his arms.

"Em, speak to me." He slid a gentle hand across her scratched face, pushing aside her matted hair.

"Dear, sweet, Em." He rested his cheek against hers, his chest tightening with emotion. She moved slightly, and he lifted his gaze, surprised to find two violet eyes glaring at him. His cruel words instantly came back to him. *I will not be forced into a marriage again.*

But was this not what he wanted? For her to hate him so he would feel free? A loathing distaste pierced him like a sword to his soul. No, he realized, he did not want this at all.

"Em, don't look at me that way, I beg you."

"Go away," she rasped, closing her eyes and turning her head. "Go . . . away."

He rubbed the pad of his thumb across a single tear that fell from her dark lashes. Holding her like this, she seemed more beautiful to him than ever.

He pulled her to a safer spot between the inn and the bookseller's. Squatting, he rested her slim body against his and took off his jacket for a blanket as he lay her on the ground, checking for broken bones.

"Sorry, sweetheart, I have to do this." He could hear her light gasp as he brushed his fingers against her skin now dotted with ashes and soot. She closed her eyes, seemingly exhausted.

Let her be all right. Please, God. Let her be all right.

His heart raced as he touched her arms, her legs, slowly turning her over to check for any cuts. A surge of protectiveness flowed through his veins. Whatever had he been thinking when he censured her actions in his bedchambers? He had been delighted when he had held her beneath him. Yet tasting her lips again had almost sealed his fate. There was no skirting around the issue. He still loved this woman.

He examined her gown and chemise that had been ripped, baring parts of her back. His hand paused when he touched a puckered scar beneath her shoulder blade. Words could not define the horror he felt when he instantly deduced the injury was inflicted by a pistol's ball.

Hell's teeth! What had happened to her?

Scurrying footsteps drew his attention. He glanced up, his eyes searching the alley, past the wisps of smoke curling in the air. A tall figure loomed before him like a phantom in black.

Every fiber in Jared's being tensed. Before he could respond, a deep, reverberating voice cut through the hazy cloud, announcing the man's presence. "What the devil is going on here?"

"Roderick?" Jared squinted, stepping forward with an unconscious Emily tight in his hold. He instantly felt the brunt of the duke's gaze and stood firm.

"I believe you are holding something that belongs to me," Roderick announced harshly, striding toward him, cursing Jared that his sister had better be alive.

Jared straightened. He would not give Emily up until they returned to Hemmingly, though he knew he had done her a great injustice, in more ways than one. However, he had already decided that she would be his, no matter what the cost.

"Your sister's fainted. She was caught up in the crowd. Believe she inhaled some smoke. A few hours and she should be much better."

Roderick's black eyes flashed with anger. "Confound it, where were you while this was going on?"

"We were separated by the crowd." *And by my foolishness.*

The chill in Roderick's glare turned icy with contempt.

Jared was glad of the shadows that hid his face. His guilt was like an iron clamp around his chest. He had failed Emily again.

*   *   *

The duchess plumped a pillow behind Emily's head and offered her daughter a spoonful of broth.

"Come now, dearest," the lady said, sniffing and dabbing a white handkerchief to her eyes. "Take some broth, Emily, dear. Agatha had it made especially for you. I cannot bear to have you in pain. Dear me, if Roderick and I had not come to visit, goodness knows what might have become of you."

Emily accommodated her mother and took a few spoonfuls of the warm liquid. She felt the heat of the beef broth starting to soothe her tense nerves. She was breathing much better now, and she closed her eyes, not wanting to think about the horrible afternoon or Jared's tender gaze when he had held her.

Swooning had been her only choice, or she would have fallen under his spell again. In the carriage ride home, exhausted from the ordeal, she had fallen asleep and she had only awaken a few minutes ago. Maybe it had been shock, too, for she could not remember being brought into her chambers.

"A little more, my dear," the duchess coaxed.

In between spoonfuls Emily glanced down, fingering her white nightgown. Her hand suddenly halted on the delicately trimmed lace beneath her breast. A cold panic swept through her. Who had changed her clothes? Had someone seen her back?

The smell of smoke still remained in her hair, and ashes from the fairgrounds still sat in the creases of her fingers. Obviously, someone had tried to wipe her down.

"You must eat, my dear." The duchess sniffed. "When Lord Stonebridge carried you in here, I thought you were dead."

" 'Tis only a few bruises, Mama." *Bruises in my heart that you cannot see. Bruises that will never heal.*

"A few bruises?" Her mother let out a long wail as she touched Emily's cheek. "Oh, my poor, dear child. I should have never left you alone."

A tremor touched Emily's lips and she tried to smile. "Truly, I will not die on you, Mama."

Her mother slid a slender finger along the black-and-blue blotch that began to appear on Emily's cheek. "You won't be out of my sight any longer. I will take full responsibility for you from now on."

Emily blinked in surprise. Was this her mother speaking? The mother who avoided any deep connection with her offspring for three long years after the duke's untimely death.

"I will have a warm bath sent up as soon as possible, dearest. I wanted to make certain you could move before you had a full bath. Agatha and her maid wiped as much grime off of you as possible. I believe you will be fine. No broken bones."

Emily sighed in relief. Agatha was the only other person who knew of her back wound. For it had been Agatha who nursed her on this very bed and tended to her injury. It had been Agatha who held her when she cried out in pain because the lesion had become swollen and pus-filled. It had been Agatha who dried her tears and coddled her like a newborn babe until she was completely healed.

"You may change into a fresh nightgown after you have bathed, my dear." The duchess stood up, smoothing her hands along her dove gray traveling gown, avoiding Emily's eyes. "I know this has been hard for you since your father passed on. But I never was good about his death, you see." Her breath hitched. "When he was dying, all he wanted was to see you, and you were not home at the time."

Emily felt the broth slide coldly down her throat. Had her mother been jealous?

Emily knew her parents had entered into a marriage of convenience, but there was no doubt the duchess had loved the duke. However, Emily's father was fond of her mother, but beyond that . . .

"You see, you were my favorite, too," the duchess went on. Watery eyes shifted back toward her daughter. "I wanted a little girl that I could talk to, shop with, go to balls with." The duchess shrugged. "But you seemed to prefer your father, and he you."

"But, Mama, I loved you both."

The duchess took her handkerchief and dabbed at her eyes. "I know that, dearest. But after your father died, I was so very angry with him. For many things." She swallowed a sob. "I was angry with you, too. I was angry with everybody, including your brothers. I drifted away from life, from my sons, from my daughter who needed me most. But now, having seen you like this, I realized I have failed you in many ways. Pray forgive me, Emily. I do so want to be a good mother."

Hot tears welled in Emily's eyes. "Oh, Mama." She opened her arms, and the duchess fell into her daughter's embrace with a heart-wrenching sob.

"Forgive me for letting you go through these past three years without me, dearest."

"Oh, Mama. I forgive you and I vow I will change as well."

Both women lifted their heads at the knock on the door.

"Come in," the duchess said, stuffing her handkerchief onto the nightstand.

Roderick peeked inside, raising a curious brow at the extraordinary sight of mother and daughter holding hands. "What's this?"

The duchess regarded Roderick's perplexed expression with a stern glare. "Is there something wrong with a mother showing affection for her daughter?"

Roderick looked at Emily, then at his mother. "Of course not," he said with smile, giving his sister a veiled wink.

The duchess gave Emily's hand a tight squeeze. "Roderick, see to your sister. I must see to a few things with Agatha, and mind you, see to the carriage being made ready for our departure." She kissed her daughter on the forehead and patted her hand. "We will depart first thing tomorrow morning. I believe you will be fine. The fresh air will do you good." Her mother gave her a questioning stare.

For once Emily was not going to argue with her

mother. She would leave tomorrow. Her heart could not endure any more pain. "I will be fine, Mama."

Her mother smiled. "Now, be a good boy, Roderick," she murmured before she retreated from the room.

Roderick knitted his brow as he watched his mother's back. "Good boy?" He almost choked out the words. "Has she a fever?"

Emily laughed. "No, Mama is quite well."

Roderick pursed his lips as if not quite believing her.

"I assure you, our mother is not insane, Roderick. But I would be very careful if you are not a good boy. You never know a mother's wrath until you step over the line."

Roderick chuckled. "I will converse about our dear mother at a later time. Now, how are you feeling?"

Emily picked at the linens. "I will recover."

There was an intense pause, and Emily felt a momentary sense of panic at the inquisitive way her brother was staring at her.

"You have a visitor," he finally said.

Emily looked up, surprised. "A visitor?"

Roderick walked toward the door and let the earl enter. "Stonebridge wishes to see you. I have given my permission."

Emily's heart twisted with pain as she pulled the blankets across her chest. "Roderick," she snapped. "I am not presentable." And never would be to this man.

Roderick exchanged glances between Emily and the earl. "You need not worry about pretenses. I am staying."

"I need a bath," she said in a low voice, feeling Jared's heated gaze burning through her covers.

Roderick glanced back toward Stonebridge, frowning. "She is not presentable."

Emily watched hesitantly as a muscle jumped in Jared's cheek.

"I need to speak to your sister. But I will not beg."

A look of annoyance flashed across Roderick's face. "Step outside, Jared."

The earl's cool gaze traveled over Emily's face before he retreated into the hall.

Roderick closed the door and turned to his sister. "The man only wishes to make things right. He worries you are more ill than we have reported. He feels responsible for what happened today, Em."

He was responsible. And for more than that, she wanted to say, but did not want to add murder of an aristocrat to Roderick's list of sins, so she consented to see the earl, only after slipping into her dressing gown.

When Jared walked into the room, he apologized for not watching out for her. She accepted this apology and glared back at him. Roderick's lips thinned as he stood near the door. Seconds of silence ticked by with increasing uneasiness.

As if sensing the turmoil swirling about the room, the duke cleared his throat. "She's quite on the mend as you can see, Jared. But we must let her rest."

Emily sank back into her pillows, able to hear every jarring word Roderick was saying.

"No doubt, she does not wish to see you," Roderick said in a harsh whisper as he jerked Jared back into the hall. "And if you were not my friend, I would call you out for leaving her to that maddening crowd. What, pray tell, were you thinking?"

Emily closed her eyes. At least she would not have to worry about having Jared around with Roderick as guard dog. Still, to have wasted so many years thinking about *that man* was too painful to even contemplate.

As she drifted to sleep, the soft padding of the maid's slippers stirred her senses. Not wanting to take a bath so soon, Emily kept her eyes shut and spoke in a tired whisper. "You may take the soup now, and please have the water sent up in about an hour."

"I am not your servant, madam."

Chapter Seven

Emily's eyes flew open in surprise. "You!" Her gaze quickly shot to the door and saw that it was closed.

"Yes, me," Jared said, his amber eyes twinkling with mirth.

"This is not funny, my lord. You do realize that Roderick will shoot you if he finds you alone here with me."

"Will he, now?"

Her jaw dropped the second he folded himself into the chair beside her bed. Buckskin breeches clung to long, powerful legs, leaving nothing in the man that seemed wanting . . . except his heart. She blushed hotly. Dark hair, still wet from his bath, curled at the nape of his neck like that of a schoolboy, making him look more innocent than he was. She could not help but notice the pair of broad shoulders stretched taut against a cinnamon-colored jacket. "Y-you better leave."

His smile only widened, and when he leaned forward, she detected the scent of peppermint from his breath. Beneath the sheets, her fingers dug into her palms. *Insufferable man!* "I will scream if you do not do as I say."

"Oh, you do that, Lady Emily. Scream loud and clear."

Her heart sped with a maddening beat when he lifted a strand of hair from her eyes. "I-I will scream, I tell you."

He flopped back in his chair and arched a devilish brow. "You do that and we will be married within the week."

Emily gasped, angry with herself for the power he still possessed over her. What was he about? Even the hint of mischief that flickered in those amber eyes confused her.

"You are a monster, sir," she said, managing to tear her gaze away from him.

"Monster or not, my sweet"—he gently cupped her face with his hands and turned her head toward him—"you are about to tell me about that wound on your back. Or should I call your brother and ask him?"

She tensed. Jared had seen her back.

"Tell me, Emily." His thumb trailed down her face, and every muscle in her body rebelled against his pitying touch. She had no wish for his sympathy. She wanted to be left alone. Wanted to forget. The man who shot her was dead, and her vow of silence regarding her work made it impossible to tell Jared anything anyway.

"Leave me be," she said, turning away, feeling the stinging tears begin to dam in her eyes. "I never want to see you again."

"Agatha is the only other one who has knowledge of your scars, if that is what you fear," he said softly.

She felt herself blush. *Agatha? Had the woman betrayed her?*

"Emily, look at me."

She turned her head and glared at him. "Leave me," she whispered hoarsely. "I never want to see you again, do you not understand the king's English?"

A muscle jerked in his cheek. "Let me change the subject, then. I'm asking you to forgive me. Is that so hard?"

Forgive him for what? Three years ago? Bowing to Roderick's request to guard her? Or quarreling with her at the fair? A knot rose in her throat and she took a deep breath, hoping he would leave after she eased him of his guilt. "I forgive you." *But I will not love you.*

He smiled then, a most devastating turn of his lips

that made her heart flutter. But she would not give him the satisfaction of knowing how much he still affected her. She wanted to be far, far away from this man as soon as possible.

He kissed her hand, and she desperately tried to dismiss the familiar aching in her body.

"Well, then," he said matter-of-factly. "Since we are on better terms, I wish to know how you obtained that wound on your back." His smile vanished as quickly as it came, and his eyes flashed with impatience. "In fact, I demand it."

"You demand? How dare you demand anything of me!"

"How dare I?" he growled, his hand coming down on hers in an iron grip, then gentling into a dangerous caress. "I daresay your brothers would not fancy that scar. Do not keep this from me, Emily."

She swallowed and tugged at her hand. "You have no right."

"Em?" They both froze at the sound of Roderick's voice outside the hall.

Emily glanced at the door. "Give me a minute, Roderick.

"Good heavens, do something," she hissed, looking at Jared. "Slip under the bed."

He stared at her as if she had two heads. "What?"

Her command surprised even her. "Slide under the bed or we will be wed before the week is out."

The man seemed momentarily speechless. He glanced at the door and lowered his voice. "The devil I will. I refuse to hide like a sniveling coward."

Another knock. "Em?"

Emily bit her lip. "I beg you, please."

He scowled. "Very well, but if Roderick—" The sentence was left unsaid as he bent over and slid beneath her bed.

Emily bit the inside of her cheeks to keep from laughing. "Of course, you know it will be much more than a wedding license that he will demand," she whispered.

The door creaked opened. "Em?"

"Come in."

"Thought you were taking a bath, but caught the maid in the hall and she said you were sleeping. Then I heard voices." He lifted a concerned brow.

"Voices? How very odd."

His wary gaze swept the room. "A male voice, if I am not mistaken."

Emily coughed. "Do be a dear, Roderick, and fetch me a glass of water." Resting a hand against her head, feigning a headache, she pointed to the pitcher on top of her nightstand.

Roderick rushed to her side and poured the water, forgetting all about the voices. Emily thanked him and downed the entire glass, all the while wondering what Jared was thinking, while being held prisoner beneath her bed and staring at the toes of Roderick's shiny black Hessians. The very idea made her giggle and spurt out some of the water onto the floor.

Jared had no idea how long he had been sandwiched between the mattress and the dusty pine-planked floor. But whatever it was, it was too blasted long. The parade of people marching back and forth from Lady Emily's chambers seemed endless.

As Black Wolf, he had done his share of espionage, but hiding under a lady's bed was not in his repertoire. If that woman thought he had not heard her stifled giggles over his dire predicament, she had better think again.

First it was Roderick asking about how the fire started. Then it was the duchess who pampered Emily like a sickly child. Then it was Jane who cried over the bruises on Emily's cheek. Now it appeared Agatha was feeling responsible for the entire mishap.

Jared's mouth twitched as a piece of dust floated to his lips. When in thunderation would they leave?

"What was my nephew thinking, leaving you in the midst of that wild crowd?"

"He did not exactly leave me," Emily said.

"What would you call it, then?" Agatha's parasol

thumped against the floor, setting up another round of dust.

Jared grimaced, feeling a sneeze coming on. Confound it. This was intolerable. The lint beneath the blasted bed was enough to give a person consumption. On the other hand, consumption would be a better alternative than his aunt discovering him in this sorry predicament. Heaven knows what kind of attack she would mount against him then. That black parasol could be a powerful weapon if used properly.

He slowly slid his fingers to his nose, pinching his nostrils to stop the sneeze. If the men at White's found out about this, he would never hear the end of it.

"Ah, hear comes the bathwater now," Agatha announced.

Jared lifted his head, hitting the rung above him. Bathwater? Devil take it! He bit back a groan when the sweet scent of roses drifted to his nose.

"I have added a few drops of rose oil, dear. I know you like it that way."

"Thank you, Agatha. You are too kind."

"If you wish, I could stay and be of some help to you."

Jared clasped his head in his hands. He had to retreat as swiftly as possible. Emily was going to take a bath, and he would have to stay prisoner under the bed while she did it. The thought was both arousing and nauseating at the same time. Roderick would surely kill him!

"No, thank you, Agatha. I assure you, no maid either. I will be able to take care of myself."

Jared let out a sigh of relief. He would look the other way. Well, perhaps . . .

"What was that?" Agatha asked, her parasol thumping closer to Jared's feet. "Thought I heard something scampering beneath your bed."

Emily coughed. "My bed?"

"Yes, I distinctly heard—"

A bark from the door interrupted Agatha's comment.

Jared groaned at the sound of thumping paws. The moment his dog pounced onto Emily's mattress, the rung above him banged against his head.

Blast it all. Nigel would surely give him away.

"Nigel, out of here," Agatha cried. "Emily cannot recover with you licking her face."

Emily laughed. "He loves the scent of rose water, Agatha."

Jared grimaced. Lucky dog!

"Off, Nigel. Off!" Agatha's parasol whacked the side of the bed. "Now, I say. Move!"

There was a bark and another thump, but this time it was Nigel's heavy paws thudding to the floor. Jared held his breath. His dog had the best nose in England and France put together. No doubt, the game was up.

"Quiet, Nigel," Agatha snapped. "Emily has had quite enough commotion for one day."

Nigel gave one last bark and whimpered.

Jared's eyes widened at the sight of a wet nose staring back at him. Praying for a miracle, he silently waved the dog away. But Nigel was not about to move an inch. Blast it to hell.

Agatha's voice boomed above him. "Ah, here comes more water, dear. You will feel so much better after a good warm bath." Jared flinched when he heard a splash. "Feels perfect."

He turned his head as the bed squeaked, and his aunt started helping Emily down. His heart stopped pumping at the sight of a shapely ankle sliding down the side of the bed.

His eyes suddenly grew round with pleasure. Perhaps he would not move for some time after all.

"Thank you, Agatha, I can do everything else from here."

So could I, Jared thought with a smile.

"Very well, dear, I will leave you two alone."

Jared felt the blood rush to his head.

"Two?" Emily squeaked out.

"You and Nigel, that is, unless you want Nigel with me?" Without waiting for Emily's answer, Agatha walked across the room to leave, closing the door behind her.

Jared stared fixedly on the second shapely ankle that

descended at his side, and he started to sweat. He was not such a sapskull that he was going to remind her he was here.

"Out!"

He jerked at the sound of the harsh voice, thwacking his head on the rungs above him. "Confound it!"

"Out," Emily snapped again.

Jared came to the realization that she was speaking to him and not Nigel. "Daresay, I prefer the view from here."

"Out!"

Letting out a dry chuckle, Jared snaked his body out from beneath the bed, eyeing more than just a shapely ankle. His gaze locked on one creamy white calf. "I take that back. Perhaps the view is better from here."

"You scoundrel!"

He smiled, lifting his gaze to her blushing face. He had an overwhelming need to pull her toward him and kiss her soundly. Well, why the devil not?

Before she knew what he was about, he wrapped a strong hand around her head and crushed his mouth to hers. Her lips were warm and sweet, just like he remembered. It ended all too soon when she hastily reared back, as if she had been scorched.

"Oh, how could you?"

"How could I?" Jared raised a mischievous brow, watching her sweep the coverlet swiftly over her body. He dropped his gaze, patting the dust off his trousers. "How could I not?"

"Will you please leave?" She swept her finger toward the door.

"I will leave only because you need a bath and more rest." He quickly spun on his heels, snapping his fingers for Nigel to follow.

"Be certain my brother is not waiting in the hallway," she bit out tartly.

He glanced over his shoulder, his gaze riveted on her snapping eyes. He knew that the scar on her back was only scraping the surface of a much larger secret. "We will continue our little talk tomorrow, *Lady Emily*."

"I do not believe so, *Lord Stonebridge*." Her tone was bitter. Yet he could not blame her, for he deserved every bit of her condemnation. But he would not let that scar go unanswered.

"I do not believe so, *Em. I know so*."

"Lady Emily to you, *Lord Stonebridge*."

"Forgive me for my informality, *Lady Emily*."

He bowed and could almost hear her grind her teeth in rage as he swiftly retreated from the room.

"What do you mean she has taken her leave?"

Jared glared at Agatha and threw his napkin onto the breakfast table, not able to believe the news.

His aunt looked up while she buttered her bread. "They took off for London early this morning."

"When?"

"Early this morning." Agatha gave a resigned sigh, reaching for the orange marmalade. "Are you deaf, my boy? I just said that, did I not?"

"No, Aunt. I meant *when* this morning?"

"When the sun rose. Thought you knew."

Jared shoved his plate forward, his knife clanking against his glass. "No, I did not know."

He glanced down at Nigel, who sat at his feet. The dog looked up, whined, and padded out the door.

Agatha waved her hand in the air and munched on her toast. "I suppose you should know I gave my permission." Another bite.

"Permission about what?"

"The duchess asked Jane to join them."

"Jane?"

"Yes, your ward." She shot him a disgusted look as if he had no idea who Jane was.

"The devil. I know who Jane is!" But how could Emily leave him like that?

"Well, you do not have to be so disagreeable, my boy. I am only a few feet away, and I am not the one who is deaf."

Jared took a deep breath, trying to calm himself. "Why did they leave so soon?"

Agatha rose to retrieve some more food from the sideboard. "You know, the Season and all."

Jared bit back an oath as he stared at his aunt's back. "And?" He waited patiently while she piled on a plate of eggs and sausage, returning to her seat.

"The Season, Jared. Balls. Soirees. Operas. Plays."

"What has that to do with Lady Emily leaving this morning?"

"Lady Emily?" Agatha looked surprised. "I thought we were speaking of Jane."

Jared stretched his neck, tugging at his cravat that seemed to have been tied too tight this morning. "I was led to believe that I was to escort Jane during the Season."

Agatha chewed and glanced up. "You know, I do believe that our dear Jane has taken a dislike to the duke. It happened after he threw her into the carriage yesterday." She shrugged. "But it was not to be helped." She buttered another bun. "And no need to fret about Lady Emily. Her brothers will see to her this Season. So fortunately for you, you won't have to escort us at all."

"What?" Had Emily's brothers found her a husband?

"Are you deaf, Jared?"

Jared glanced at his aunt in frustration. "Could you please explain about Emily's brothers?"

Agatha stopped eating, staring at him with an expression that he could only interpret as worry. "Emily's brothers have decided to take the matter of her future into their own hands."

"And?" His heart beat a little faster.

"And they are going to choose a husband for her before the Season is out. It seems Lady Emily has a list of suitors a mile long vying for her hand."

His face tensed. "Like who?"

"Like Mr. James Fennington, for one."

Jared shot from his seat and paced the room. "Fennington? The man is flat broke and a drunk."

"He may be flat broke, but . . ." She waved her hand in the air as if the rest of the words were of no importance.

He spun around. "What?"

His aunt eyed him with concern. "They say he is more handsome than—"

He leaned forward, his knuckles on the table. "Than who?"

She gulped and glanced down at her plate, picking up her fork and shuffling the sausage around the eggs. "Than you."

Jared scowled. Fennington was a dog. "Who says so?"

Agatha looked up and coughed. Her eyes were half closed as she spoke. "Why, Lady Emily, for one."

Furious, Jared closed his fingers into a fist. Emily could not be infatuated with that man. Roderick would not allow it.

"And," Agatha went on, "the duchess told me that on one occasion her sons found Mr. Fennington hiding in Emily's bedchambers ready to escape with her to Gretna Green."

Jared stilled. "*That* is the most preposterous thing I have ever heard." Roderick had told him about Fennington sniffing after Emily, but the duke had failed to mention Emily's bedchambers and Gretna Green in reference to the man.

What other news had Roderick withheld from him? No matter, Jared reasoned, Emily belonged to him. The sudden notion filled him with a joy he had not felt since his daughter was born. Emily might not deserve him, but he would make it up to her.

"Jared?"

He glanced at his aunt, hoping he had not cut all ties to whatever feelings Emily had for him.

"Hope you don't mind"—Agatha stood, grabbing her parasol—"I will be leaving in a week as well, and since I am having my place refurbished, the duchess invited me to stay with her . . ."

His aunt went on talking, but Jared had barely heard anything she uttered past the words Gretna Green.

"Jared, are you ill?

"No, I am not ill." *I am quite insane, thank you.*

"Then, of course, you are going to accept the invitation and come along with me? But you do realize that poor Nigel will have to stay here, I fear."

Jared felt momentarily stunned. "What invitation?"

"To stay with me at the Elbourne townhouse. You have already told me your townhouse is not fit to live in for a few weeks, and I am using the same workers to redo mine."

Not fit for at least a few weeks. How fortunate. He would accept the offer to stay at the duke's London home. No doubt the duchess and Agatha made plans without Roderick's approval. But so be it. It would give him more time with Emily, whether she liked it or not. "Of course, I will stay there."

Agatha clapped her hands and smiled. "Wonderful! You may inspect the suitors who come to call on Jane, and the duke will be there for Emily. His Grace is more determined than ever to see his sister set in an agreeable marriage."

Jared's brows slammed together in annoyance. Agreeable marriage indeed.

Chapter Eight

Emily had been in London for five days, and this morning she found herself among the crowd of women vying for Madame Claire's attention. Female giggles wafted above the bolts of muslin and silk in the dressmaker's shop. Emily stood with Jane beyond the window near the front counter. Roderick had escorted them to the shop thirty minutes earlier, quickly retreating to accompany his mother to the nearby milliner.

Clad in a lilac gown with tiny blue flowers, Emily paged through the dress patterns more determined than ever to remove Lord Stonebridge from her mind. But her thoughts kept going back to his devastating kisses. The touch of his warm lips upon hers had left an indelible imprint on her mind, planting hope into her soul, tormenting her heart, making her realize that keeping a safe distance from the compelling man was the only hope of saving her sanity.

He never loved her.

"Emily, I do believe that someone is staring at you through the window. A fair-haired gentleman with a rather comely face. Wait. Wait. He is putting something to his eye. I believe it a quizzing glass of some sort," Jane chuckled. "A very huge one, in fact."

A huge quizzing glass? Emily's throat constricted with dread as she slapped the pattern books closed and threw a hand to the golden locket resting upon her neck. "Good heavens, I cannot believe *he* has followed me here."

Smiling, Jane casually turned and showed Emily a bolt of crimson red material. "Do you think the handsome gentleman would prefer to see you in this color?" She picked out a flimsy purple concoction and giggled. "Or this one?"

Emily groaned, pulling Jane's arm and shuffling past a mother and daughter fussing over a piece of French lace.

"Jane," she hissed, "this is no times for jests. *That* is Mr. James Fennington. It seems he has decided it is me or nothing. I had once thought of choosing a fop like him for a husband to ensure my freedom, but, good grief, I simply could not do it."

Jane's eyes flitted mischievously. "How utterly romantic."

The corners of Emily's mouth began to twitch. "This is not amusing, Jane. Whatever am I going to do? You do not know the half of it. Roderick will surely shoot him if he sees the man here."

Jane skirted her friend around a row of pink silks, their gowns rustling against the wall. "I must tell you, Emily, that I have heard about Mr. James Fennington, so you need not tell me a thing."

Emily frowned as she met her friend's twinkling blue eyes. "Agatha?"

Jane nodded. "But you may depend upon it, she has not told anyone but me."

Somehow, Emily doubted that. Her eyes darted about nervously. Good gracious. The man was a nuisance. "Oh, Jane, what are we to do? Roderick will be returning in a matter of minutes. I do not fancy seeing Mr. Fennington killed before our very eyes."

Jane laughed, scooting them behind a tall stack of cream-colored muslin. "Surely your brother will not shoot the poor man."

"You do not know Roderick. He is the most disagreeable person in all of England."

Jane gave her friend a pat on the hand. "Stay here. I am going to peek and see if Mr. Fennington has taken his leave."

Emily waited, becoming more uncomfortable by the minute. She paced back and forth in the small space allotted her. A wave of flowery perfume sailed her way as a rather large-sized woman squeezed in between her and the muslin.

Within a minute Jane's slippers came slapping around the corner. Emily looked up in dread when Jane put her hand across her breast and let out a distressed sigh.

"Emily, you will not believe it."

Emily tensed. "Tell me he is not dead, or worse, entering the shop."

Jane bit her lip, her eyes sparkling. "Very well, then, I won't tell you that the gentleman in question is entering the shop, and I won't tell you that every female here is watching him make his way toward you, and I won't tell you that, indeed, the wretched fop is carrying the most horrendous quizzing glass I have ever been subject to witness."

A low murmur of female voices drifted through the shop.

Emily grabbed her gloves from her reticule, wishing she could melt into the bolts of fabric and disappear. "Very well, then. I need to leave by another way. Do you know—"

"Ah, Lady Emily." The deep baritone voice of Mr. Fennington made Emily stiffen. "What a miracle I have found you." Without a second to lose, he grabbed her naked hand, raising it to his mouth for a kiss. Cold, wet lips hit her skin like a slab of ice. She jerked her fingers out of his grasp.

"Sir, you go too far."

Jane tried to hide her snicker.

Mr. Fennington glanced at Jane, then tilted his head, giving Emily a saucy wink. "Ah, forgive me." He leaned over to whisper in her ear. "I forgot, we are being watched."

Emily blinked against the smell of spirits on his breath.

"Mr. Fennington, how on earth did you find me? My brother will be here any minute." She hoped the man would take the hint to exit before Roderick showed his face.

But the man seemed to ignore her warning. "I declare, I find myself drifting on a heavenly cloud whenever I catch sight of you, dear lady. But who may this beautiful angel be?" he asked, bowing to Jane.

"Forgive me, Mr. Fennington. May I present my friend, Miss Jane Greenwell."

Emily could not help but send Jane a smile at the vexing predicament they found themselves in. Emily rolled her eyes when Mr. Fennington took out his quizzing glass, stared back at Jane, then proceeded to kiss her friend's hand in the same fashion as he had hers. Jane towered over the man's bent head and stared back at Emily, her delicate brows lifted in shocked amusement.

"Roderick, dearest, would you mind terribly if I waited in the carriage while you attend to your sister and Jane? My feet are vexing me to no end. I believe my gout may be acting up again."

"Certainly, Mother. I will return as soon as possible."

A row of shiny black coaches lined the cobblestone streets as the servants waited for their masters to return from their shopping. Roderick took the duchess's hand, gently guiding her into the Elbourne carriage situated a half block from Madame Claire's shop.

The duchess leaned forward from her seat, patting her gloved hand across the back of Egypt's white coat of fur. "Do let the girls take as long as they wish. Emily is choosing a new wardrobe, and I want her to have as much time as she needs. Jane is knowledgeable on the subject, and I trust the girl completely. Do not worry about me. I will wait here and rest."

Roderick groaned. "I daresay, it won't be anytime soon before I return with them, madam. An entire wardrobe, you say? Perhaps we could have Madame Claire make a visit to—"

"Your Grace!" a lady's voice called out to the duchess, interrupting Roderick's plea.

The duchess peeked around the open door.

Roderick glanced over his shoulder, a frown flitting across his face. "It appears Miss Appleby and Stonebridge seem to be in Town. Imagine that."

"How exciting," the duchess said as she slipped out of the carriage. "I was not certain that they would accept my invitation to stay with us, you know. I hear the earl can be such an obstinate sort of man—somewhat like you, Roderick."

Roderick gave a grunt. "What about your feet?"

"Of course, I have heard that the man can be accommodating as well," she said over her shoulder as she strode toward her friend, ignoring Roderick's question.

Jared and Roderick exchanged curt nods.

"Anne," Agatha cried, giving the duchess a hug. "It has been too long."

"Too long?" Jared and the duke both said in unison, raising their eyebrows in bewilderment. Evidently the ladies had not heard them, for they had moved toward the milliner's shop to view the latest creations the duchess had ordered.

"I have just been informed that you accepted my mother's invitation to stay with us," Roderick said to Jared, then lowered his voice. "I thought you might have possible business in St. Helena soon."

Jared scowled. "You have information to pass on, *Your Grace*?"

"Your Grace? Has our friendship come to that? It seems I may have to accompany you, if we have to go at all."

A shadow of annoyance clouded Jared's face. It was obvious Roderick had not forgiven him for letting Emily be trapped in the fire. Jared had not forgiven himself.

Jared glanced down the street, waiting for a pair of gentlemen to pass. "Sources say Boney's not happy."

"Why should he be? The man was exiled."

"There is some concern about an uprising."

Roderick grimaced, stuffing his hands into his pockets

and walking a bit past the carriage. "Will this blasted fighting ever be over?"

Jared wondered the same thing as he followed beside the duke. "For England, it's over, but to the remnants of Napoleon's followers, it will take a long time to end." Monsieur Devereaux came to Jared's mind, but he was not about to bring the man's name up to Roderick. For it was the duke who had emphatically pronounced that the man was dead.

Roderick's boots halted. "Ah, here we are." He frowned, leaning into the shadows of the dressmaker's shop.

Jared lifted his head and quirked an amused brow. "Never thought Headquarters would go so far as have you wear one of Madame Claire's latest creations," he said sarcastically. "But as you say, orders are orders."

Roderick sneered. "My sister and your ward are the ones choosing the latest creations, not me, and I refuse to wait for nightfall before they are done."

Jared pictured the duke waiting hours beneath the dressmaker's sign and laughed.

Roderick seemed to read his thoughts and leaned against the red stone front, crossing his arms against his chest. "I would advise you not to push your luck. I have not forgiven you for leaving my sister with that maddening crowd."

Jared stiffened. The man had every right to be angry.

"However, from this moment on, we must work together." Roderick's eyebrow lifted. "We are now entering into the den of the most dangerous places in all England."

Jared pursed his lips. "And pray tell, what den is that?"

"The female den. The most dangerous of all God's lairs." Roderick pushed himself off the wall and opened the shop door. "Not to mention mothers, Jared. Diabolical, conniving, devious mothers looking for the richest son-in-laws on earth."

Jared laughed. "Indeed." He bowed to the duke. "Though I have a duty to see my ward clothed in the highest of fashion, you must proceed before me, Your Mighty Grace. You are far above me and should enter the den first. I insist."

Jared heard Roderick mumble a curse as the bell above the entrance jingled, announcing their presence.

Jared stopped short as he looked around, taking in the ghastly sight. "I will never forgive you for this, Roderick."

Roderick stood, dumbfounded. "Believe me, I had no idea. It was not like this when I left."

The shop was filled to capacity with every female in London fancying a new gown. Jared grimaced when everyone turned their way. At least ten ladies and their mothers immediately rushed toward the two most eligible bachelors in London.

Jared spoke through stiff lips. "Should have worn the gown, *Your Grace*. We would have been able to slink into this shop without such a commotion."

"This is insufferable. Worse than Almack's."

Heady scents of perfume assaulted their noses. Jared smiled to the gathering crowd of tormenting females, inwardly vowing to kill Roderick before the day was out.

"Lord Stonebridge, I had no idea you would be in London."

"Lord Stonebridge, however do you stay so trim?"

"Lord Stonebridge, would you do me the honor of attending my little soiree tomorrow?"

Roderick would pay dearly for this! Jared had quite enough when he became crushed between a bolt of copper-colored muslin and a tray of tiny porcelain buttons that clattered to the floor. He gave his friend a scowl, which immediately turned into a smile when he saw the duke pushed into a table containing a stack of very long embroidery needles. Served him right.

As the minutes passed the mass of ladies competing for their attention was staggering. Jared could barely breathe. The situation was hopeless.

"Ah, but Lady Emily, you seem to forget I will never give up." Both gentlemen snapped to attention at the sound of the only other male voice in the crowd.

"Fennington," Jared mouthed to Roderick.

There, in the corner of the shop, where muslin met silk, James Theodore Fennington could be seen in a dark brown jacket and bright white cravat crooning over two ladies, Lady Emily and Miss Jane Greenwell.

Jared narrowed his gaze on the ladies. His nostrils flared at the sight of Fennington's beady eyes fixed precariously on the creamy expanse of skin where a golden locket rested.

Jared immediately excused himself from the ladies present and made his way past the rows of lace and silk, his long strides unwavering as he knocked down a bolt of blue brocade trim. He wondered how he should knock Fennington to the ground, with one fist or two. It seemed that Roderick had already broken through the swarm of ladies as well, but Jared was a yard ahead of him.

When Emily looked up to find her brother and the earl barreling in her direction, her pulse skittered alarmingly. The gaggle of surrounding ladies erupted into low murmurs once again. Emily glanced back at the smiling but odious man in front of her and felt a pang of regret for what was about to happen to him. He was an insufferable pain, but he did not deserve both men at once.

"Mr. Fennington," she said, touching his arm.

He bowed to her, flashing a set of white teeth her way. "Your slightest wish is my command, my lady. Just one word from those ruby red lips and I am yours forever."

What a peagoose! How could she ever have thought of wedding such a popinjay?

"Mr. Fennington, I do implore you, if you have the slightest wish to see the sun rise tomorrow, I suggest you exit by the back door before my brother kills you."

Fennington laughed. "His Grace is only jesting, my dear lady. He would never—"

Emily grabbed the man's arm. "He would never give you another chance. Please, he is only ten feet from your back."

Fennington turned as white as the lace behind him. "Eh, ten feet, you say?"

"Five feet," she replied as she pushed Fennington aside. "Stop, Roderick! I beg you, do not harm him."

Boxes and buttons rolled and thumped onto the floor as Fennington escaped through the back door. To her shock, it was not Roderick, but Lord Stonebridge who was but a step away from her brother, glaring at her.

"What the devil do you think you are doing with that conniving snake?" he snapped.

Roderick obviously decided not to pursue the gentleman and, instead, stared at his friend. "I appreciate your concern, Jared, but I will see to my own affairs."

"This is my affair," he growled.

Roderick grimaced as he took in Jane's amused expression. "Indeed, your ward seems to be rather fond of Fennington herself."

Jane's blue eyes narrowed on the duke. "How would you recognize any fondness at all, Your Grace. It seems to me that your heart is as cold as your kiss."

Surprised, Emily stared back at her friend. Kiss?

"My kiss, madam, is not cold."

Emily watched in fascination as Jane and Roderick went back and forth muttering snide remarks. But it was Jared who finally pulled Jane from the pressing crowd, back through the bolts of muslin and silk to the front door. Roderick followed, towing Emily past the buttons and lace, clattering everything in their path.

Voices whispered as the foursome finally retreated from the shop. After the door jingled, announcing their departure, the gossip about the Earl of Stonebridge, the Duke of Elbourne, Miss Jane Greenwell, and Lady Emily began.

However, in the small dressing room, off to the side, a certain Miss Susan Wimble stood, glaring into the looking glass, her eyes glazed over with hatred. She slipped off her wedding gown and turned to her maid.

"Find out everything you know about that dark-haired lady speaking to Stonebridge, do you hear? I will not have the chit taking my place! I will be a countess before the Season is out, and no one is going to upset my plans!"

Outside the shop, Jared dropped Jane's hand and scowled. "I am dismayed at your manners, Jane. What is going on between the two of you?" He glared at the duke.

Jane looked up with tears glistening in her eyes. "I did nothing to offend you, Cousin Jared. It was *his* fault." She, too, glared at the duke.

Roderick frowned back, his eyes darkening.

Before Jared could obtain an explanation, Jane flew into the duchess's carriage with a heartfelt sob.

Emily glared at Jared, then at Roderick. "I cannot believe you would speak to Jane like that. It was not well done of either of you."

Roderick's expression was cold and tight with strain. "You, little sister, have no right to tell me what is well done and what is not. Fennington was to stay away from you, and here I find the man slobbering all over you . . . and Miss Greenwell."

"Good gracious, the man followed me into the shop, but I have not set my cap for him, if that is what you think. Besides, it was nothing but a chaste kiss on the hand."

Jared stepped between the two. "I beg to differ."

Emily's eyes flashed with anger. "I beg to differ with you as well, *your lordship*."

Jared's face hardened into a mask of fury. "You are not in a position to argue with me or your brother."

Roderick's lips thinned. "Fennington is an idiot. It's obvious he followed you into that shop, but you cannot let your heart be used by such a rogue. You are too softhearted, Em."

Emily shrugged, avoiding his gaze. Her brother was correct on one fact, she was too softhearted. Jared was proof of that.

"You must let men like Fennington know you are not interested," Roderick snapped. "Give the fop the cut direct in no unlimited terms. No hands! No kisses! Not even a gaze! That is how it is to be done! Do you understand me?"

Emily looked up at Roderick's hard expression and had a sudden urge to laugh. How had she let her brothers push her around so? All she had to do was say no, and they could do nothing about it. The thought was exhilarating. They would not dare to touch her. If she did not put her foot down now, there was no telling what her life would be like the next few months.

"I understand you perfectly. Though you are my guardian, you are not my conscience. I am not interested in Fennington, however, I will do as I see fit."

Roderick's face turned red. "Indeed you will not. In fact, you will not attend the ball tonight, and that is final."

"I agree," Jared said with a stern glare. "For once, Roderick, you are doing something right."

Roderick turned a scowl upon Jared. "I don't know whether to box your ears or thank you."

Emily tightened her hold on her reticule, trying to subdue the urge to box both their ears. "I do believe that you two are the most pompous gentlemen I have ever set eyes on. For my part, I will attend the ball. And you two can do nothing to stop me. Besides," she smiled, "Mama would not allow it."

With those last words she tilted the brim of her hat over her eyes and entered the carriage.

Jared stared at the duke. "What have you done to her the past few days?"

"Me?" Roderick asked incredulously. "She has not been the same after that blasted fire, and what say have you about my sister anyway? Your duty is done."

Jared glared back. "I'm Jane's guardian. She has been traveling with Lady Emily. It is my duty to watch the coming and going of her friends."

The tense lines around Roderick's mouth loosened. "Daresay, thought for a moment you had your sights on Em. Believe I am going mad."

Jared stared at the shiny black hair that bobbed beyond the window of the carriage. Mad indeed. He turned his gaze back to Roderick. And what the devil had Jane said about a kiss?

Chapter Nine

"Clayton and I have a small list of suitors that meet our requirements." Marcus slapped the paper onto the leather-topped table at White's.

Across from him, Clayton sipped his wine. "Daresay, we have gone all out. Quite hard to find a suitable husband for a sister, you know."

Roderick glanced at the list, his eyebrows gathering into an intense "V." "Small list indeed. I presume you have researched these men concerning their suitability." A mocking twinkle appeared in his eyes. "And I dearly pray that you do not have one with a monstrous quizzing glass stuck to his brow."

A hint of a smile tipped at the corner of Clayton's lips. "What do you take us for? A bunch of addlepated nincompoops?"

"We do not speak like that Clayton," Stephen said in a high-pitched voice as he tugged at his cravat. "Pray now, you will do the right thing and wash your mouth out with soap."

Clayton laughed, tipping himself back in his chair. That gave Stephen the few precious seconds he needed to wrap his Wellington boot around one of the chair legs and dump his brother with one quick jerk.

Clayton bounced to the floor with a thud. "What did you do that for?"

Stephen raised a dark brow, shuffling a deck of cards for their game of whist. "Felt like it."

Marcus and Roderick burst into laughter.

As Clayton staggered back to his seat, Roderick tilted a raised eyebrow toward Stephen. "Where's your list?"

Stephen shrugged. "Still working on it. What about yours?"

Roderick sighed. "It's coming along quite nicely." He lowered his gaze to the list of names given to him by Clayton and Marcus. After a few seconds, his eyes widened in outrage. "What do you mean by including Lord Durham? The man's a womanizer of the tenth degree."

Clayton's jaw dropped as he turned a hardened glare on Marcus. "You were supposed to check the man's background. How could you make a mistake like that?"

Marcus's eyes fell into a pair of challenging slits. "Me, I daresay you were the one who said you would have the man investigated. I already took the initiative to look into Mr. Glover's background."

"Mr. Glover?" The cards in Stephen's hands flew haphazardly into the air. "Hell's bells! How can Emily marry a man with no title?"

Roderick slapped a hand to the table. "Those two are out as are the rest of these." His dark eyes drifted to the last name. "But wait. Lord Bringston?"

"Bit older man," Marcus added. "Forty-five, I believe. Seems he decided to marry after all these years. In the market now. The man is rich, too. Has some plantation in Jamaica."

"Quite a decent chap," Clayton said. "Older man might be just the thing for Em. Heard he's brilliant. His appearance is quite acceptable as well. Handsome, they say."

Roderick pursed his lips in thought. "Looks like we have only one eligible suitor so far. But the more I think about it, the more the idea of an older gentleman might suit our needs perfectly."

Stephen cocked his head to the side. "One eligible suitor? Have you seen the betting books?"

All three brothers looked his way, their expression

curious. "Why the blazes would the betting books have anything to do with Em," Roderick asked incredulously.

Stephen stared at Roderick. "I daresay, you should know. You were there they say."

"Where?"

"Good grief, Roderick. You were at Madame Claire's earlier today when Stonebridge took Emily to task, were you not?"

Roderick straightened, stretching his shoulders taut against his navy blue jacket. "And what, pray tell, has that to do with the betting books?"

Stephen rubbed his hand across his mouth in agitation. "Are you blind and deaf? You do recall that the earl's marriage was on the books with a certain Miss Susan Wimble?"

"Go on," Roderick replied, his eyes fixed.

Stephen shook his head. "Before you three entered the club, I wanted to place a little bet on our friend myself."

Clayton glared at his brother. "Confound it, Stephen. How much this time? I pray it was not ten thousand pounds again."

"Certainly not."

Roderick cursed. "Never mind the money, what are you saying?"

Stephen leaned forward. "It seems Miss Susan Wimble has dropped in the running, and the odds are now two to one that Stonebridge will marry Emily before the Season is out."

"What?" All three siblings yelled in unison.

They did not wait for Stephen's explanation before pushing back their chairs and marching toward the betting books. A wave of curious gentlemen parted at the sight of the three brawny men coming their way.

Meanwhile, Lord Stonebridge was unfortunately entering White's at the same time, his mind set on approaching the Duke of Elbourne about the man's intentions toward Miss Jane Greenwell. Jared had been so fixed on Fennington's approach of Emily, he had turned his anger on Jane when she began arguing with the duke. But after a few hours of sorting out what had happened at the dressmaker's shop, Jared began to assimilate the situation more clearly. Roderick had taken liberties with Jane.

As soon as one of the servants took the cloak from his back, Jared noted a large crowd gathering in the room where the betting books were kept. He could see the four brothers clearly, and his lips dipped into a foreboding scowl.

"By Jove," Clayton said as he pulled at the famous betting book. "Look at this, would you, Roderick? You are put in the books as well."

Roderick grabbed the ledger, his gaze hardening like ice. "Miss Jane Greenwell and me? Preposterous!"

Grinning like a jester in the king's court, Clayton slapped his eldest brother on the back. "Busy again? And we thought you were working on suitors for Emily."

"Indeed, Your Grace. You are a busy man." The soft, hushed tone of Lord Stonebridge's voice cleared the floor.

Roderick spun around, backed by his three siblings. "Ah, the man all of London is betting about." He raised a right brow in challenge. "What say you of the odds?"

"Not here," Jared hissed and turned on his heels, proceeding into the next room. He was not about to air their doings for all of London to see.

Four grim-faced gentlemen followed Jared into a more private alcove, their footsteps echoing from the paneled walls as the rumble of voices began once again.

Jared casually leaned against the back wall. He glanced at Roderick and his three brothers, who stood with hands on hips, their feet planted solidly on the floor. "You asked me about the odds. The odds on you marrying Jane, Your Grace?"

"No," Roderick growled. "The odds of you marrying Emily."

A muscle twitched in Jared's jaw as he took in the chilling eyes glaring at him. "Ah, have you put me on the barbaric list of suitors?"

"You were her protector and nothing else," Roderick bit out. "You have never been on the list."

"And never will be," Clayton added curtly. "Our Emily—"

"Your Emily?" Jared interrupted. He thought about the late duke, and anger began to spurt from his veins. He could have pummeled all four brothers at once. "How dare you make her *your Emily*. The lady in question has a mind of her own. She does not need an arrogant foursome to make her decisions for her, especially when it comes to finding a husband. Give her the credit for having some brains."

"Indeed?" Roderick said with a menacing sneer. "If it is not one of our choices, whom should she marry? Fennington, perhaps? You heard her today. No telling what she will do. She is a stubborn female set on her ways. Should she have her money run dry after only one year of marriage? Is that what you suggest?"

Clayton took a threatening step forward. "Yes, and were you not the one who was to guard our sister while we were in London?"

Jared's eyes darted toward Roderick. "I have come to speak of Miss Jane Greenwell, not your sister. What about that kiss a few days past, Roderick? You do remember, do you not? The day you left Hemmingly and stopped at the posting inn to dine?"

Stephen, Clayton, and Marcus turned their bewildered gazes upon their eldest brother.

Roderick glowered at Jared. "We need to talk."

"Talk?" Jared said with a sardonic smirk, his annoyance evident. It grated on him the way these four barbarians battered Emily's life about as if it were a ball in a cricket game. And now it was Jane's life as well. "We need to do more than talk."

Roderick's challenging gaze did not go unnoticed. "Indeed?"

"I will meet you at Gentleman Jackson's in one hour."

"One hour," Roderick snapped as his brothers gave each other a broadened smile. A boxing match was something they would never miss, not between the two best fighters from Oxford.

Minutes after the departure of the Earl of Stonebridge and the Duke of Elbourne from White's, the rustle of voices in the club escalated to mounting proportions, especially at the betting books.

Emily stood in her bedchambers and glanced at the letter from Headquarters one more time. Excitement flowed through her. The coded message conveyed that she was to meet with her two secret contacts in the conservatory during the Garrick Ball. The objective—to finally be introduced to one another.

She stepped toward the hearth, threw the missive into the fire, and walked across the room to peer at herself in the looking glass. The light green gown fell against her curves in a gentle wave of silk and lace. It held a daringly low-scooped neck that Jane insisted was quite proper. Her dark hair was piled on top of her head in a nest of springy curls that brought attention to her violet-blue eyes.

She turned at the scratch on the door.

"Come in."

Jane entered, smiling. "You look splendid, Emily."

"And you, Jane. You are beautiful." Jane's pale blue gown brought out the color of her sapphire eyes, which were matched by a silk ribbon intertwined through her golden curls.

"No, these are beautiful, dearest." A grin spread across Jane's face as she pulled out a strand of snow-white pearls from her reticule. "Your grandmother's, I believe. Your mother would have brought them herself, but the maid is still dressing her hair and I promised I would come here straight away."

"Oh, Jane. My grandmother's? Truly?"

Jane nodded and rested the pearls against Emily's skin, clasping the hook behind her neck. "They are beautiful, are they not?"

"Beautiful." Emily brought her hand up to her neck,

and her throat ached. Jared had promised her a similar set when they wed. Oh, why could she not forget him?

Jane placed a hand on Emily's and peered at her reflection in the mirror. "Do you love him so very much?"

The question took Emily by surprise, and she blinked, turning away from the mirror. "Him?"

Jane crossed her arms over the lace bodice of her dress. "Do not play with me, Emily. I am no fool. You have been acting oddly since you came to Hemmingly. I believe Cousin Jared is the reason, am I correct?"

Emily turned to her friend and sighed. "He . . . is impossible."

"Well, now we are getting somewhere. Come sit down and tell your best friend everything." Jane pulled Emily toward the bed, her grip determined. "And I mean everything."

Emily gave a nervous laugh. It was suddenly all too much for her, and she finally let down her guard, telling Jane about her relationship with Jared and how he had left her for another woman.

Jane sat wide-eyed, her expression changing from surprise to utter fascination. "And then your brothers had him serve as protector for you at Hemmingly?"

Emily nodded.

Jane's face glowed with indignation. "Of all the barbaric things to do! It must have been dreadful, since you are still in love with him."

Emily clamped a pillow to her stomach. "I am not in love with him, Jane."

Jane patted Emily's hands affectionately. "Of course you are, dearest. Though it does not mean the man has not been an idiot."

Emily paused, then burst out laughing. "Oh, Jane. What in the world am I to do? How can I avoid him when he is living under the same roof as I?"

Jane sighed. "You cannot avoid your feelings, dearest."

Emily frowned. Yes, she could. The last time she had paid attention to her feelings, she had lived to regret it, and she never would be placed in that position again.

* * *

Jared found his ward in the hallway of the Elbourne townhouse an hour before he was to leave for the Garrick Ball. His protective instincts plunged into full alert at the sight of Jane wrapped in a confection of blue satin with ribbon trimmings, looking like some dazzling gift to be unwrapped.

Blast! More than one gentleman would be looking at her through lecherous eyes, including the duke. He knew he had a responsibility to watch over her, but how in the blue blazes was he going to do that, along with his plans for Emily.

"A minute, Jane."

"Yes?" Jane answered, glancing over her shoulder.

Jared narrowed his eyes in confusion. If he had not known better, he would have thought she was still angry with him about the incident at the dressmaker's. But he had apologized.

"A word with you, please."

Her lips seemed to thin. "Now?"

"Indeed, now." When had Jane become so beautiful? Frowning, he took hold of her elbow and escorted her into the duke's library. Roderick and his brothers had left for the club an hour previously, so he would have the room to himself.

Jane took a seat in the leather-backed chair near the hearth, studying his face. "What happened to your eye?"

"Nothing," he said. Nothing but Roderick's right jab.

She pursed her lips, obviously not satisfied. "Hmmm."

He leaned against the mantel and cleared his throat. Now, how to tell the girl to stay away from rakes such as himself? "I am your guardian, as you well know."

She arched a brow, and he was instantly assaulted with an icy blue gaze that could freeze the Thames.

"My misfortune, is it not?"

"Misfortune?" This girl had loved him like an elder brother. Had Roderick poisoned her brain against him? No, the duke would do many things, but that was not his way.

Jane folded her pale arms across the lace bodice of her dress and looked up at the ceiling. "I would rather not speak about it."

Jared quickly crossed the distance between them. Her haughty tone enraged him. "And when will you speak of it?"

She glanced toward the door and pushed her hands against the chair, starting to rise. "Pray, excuse me. I do have a few finishing touches to attend to before I depart for the ball."

"Sit down, young lady." It was not a suggestion.

Jane's forehead creased into a wary line, and she sank into her seat, her expression strained.

Jared clasped his hands behind his back. "I realize there is no easy way to say this, Jane, but as your guardian I must make myself plain." He noted the flash of anger in those sapphire blue eyes, not able to believe that this sweet, little female had the impertinence to defy him with such a surly gaze. If he did not love her like a sister, he would stand back and let her continue her liaison with the duke and enjoy watching her break Roderick down like an obedient puppy.

"What do you want?" she asked curtly.

Jared dragged his mind in an effort to recall anything else he had done to offend her. Had she found out about his boxing match this afternoon at Gentleman Jackson's?

"Is something amiss, Jane? Have I offended you?"

"Offended me?" She shot from her seat, her hands clenched at her sides. "Offended me? If that were only the case, I would not be so angry with you."

Jared watched in shock as Jane started to turn about the room, her hands flapping in the air like a maddened seagull. He became dizzy just watching her.

"How could you?" she shrieked. "How could you be so heartless?" She whirled around, wiping the tears from her eyes.

Jared shifted uncomfortably and swallowed. "What?"

"How could you do that to Emily?"

Ah, Emily. He squared his shoulders. "My relationship with Lady Emily is my business," he warned. "Do not interfere."

"Business? How can you say that? She loved you and you act as if it had never happened." Her voice softened, losing its razor-like edge. "Emily is devastated that her brothers are looking for a suitable husband, and now I cannot fathom that you are a partner in that crime."

Jared was not going to delve into his relationship with Emily, though it seemed Emily had confided in his ward. However, Jane's outburst had angered him so, his patience snapped. "Speaking of her brothers, the duke, in particular"—he closed the gap between them—"I forbid you to go anywhere near the man."

Jane glanced up, her eyes flashing with contempt. "Y-you forbid me?"

"I realize you will be living here for the Season, and as your guardian I will act as a chaperon, along with Agatha, but besides the occasional meal when His Grace is present, you should not have any trouble avoiding the man. Do I make myself perfectly clear, young lady?"

He picked up the door key resting on the massive mahogany desk and tapped it against his palm.

Jane glanced at the key, her blue eyes narrowing in fury. "Oh, yes. Key, lock, prison. You have made yourself perfectly clear. As clear as an addlepated nincompoop!"

Jared grimaced. Now, where the devil had he heard that before?

Chapter Ten

Dumbfounded, Jared watched his ward leave the library. With a muttered oath, he stalked across the Aubusson rug to the rosewood sideboard, where the duke kept a bottle of Madeira. He downed a glass and strode toward the Chinese silk screen in the corner of the room and gazed out onto Grovesnor Square.

He turned with a start when the clatter of footsteps sounded behind him. Thinking it was Jane coming back to apologize, he stepped from behind the screen and stopped short. His eyes focused on the curvaceous backside of Emily's green gown. She seemed to be looking for a book and had no idea anyone else was in the room.

A slow smile spread across his face. He had wondered when he would have a moment alone with her.

Shoving his hand into his jacket pocket, he fingered the door key and took a quick glance toward the hall. Key, lock, prison, and Lady Emily. How delightful.

Emily peered up at the fourteen-foot bookshelves lining the library wall, grabbed hold of the ladder, and started to climb. Though, why her mother wanted the new Radcliffe novel to read before the ball was beyond her. They were leaving in an hour.

Halfway up, Emily stopped and peered over the collection of Minerva Press novels four rows up. There was the book, three feet to her left. She carefully pushed the rolling ladder to the desired destination and leaned over to reach for the book, when a deep voice rang in her ears.

"A dangerous position to be in, my dear. Especially with a rolling ladder."

Emily swirled around, stunned to find Jared standing beyond the library doors. His looming presence stole her breath away. She hated to admit how much he meant to her, though she had tried to deny it. Even now, his presence captivated her.

He was clad in a midnight black jacket and a green velvet waistcoat and looked too desirable for any woman, let alone one who recalled his kisses all too clearly. The memory of his passion surged through her blood like an elixir.

"Go away." Her voice was harsher than she intended, but she had a much stronger guard up now and was determined he would not have the upper hand. She had no intention of falling under his spell until she was good and ready, if at all, and conquering her emotions at this time seemed the best place to start. Drat. If only he were not so attractive.

"And good evening to you, too."

She suddenly found herself squinting at his face, noting that one of his eyes was half-closed. Roderick's doing, no doubt, for her brother had come home from Gentleman Jackson's with a similar ailment, except double the damage.

Still, there was a lethal calmness in the earl's expression that sent her heart racing. But she was safe. She was in her own home. However, it was when he turned his back on her, shutting the library doors closed with a thud that her grip on the ladder tightened and her eyes widened in stunned astonishment.

"Open those doors immediately."

He slowly peered up at her, his smile sparkling with an unholy glint. "No." He then turned back toward the doors and proceeded to pull out a key and insert it into the lock with a resounding click.

A soft gasp escaped her. Good heavens, the man had her under lock and key in her very own home. *Safe* was an understatement. "You cannot lock me in here like some trapped animal," she hissed.

His brows lifted suggestively as he walked farther into the room in long purposeful strides. "No?"

"No, you cannot." She scrambled farther up the ladder, glancing over her shoulder. "You best unlock that door before my brother comes in here."

Jared laughed. "Your brothers, including Roderick, have left for the club and won't be seen until the ball."

He stood there with his hands planted on lean hips exuding such an air of self-confidence that she was momentarily stifled with shock. She was determined to hold the upper hand here. She would not love him. She would not.

"Well, I daresay, someone is bound to come looking for me, so you best open that door."

"Or what?"

Her eyes widened. "Or I will scream."

He took another step and lifted a foot onto the bottom rung of the ladder, dragging his eyes up to hers.

"Come down here, Emily."

The warmth of that endearing smile echoed in his voice, and she blushed. Oh, he was an insufferable rogue. She needed to think. Her chin lifted only slightly, so she could still keep her eyes fixed on his movements. "I refuse to come down until you take your leave, sir."

His eyes drank in the sight of her, gleaming with purpose as they raked her body from head to toe. "You leave me no choice than to join you, Emily."

His words were like an enticing caress, and her knees began to feel like jelly. She merely blinked in awe as he started ascending the ladder. A powerful set of shoulders blocked her view of the ground, and she immediately awoke from her shocked state, scrambling farther up the ladder.

When she reached the highest point she could go, she panicked. "Jared, please get down! This is becoming ridiculous."

He lifted his amber eyes, which were now even with her green slippers. "Get down? And pray, my dear girl, why would I do such a fool thing as that when I find myself enjoying the sights." Before she could retort, he traced a light finger across her ankle. "Immensely, in fact."

A prickling heat shot through her leg at the mere touch of him, and she jerked her right foot off the ladder, tightening her grip on the sides. "Oh! You are not a gentleman."

He wrapped his hand gently around her afflicted ankle, kissing it lightly. "Come here, sweetheart."

The endearment sent her heart fluttering. How could she stop loving this man? She closed her eyes, heedlessly easing her grip on the ladder. She immediately realized her control was slipping and not just in her mind.

She tottered precariously, spinning off the ladder and bumping into the shelving. "Jared!"

She groped mindlessly, falling in midair when a strong hand grabbed her around the waist, heaving her upward, knocking the breath right out of her.

"For the love of heaven, woman. Stay still."

She froze, feeling herself dangling about ten feet off the floor. To her astonishment, the earl carried her like a sack of flour on his hip as he maneuvered himself down the ladder. When his shoes hit the ground, he stood her upright, his hands still wrapped tightly around her waist. He glared at her, his mouth clenched tight. "Don't ever try that again. It was a stupid thing to do."

Emily fell back, gasping for breath, stunned by his criticism of her for *his* wrongdoing. How dare he treat her in such a fashion! The blood rushed to her face, and suddenly everything inside her finally snapped.

"You pompous idiot!" She pummeled his chest with her fists, her breathing still labored. "How dare you accuse me! Never . . . in my life . . . have I met anyone like you." He clamped her hands to his sides, but she was too far gone to stop her tirade. "Of all the unmitigated, insufferable—"

Her words were muffled against the warmth of his lips. "Emily, sweetheart, I never meant to hurt you."

The tenderness of his whispered kiss awakened her soul. She fell against him, melting into his embrace. He trailed kisses down her neck, and she shivered, knowing she loved this man and would never love another. How could she not? Whatever happened three years ago had an explanation, she was sure of it. He would tell her soon.

"Emily Anne, are you in there?"

Emily fell back from Jared's passionate embrace and gasped, frantically pushing her hair back into place at the sound of her mother's voice. "Gracious, I must look a fright."

Jared smoothed his fingers against her lips and proceeded to replace the pins in her hair. Smiling, he kissed her, raising the door key in his hand.

"Take this. Tell her you needed some privacy. I can step behind the screen near the window."

"Don't be a fool," Emily hissed. "She's not an idiot."

He lifted an amused brow. "Very well, then. If you wish, I can open the door for you."

The door rattled. "Emily?"

Emily jerked the key from his hand. "Very well. Move behind the screen."

He kissed her hand and bowed. "Your wish is my command, sweetheart."

Emily felt a severe tightening in her chest when she reached for the door. The man had stolen her heart . . . again.

Candlelight dripped from a string of crystal chandeliers above Jared as he leaned against a pillar in the Garrick ballroom. His gaze followed the back of Emily's green gown as she stopped to converse with a couple of dandies who were dressed to perfection, their waterfall cravats and bright-colored waistcoats portraying them like strutting peacocks. A small orchestra played a waltz in the far corner of the room. A peal of laughter echoed near the refreshment table, where two young debutantes stood surrounded by a group of young bucks vying for their attention.

At that moment Emily glanced toward the sound. Jared caught her eye and winked. A blush stole across her face and he smiled.

"What the devil are you grinning about?" Roderick growled beside him, his arms folded across his chest. "Makes that ghastly eye of yours look wretched."

Jared raised his good brow. "At least I have one good eye. You, on the other hand, have no good eyes."

It was true. Both of the duke's eyes were half shut from Jared's bout with him in the boxing ring that afternoon. Nothing about the two women had been settled. Nothing except that each one had ordered the other to stay away from their respective relative.

Roderick grimaced. "You may not have the other eye available if you seize another dance with my sister. Her future husband would not care for you snatching three dances with her this evening. You have already gone far and above the call of duty with two, and I daresay, the way you held her in that waltz made me want to shoot you point-blank." He tilted his head toward the opposite side of the floor where the musicians played. "See there, how very good they look together. And a waltz. Nothing more intimate than that, is there?"

Jared pushed off the wall, his gaze flying across the room. Something primitive shot through him at the sight of Emily in Lord Bringston's arms. The marquess was a perfect gentleman and good husband material. That fact did not sit well with Jared at all.

Roderick waved his hand in front of Jared's face. "Suffice to say, we do have other matters to attend to tonight than my baby sister."

The strains of the waltz pounded in Jared's ears. He became increasingly uneasy as he noted the smile blanketing Emily's face while she was swirled around the ballroom by Bringston. It was all Jared could do not to march across the floor and sweep Emily into his arms, announcing she was his. But he had a job to do tonight, and the meeting of the three most prominent secret agents in London was going to take place, Emily or not.

"Jared?"

Jared shifted his gaze back to the duke, and they walked back into the shadow of the pillar, away from the crowd. "At fifteen minutes to twelve," Jared said, "I will make my way to the designated rendezvous point. You follow in ten minutes."

Roderick nodded. "Heard the fellow took a ball to his back to stop the missive informing the enemy of your location."

Jared grimaced, hating to owe any man, let alone a man who almost died saving his life. "I have not forgotten. I owe the man a debt I cannot repay. Any more words of wisdom, Duke?"

Roderick broke into laughter and held up his hands. "Truce. Have you not considered the fact that this legendary man may be as big as the two of us put together?"

A sliver of softness squeezed into Jared's expression. "Truce, but only for tonight . . . as long as you stay away from Miss Greenwell."

Roderick's lip curled. "A mere half truce then, since you will stay away from my sister."

"Call it what you will." Jared shrugged, moving a few feet and leaning his back against the pillar. Boney would have to take over England before Jared would stay away from Emily. "I have made my orders plain to Jane on this matter."

While Jared's roving eye searched for Emily, he missed the duke's intent gaze locked on a pale blue gown located near the refreshment table.

Jane stood near the punch bowl, waving her fan about her face. "I simply do not know if I can make it through the night, Agatha. That colonel with the big red nose stepped on my toes twice, Lord Goodley tried pulling me into the gardens, and Lord Sunbury breathed so heavily on my neck I thought I might wilt."

Agatha laughed. "What about Emily's brothers?"

Jane's face brightened. "Oh, I have danced with each one of them."

"Except me."

Jane whirled around to find the duke towering over her. "I believe this next dance is mine, Miss Greenwell."

Jane frowned. "I fear you are not on my dance card, Your Grace. The next dance has been given to Lord Hanley." She tilted her head toward a homely gentleman with a hooked nose and buck teeth walking toward them.

The duke sent the man in question a stern glare. "I believe this dance has been taken, Hanley."

"T-taken?" The man's eyes bugged out from his head.

"Yes, taken," the duke repeated curtly.

Hanley's face turned a deep pink as he stared at the duke's swollen eyes. "Your servant, madam." He gave Jane a swift bow and departed before she could gather a reply.

Furious at the impertinence of the duke, Jane gave the man her iciest stare. "*That* was not at all gentlemanly."

The duke had the audacity to laugh, turning Jane's cheeks red.

"Oh, fustian, child." Agatha tapped her trusty parasol against the table. "Go with him. He won't bite." She shot the duke a questioning smile. "Or will you, Your Grace?"

Roderick raised two swollen brows. "I do not make promises I cannot keep, Miss Appleby."

Agatha dropped her gaze, hiding her smile. "I see. Then perhaps it would not be wise if she danced with you after all."

Jane snapped her fan closed. "I daresay, Agatha, I will be able to withstand one dance with His Grace." She inclined her head toward the duke, her blue eyes narrowing suspiciously. "And pray, what happened to your face?"

The music began for a waltz, and Roderick swiftly took hold of her hand, smiling mischievously. "Nothing that a dance can't cure, Miss Greenwell."

*   *   *

Emily's green slippers padded softly along the dimly lit hallway as she made her way from the ballroom to the conservatory of the Garrick mansion. It was a few minutes before twelve. She was giddy with excitement. Tonight she would finally meet the Black Wolf and his partner.

She rested her ear lightly against the door to the conservatory. Nothing. Slowly she pushed the door open, its hinges creaking in the darkness.

She froze, waiting, listening, but heard only the mingling of violins and laughter coming from the dance floor at the other end of the home. She hastened inside, her eyes trying to adjust to the dim light given off by the moon as it fingered its beams through the tall panes of glass on the far side of the room.

The large chamber was hot and humid. Plants of every kind reached out, rubbing against her arms. Pint-sized rhododendrons brushed at her skirts. The sweet smell of roses teased her senses. If it were any other time but now, she would have taken a leisurely stroll about the hothouse to inspect the flowers that grew there.

Her neck prickled at the sound of clacking footsteps drawing near. She skirted behind a statue of an angel and waited.

"Lady Emily, are you there?"

Emily bit back a groan of disbelief. Not now! Mr. Fennington's voice was beginning to grate on her nerves. She pushed herself further against the warmth of the wall behind her, holding her breath, listening intently as a pair of black buckled shoes clapped hard against the conservatory's marble floor.

"Come now, Emily. I know you are hiding." The man's staggering footsteps gave her the uneasy feeling that he was foxed to the gills . . . again. "Do not play coy with me, my little cabbage." Emily cringed. "I saw you escape the ballroom after looking in my direction. Your timing was perfect, my dear. No one will suspect our little rendezvous here."

Emily clasped her hands together in horror. The impudence of the man! What if her counterparts showed themselves? The thought of Fennington meeting up with England's most prominent but dangerous agents sent a cold shiver down her back.

She became more uncomfortable by the minute as the man began to march up and down the aisles of plants searching for her, thumping around like an elephant on the hunt for food.

"Emily, I say, you little imp, having me look for you? Making a game of it, eh? But I will find you, and then we will have quite an amusing time."

Emily started, catching sight of Fennington's tall shadow about ten feet away. He hiccuped, stumbling against one of the countess's prize roses. There was a crash. Pink petals and dirt fell everywhere. Emily swallowed a bubble of laughter.

"Come now, my lady. I daresay I have had enough of these childish pranks." His voice rose in anger.

Silence blanketed the room like a heavy shadow. Emily peered toward the door, measuring her escape. She had to take her leave. She was putting her counterparts in danger with this ninny. Her musings had made her temporarily lose sight of Fennington. Drat. Where was the idiot? Her heart thumped in her ears, and she hastened back a step, accidentally slipping against the statue. It teetered precariously. With a gasp, she reached out to grab it.

"Aha! There you are, you little termagant!"

Fennington's hand snaked around her waist and squeezed. His hot breath hammered against her ear. "Alone at last, my little one."

Emily felt a momentary alarm. "Mr. Fennington, I implore you, this is not what it seems. I did not, I repeat, did not come here in hopes of a tryst with you."

"Ah, my shy, little Emily. You are even more beautiful than I remember. I saw you one day at the lake near Elbourne, and I must say, you showed quite a pretty leg."

Had this odious fop been spying on her? She pushed him away and lifted her chin, daring him to touch her.

"I am leaving now, Mr. Fennington. Pray, sir, do not ever touch me again or it is I who will kill you."

The man dared to laugh, and with a jerk of his hands flattened her shoulders against the wall.

Emily's eyes grew round at his determination. "What do you think you are doing?"

A moonbeam struck his face, and all at once Emily saw his handsome features marred by an infuriating rage. This was not the Mr. Fennington she knew.

"I believe it is time you call me James, my lady. For soon we will be wed, and I won't have any wife of mine calling me *Mr. Fennington*." He ground out the words against her cheek.

"Wed?" Emily was stunned. "You must be mad!"

"Not mad. You have teased me long enough, my girl."

Emily winced as his grip on her tightened.

"I have a carriage to take us away to Gretna Green tonight."

"Gretna Green? Preposterous."

He let out a mocking laugh. "But of course, my dear, since it will take a few days to arrive to our destination, we will have to put up at a few posting inns."

With one hand still on her, he pulled out his quizzing glass and peered at her, a malevolent glint in his eyes. "So you see, even if one of your arrogant brothers deems it necessary to rescue you, your reputation will be in rags, and alas, you will be mine, dear Emily. Mine forever." He flicked a finger across her lips. "I fancy you have finally deduced that I am not as stupid as you may have once believed."

Mad was more like it. Emily felt her frustration build. "On the contrary, I find you quite the most interesting man I have ever come across, *James*." She batted her lashes at him, and to her surprise, the man loosened his grip on her.

His expression changed to one of delighted eagerness. "Then you won't scream if I kiss you?"

"No, but I mind," a commanding voice rang out.

Emily's eyes flew to her right. Glittering amber eyes leapt out of nowhere. Fennington was instantly picked off his feet and thrown across the room. A row of hydrangeas slammed to the ground. Fennington groaned as he rolled off the dirt and cracked pots.

"If you dare even look at Lady Emily again," Stonebridge said in a dangerous tone, his menacing form hovering over the shocked man, "I will hang you by your cravat until you are dead." A shiny black shoe pressed against Fennington's chest. "Do hope you understand, dear fellow."

Fennington nodded, not daring to look up as he snatched his quizzing glass from off the floor. The earl then proceeded to pick the man up, throwing him toward the door.

"You have exactly one minute to leave these premises, and then I will come after you with this." A small black pistol glinted against the night, and Fennington swallowed hard. He was gone without a word.

Recovering from her shock, Emily stared at the pistol in Jared's hands. Her knees were about as solid as the marmalade Agatha ate that morning. "H-how did you know I was in here?"

His glittering stare burned into her, gnawing away at her self-confidence. "You, madam, should never have left the ballroom."

Emily lifted her chin. "You, sir, are not my guardian or my husband."

"It is merely a matter of time."

Emily's heart leapt to life. He wanted to marry her? His gaze swept over her, and her pulse skittered. She knew there were things they needed to talk about. He had said something about being forced to marry Felicia. Surely, he would tell her all, and she did love him.

She paused as a sudden thought occurred to her. Good heavens, what if Black Wolf decided to show himself at this very minute?

She watched in silence as Jared slid his pistol inside his jacket. Her mind began to spin as she considered her predicament. If she were meeting someone, mayhap

Jared was meeting someone as well. Her confidence plummeted like a lead ball dropped from the tower.

She instantly recalled seeing Miss Susan Wimble paying quite a bit of attention to the earl at the refreshment table. A sudden burst of fury filled her. "I daresay, that the only reason you came here was to meet someone."

She saw his jaw stiffen, and her heart deflated. So, it was true. What was his game?

His gaze hardened. "What about your intentions? I could say the same about you."

The shock of his words stifled her. She could not tell him whom she was to meet. She would never divulge that information.

With a mumbled curse, he inclined his head, directing her to move to the end of the conservatory where it was pitch-black. "Over there."

Emily glanced toward the darkened alcove, her eyes widening in outrage. She may enjoy his kisses, but if she moved toward the darkness, her senses might completely leave her and then where would she be? "I certainly will not."

"You can walk or I can carry you. Your choice."

There was a stern expression on his face, which broke no argument. It reminded her of Roderick when he was cross, but more intense. "Very well," she snapped, "but I do not condone this caveman-like attitude of yours."

She picked up her skirts and started for the other side of the room, her slippers dodging the broken pots and debris left by Mr. Fennington's fall. She hoped that Black Wolf had been alerted to the commotion with Fennington and had retreated.

She halted near a rosebush and glanced at the man behind her. When she looked at him now, drops of moisture clung to his damp face and his eyes glittered with an almost wolfish look. Her gaze froze on his rugged profile.

No, her heart cried. No. No. No.

"Have you hurt yourself?" His cool gaze pinned her to the floor as he closed in on her like a wolf advancing on his prey.

"N-no, I'm not hurt." Only stupid, she thought, turning around, fumbling with a pot beside her as she pushed it farther onto the table. What a ninny she had been. "Mr. Fennington was quite a menace, and I must thank you for rescuing me."

"Emily, look at me."

She spun around, her heart pounding, and for every step he took toward her, she took two steps back until the warm wall of the conservatory rammed into her shoulder blades. Moonlight suddenly struck the harsh planes of his face, and she closed her eyes, everything becoming all too clear. Yes. Jared was the Black Wolf. She had no doubt about it now.

"The devil, Emily, I am not Fennington. Did you come in here to avoid the fop?"

She slowly lifted her lids, too astonished at her discovery to speak. She swallowed past the tightness in her throat, her violet eyes locking in recognition with his amber ones. "No." She paused. "But I know who you are."

A smile flitted across his face. "Really, you don't know who I am already?"

The question only strengthened her resolve to find out for certain. She felt trapped, yet she could use one phrase and he would know who she was as well. It had been sent in the missive. She chewed her bottom lip, determined to see this through. "May I ask you a question?"

"Ask." He took a step back, placing his hands on his hips.

"Very well, then." She glanced briefly at the conservatory door, then back to him. "Tell me, can a fox and a sheep befriend the wolf?"

His hands fell from his sides, his eyes pinning her with a cool, disbelieving stare. "What are you saying?"

Emily thought he would be relieved to know she was not meeting anyone, but he seemed to be incensed that she knew his secret. "I cannot see that your question matters, my lord."

"Jared. My name is Jared."

"Is it?" she asked, irked by his indignant manner.

"You have no idea what you are saying, madam."

They stared at each other in the hushed tones of their breathing, but she would not let him make her feel guilty. "I am who I am, *Jared*, and if you do not like it, you may leave your precarious employment anytime you please."

His eyes widened in shock as if he finally understood the implications of her little speech. "The devil you are!"

She lifted a challenging brow. "No, the devil I am not."

He took hold of her shoulders and shook her. "You little fool. How could you have put yourself in such danger?"

Fury drowned any resolve to stay calm. "I saved your life, and this is how you repay me?" The bold words spewed from her mouth before she could stop them.

His hands dropped like a dead-weight from her shoulders. Even in the dim light, his face appeared to drain of color. His body stiffened as he turned his back to her, his hands fisted at his sides. "Confound it, Emily. You could have died."

Emily touched his shoulder. "But I survived."

He spun back around. "You must have suffered terribly." He brushed a stiff hand across his face. "To think that I was the cause of your pain . . ."

"Agatha took care of me."

"Emily, Emily." His eyes swept over her face, and he pulled her to him. The simple touch of his hand against her cheek sent a warm shiver through her. "I lost you once"—he drew her to him and kissed her long and hard—"I could not bear to lose you again." He pulled away, tracing her lips with his thumb.

"Oh, Jared."

"I have always wanted you, sweetheart. I wanted to marry you three years ago. Believe me, I did everything in my power to convince your father to give me your hand. But he had his reasons and denied me."

"He refused you?" Emily glanced up in shock. "But I never knew. My father said nothing. You never wrote."

"I did write, but you obviously did not receive my letters. When your father first rejected my suit, I had no wish for you to know about it, not until I had decided on another course of action." He paused for a few seconds, and his hands clenched.

Emily watched his amber eyes close, as if he were debating whether to say something else, then decided against it. "Jared?"

He avoided her gaze and turned to stare at the darkened room. "Before I could devise a plan to see you again, I was found in a compromising position with Felicia Fairlow at Lady Rosalind's ball. I had thought you were to be in the garden, but I found myself holding a swooning woman in my hands instead, and soon I was wed. Felicia's reputation would have been tarnished, sweetheart. My honor was at stake along with her reputation. You have to understand why I married her."

Though it hurt her deeply and there were still questions left unanswered, Emily was finally able to begin to understand what had happened to their love three years ago. Her father must have misunderstood or misjudged Jared's intentions. Tears welled in her eyes. Jared had wanted to marry her all along.

He turned and touched her cheek. "Marry me, Em." He buried his face in her hair. "Please, sweetheart. We've waited too long."

Emily lifted her gaze to his. "Yes, I'll marry you."

Laughing, he swept her into his arms, locking his lips to hers in a crushing kiss. His hands moved gently down her spine, and a deep feeling of peace filled her.

"How very cozy."

The cool, clipped voice was like an icy finger against Emily's neck. She slipped from Jared's arms and spun around. "Roderick?"

Chapter Eleven

"Roderick," Emily said again, but this time it was not a question, it was a hideous fact.

"Not quite," the duke drawled. "I was wondering . . ." He shot Jared a chilling glare, then moved his icy gaze back to his sister. "Tell me, Em, can a fox and a sheep befriend the wolf?"

Emily paled. Roderick was Black Wolf's partner. The very notion was like a kick to her stomach.

The duke stepped closer, jerking her to him. "If I had known what you were about the past three years, little sister, I would have imprisoned you at Elbourne."

"Leave her be," Jared snapped.

Without warning the duke pulled Emily into a slash of moonlight, grabbed hold of her gown, and spun her around. Before she could protest, he gazed down the back of her dress and cursed at the scar he saw. "The devil, Em! What the blazes were you thinking! What kind of fool are you?"

Fool? Tears sprang to her eyes. "I did my duty, Roderick. Is that so hard to understand?"

His strong hand guided her toward the door. "We will speak of this later. Go back to the ballroom."

"I will not be dictated to."

"You will obey me, Emily Anne."

Humiliation filled her. Pressing her lips together, she

avoided Jared's face and strode from the room, knocking down a tall rhododendron in her wake and slamming the door.

Roderick turned a hardened gaze back toward Jared. "Blast Headquarters for allowing this!"

"She saved my life, Roderick."

"Then you of all people should be horrified."

Jared glared at the duke. "Horrified? You astound me. I am privileged that anyone, let alone a woman, would put her life on the line so that I may live. You, Your Egotistical Grace, are the one that should be horrified with your atrocious behavior. That sister of yours has been hiding that dreadful secret all these years, and you were too blind to see it. You, one of the most prominent agents in England, known to steal secrets from the most cunning enemies in the profession, had under your very roof the one invaluable person who had been helping us cross the French lines."

Jared recalled the pain in Emily's voice, and his anger intensified. "How dare you treat her like . . . like a piece of chattel."

"Wait just a minute," Roderick growled. "How would you feel if that was your sister and you saw the scar from a ball marring her body?"

Amber eyes struck back. "I, for one, would hope I would feel proud. Proud that my sibling had the gallantry to serve her country in the most precious way she could . . . with her life."

"She almost died in that attack!"

Jared let out a deep-seated sigh. "Don't you think I know that?" She could have died saving his thick, stubborn hide. The hideous thought ate at his soul.

The moon glowed brighter as Roderick began to pace in frustration, his heels clacking loudly against the floor. "Confound her. She best not think of doing anymore jobs."

"I agree."

"You do?"

"Indeed, I will not have my future wife gallivanting about England and who knows where as a secret agent.

Headquarters will understand now that we know each other. And we won't have to worry about St. Helena either. Moments ago I was delivered a coded missive via one of my aides. We are not needed at St. Helena after all."

Roderick's head jerked. He ignored the comment about St. Helena and went straight for the jugular. "What do you mean, *your* future wife?"

Jared realized this was not the time or the place to discuss his wedding plans. After a long pause, he spun on his heels to leave. "You must have heard us, Roderick."

Roderick grabbed his shoulder. "I forbid you to marry her!"

Jared turned, meeting Roderick's icy gaze with one of his own. *Not again. Never again.*

"Forbid away, Your Grace. But if I were you, I would add a tidy sum to those betting books at White's. A man like you could make a good profit with your inside information."

Roderick raised his right eyebrow in fury. "Take your belongings from our home. You are no longer a guest, *Stonebridge.*"

"No, I won't be a guest much longer, will I? Mayhap you will have room for me in a month or two when I become your new brother?"

Emily had never been so humiliated in her life. She ran down the hall into the darkness of the green room, sinking into the first chair she saw. Wrapping her arms tightly around her stomach, she fought back the sobs that sprang to her throat. How long she sat there she did not know. But the horrid incident that had caused the scar on her back was nothing compared to the disgusted look in Roderick's eyes.

"Jared, dear. Where on earth have you been?"

Emily stiffened at the sound of a lady's sultry voice directly outside the door.

"Jared, I missed you. Where have you been off to, you naughty boy."

Emily carefully wiped the tears from her face and listened intently as two shadows fell into eerie shapes against the opposite wall.

"I needed some fresh air." At the sound of Jared's voice, Emily felt as if she would lose her dinner.

"Out here?" the woman laughed, and Emily saw the two shadows come together.

"No, I took a walk in the conservatory."

"I know a better place than that, darling. Through the ballroom and past the French doors. Now, there is a perfect place for us."

Emily pressed a shaking hand to her throat. An intense sense of betrayal coursed through her. Again. The tears she desperately tried to stop earlier began to flow silently down her cheeks. How could she ever have thought that Jared loved her? He pitied her. She had almost died for him, and now honor and duty made him propose.

"Do you never stop, Susan?"

"Not with you, darling."

Miss Susan Wimble. Emily heard nothing but the rustle of clothing. Her face grew hot with humiliation, her cheeks burning with the memory of lips that kissed hers only minutes ago were now kissing another woman's.

"Why should we wait, my lord? Why not announce our engagement tonight?"

"Not tonight."

"Why not?" the lady whined, and Emily sank deeper into the chair.

"I have business to attend to in the next few weeks," Jared replied matter-of-factly.

"Very well, but you promised me a dance tonight."

"Had I known you were coming, I would have prepared for your overbearing welcome."

The woman giggled.

A raw and biting grief overwhelmed Emily.

"I had believed you in the country aiding your ailing cousin?" Jared uttered.

"Oh, did I not tell you? Bess is much better."

"Is she now?"

"Darling, do not look at me like that," the lady snapped. "I cannot bear to have you angry at me."

The words drifted beyond Emily's ears. A deep and aching pain lodged in her chest. Could she ever face the man again?

She glanced at the window, where outside it had begun to rain. The drops pattered against the pane like rocks to her soul. She clasped a fist to her breast. Oh, Jared, how could you do it to me again?

"Have you seen Emily?" Jane asked her aunt as the strains of a cotillion floated above the dance floor.

Agatha tapped her parasol, sending a frowning glance in the direction of the ballroom entrance. "No, dear, I have not seen her for at least an hour."

Jane patted her fan against her chin. "Have you seen Cousin Jared then?"

Agatha looked over the crowd. "Believe he took to the card room. I suspect he will return momentarily."

Once again, Agatha's gaze drifted to the entrance to the ballroom. "Ah, there he is now."

Jane scowled. "And that Miss Wimble is hanging on to him like a bloodsucking parasite."

"Shhh. I told you, we are not to know a thing."

Jane bent her head and whispered, "How could he do that to Emily? How could he prance that little tease about the ball tonight when Emily had such high hopes?"

Agatha tapped her niece's powder blue slipper with the end of her parasol. "Listen to me, if you do not stop staring at him as if your eyes are about to fall out of their sockets, everyone in the *ton* will suspect something."

Jane pulled her fan up to cover her face as she spoke. "The lady in question is most inappropriate for him. Most inappropriate indeed."

"If I were you, young lady, I would keep that mouth of yours closed for the time being."

Jane's brows drew together as Miss Susan Wimble

pulled her guardian onto the dance floor. "Why, I should like to say a few words to that . . . that woman. Only an hour ago I saw her flirting with Mr. Fennington."

Agatha let out a low chuckle. "Yes, those two would fit together quite nicely." There was a slight pause. "Ah, there is your duke, dear."

With her fan lifted just below her eyes, Jane tilted her head to her side. The Duke of Elbourne was leaning against the far wall, talking to the host. "Good gracious, why would you say he is *my duke*?"

"Come now, child, do not think me a simpleton."

Jane's head snapped around to meet Agatha's amused gaze. "I do not think you a simpleton. I am merely saying—"

"Jane, your heart is not as invisible as you think."

Jane blushed.

"But it would be in your best interest," Agatha went on, "and the duke's, mind you, if you kept your little meeting in the garden a secret. It seems His Grace is not looked upon with much favor from your guardian. And do not forget, it is your guardian who will have to sanction your future husband."

"No," Jane admitted with a frown. "It would be best not to say a word on the matter. Not a single word."

Agatha rose. "I will make my way toward the refreshment table, dear, and see to the duke. Mayhap he has seen Emily."

"Pray, do not get up, Aunt. I can ask him."

"No." Agatha's voice was firm. "You will not cause any more excitement tonight with those two hotheaded men. I am going to speak to His Grace, and you may search out Emily's brothers to inquire if they have seen her."

Agatha hastened to meet the duke before he was pulled onto the dance floor by the hostess. "Your Grace, I have not seen much of you tonight."

Roderick turned toward Agatha. "Ah, can you see enough of me now?" He gave her a teasing half smile, stood back, and bowed, showing off his full form, two swollen eyes and all.

Agatha glared at him, tapping her parasol on the floor.

"You are an impertinent young man," she hissed for only him to hear.

"Well now," Roderick said as he glanced at Jared across the way. "Impertinent? I must be growing in your estimation. Let me see the last time you addressed me as such, I was an overbearing, contemptuous—"

"Impertinent young man," Agatha snapped. "Now, escort my old bones to a chair and fetch me some punch."

The corner of Roderick's mouth turned upward. "Fetch you some punch? Dear lady, if I did not know better, I would think that you are asking a duke, a high peer of the realm, to fetch you some punch."

Agatha gave him one of her famous smiles. "Oh, no, Your Grace, I am not asking you, I am telling you."

His smile twisted. "Telling me, eh?"

Agatha flipped her hand in the air. "We have matters to discuss. Important matters."

Roderick's jaw tensed. "About what?"

"Not about what, but about *whom*?"

"I am not going to speak to you about your nephew, Agatha. He should never have come to stay at the townhouse this Season. He has caused a great deal of distress in regards to Emily."

Agatha pursed her lips. "And what about Jane, then?"

His mouth softened. "Ah, now Miss Greenwell is another matter entirely."

"You forget that Jared is her guardian and unless you reconcile with him, you won't have a chance to marry his ward."

Roderick's mouth dropped opened in shock. "Marry? When, pray tell, have I ever mentioned a word about marriage?"

"Do not play me the fool, young man. Whether you wanted to or not, you inadvertently proposed marriage when you stepped out onto the terrace with my Jane."

The duke's forehead creased into a furrow of tiny lines. "And I suppose you would be the one to tell your nephew?"

"Serve me that glass of punch, and we will talk some more."

"Blackmail does not become you Agatha, not at all."

"Yes, so people have said." Agatha smiled as the duke retreated to the refreshment table. But her smile soon soured as Miss Susan Wimble swished off the dance floor in a rustle of pearls and silk, disappearing into the hall.

"Here you are," Roderick said a minute later as he bent down to deliver Agatha a glass of red wine.

"I said punch," she scowled, handing it back to him.

Roderick smiled and took a seat next to her. "Ah, but if I am an impertinent young man, as you say, I should not do your bidding."

"Where is your sister?"

He looked across the crowd. "I have not seen Emily. She should have returned by now. No doubt she's probably with Mother."

Agatha frowned. "Fetch Jared this instant. Over there, by the violins."

Roderick shot from his chair. "I believe this is where I do become the impertinent duke, madam. I will not—"

The parasol hit his leg, and he jumped. "You will fetch my nephew this minute or I will share with him my comments about the French doors and your lovely Jane."

Roderick's face hardened as he lowered his voice. "That is despicable, Agatha, even from the likes of you."

"I have been called worse. Now, off with you." She clacked her parasol against his shiny black shoes. "Hurry now. This is of the utmost importance."

"A matter of life and death then," he said sarcastically, bowing to her.

Agatha's eyes narrowed as the duke retreated into the crowd. "More than you will ever know," she murmured.

A faint shaft of light filtered from the hallway through the open door, stopping at the toe of Emily's slippers. She needed to return back to the ballroom before someone missed her. But she had no intention of giving Jared the satisfaction of seeing her cry. A metallic taste rose in her throat at the thought of Miss Wimble wrapped in his arms. What a fool she had been!

She would enter the ballroom with her head held high,

her face wiped clean of all tears. She vowed to show him how indifferent she felt about his false proposal. She would prove to herself that she was immune to him after all.

"I see you are still here."

Emily flinched. She glanced up at the doorway, where the silhouette of a woman stood. Miss Susan Wimble. Even in the dim lighting Emily noted the pale yellow gown with its low-scooped neckline, showing more than enough bosom for two women.

Hopefully the darkness hid the wetness on her cheeks. She assured herself that this woman had no idea who she was or what she was to Jared. Emily drank in the sight of the attractive lady and felt her heart break in two. "Good evening."

"I had wondered where you had run off to after scurrying from the conservatory like a frightened little mouse."

Emily stared back in shock. Had the woman overheard her conversation with Jared, or even with Roderick for that matter? She spread her hands against her skirt. "The conservatory?"

The woman stepped into the room. "I happened to be taking a tour with the countess when I saw you run from the room."

Emily was momentarily speechless. Had the countess seen her with the other two men? Then, as if knowing her very thoughts, the woman snapped back.

"No, the countess did not see you. She turned into the blue room before you made your escape."

"I had been interested in the plants," Emily countered.

"Oh, I daresay, Lady Emily, you were interested in more than plants. And, yes, I know what you want. I saw you dancing with Lord Stonebridge, and I do not appreciate you smothering my fiancé with your girlish flirtations. If I were you, I would stay away from him. Far, far away."

"Is that a threat?"

"A threat?" The woman threw her head back and

laughed. "No, take it as fact. You will stay away from him or I will make your life a living—"

"Hello, Susan."

Susan spun around, her eyes wide. "Jared. I thought you were still in the ballroom."

"Obviously."

Emily sank deeper into her chair as the dark shape of Jared's tall body came into view. The very way he stood there told her he was angry with the woman. His massive shoulders blocked any light shining into the room, and Susan shrank in his presence, yet her flowery perfume seemed to seep into every crevice in Emily's chair, making her ill.

"Lady Emily," Jared said curtly, looking down at her.

Emily felt a mounting fury so intense that she thought it might choke her. "Yes, my lord?" She unfolded her body from the chair and stepped forward.

"Emily—"

"Was just leaving," Susan interrupted. "Were you not, my dear?"

Emily lifted her chin and stared at the man beside her. "Indeed," she said stiffly and moved toward the door.

"Emily." Jared detained her departure with a firm hand to her elbow. "Miss Wimble and I—"

"Are more than friends," Emily spat out. She leaned away from him, her gaze still misty with tears. "Do not take me for a simpleton, my lord. I have two eyes." And only one heart, she thought, and you have broken it one too many times.

"Wait for me in the ballroom," he commanded, letting her arm drop to her side.

Emily pressed her lips together, not trusting herself to speak. She took one last glance at Miss Wimble's smiling face and retreated with unyielding dignity, her chin lifted, her steps unfailing, while inwardly, her heart felt sliced in two.

As soon as Emily entered the ballroom, Clayton, Marcus, and Stephen surrounded her like a gathering of grumbling hyenas.

"Dash it all," Clayton said in exasperation. "Where have you been?"

Stephen slid beside her. "By Jove, you have been gone over an hour. At first we thought you with Mother. But we just discovered she had not seen you the past hour either. Had we known, we would have been searching for you earlier."

Marcus moved in front of her, blocking her way to the hall. But Emily was not about to cater to their pompous attitudes now. She stared at them defiantly. "I appreciate your concern, but I daresay, my whereabouts tonight are none of your affair."

Horrified at her outburst, Clayton and Marcus stared back at her as if she had a wart on her nose. But it was Stephen who smothered a chuckle, his eyes sparkling with surprise.

"None of our affair, is it now?" Marcus growled. "I will have you know that your welfare is our affair, little sister."

"Roderick," Clayton said, glancing over his shoulder as the duke approached. "Set her right, will you?"

Emily had no intention of letting her brothers bully her tonight. She had experienced enough of that from one man already. She decided that her only way to take her leave without them giving her another one of their pompous speeches was to hasten to Lord Bringston's side.

Her brothers had already picked the marquess for the top spot on the list of suitors as her future husband anyway. Just as Roderick made it to her side, she broke through the towering male forms and hastened around the perimeter of the room.

"Em, come back here," Roderick hissed.

Emily dismissed her brother with a contemptuous glare as she continued on her path to Lord Bringston. She felt quite relieved when the marquess took her hand, leading her past the refreshment table and onto the dance floor.

She held her breath when she caught sight of Roderick's flashing gray eyes. Feeling daring, she answered back with a brilliant smile and watched with pleasure as four male mouths dropped open in shock.

"By Jove, she is not our little Emily anymore, is she?" Stephen replied.

Clayton frowned. "Look at Bringston drooling over her like a sick puppy. It's enough to make a grown man ill."

Stephen lowered his voice. "If I am not mistaken, Clayton, you had that same drooling face only fifteen minutes ago when you were dancing with Lady Eugenie."

"Lady Eugenie now, is it?" Marcus said with amusement. "I thought it was Lady Cassandra."

"No," Roderick interrupted. "That was an hour ago. Clayton's tastes change like the wind."

"Aho," snapped Clayton. "Speaking about tastes, what say you about Miss Jane Greenwell? I thought she was rather fetching in my arms."

Roderick pushed Clayton against the wall while behind them Stephen and Marcus began to chuckle.

"Boys." Their mother's voice sounded in the distance.

"Mother," Stephen drawled, turning toward her, smiling. "What can we do for you?"

"Have you seen Emily? I need to speak to her about an invitation I just received from the Duke of Wellington."

"Wellington's here?" Roderick asked.

"Over there." His mother pointed across the room. "The man has been here only five minutes, and as luck would have it, I met him at the door just as I was speaking to the countess."

She sighed in delight. "Oh, what a hero. I want our Emily to meet him." She looked about. "Have you seen her about?"

"Over there." Stephen tilted his head across the dance floor. The duchess picked up her spectacles. "I daresay the man beside her does look familiar."

"Lord Bringston," Stephen offered.

The duchess gave a tremulous smile. "Ah. You have

done well with your choice, dears. Why the man is known throughout all of England as a positively handsome specimen, not to mention a very honorable gentleman indeed."

She let her spectacles fall to her bosom and cleared her throat. "But he is much older than your sister, is he not?"

"Five and forty, Mother."

"Four years younger than myself," she said, frowning. "Do you believe he is in good health?"

Stephen raised a sardonic brow. "Well, Mother, we have not yet given him the physical."

"Physical?" the duchess asked warily.

"Yes, he will have to beat Roderick at boxing." Stephen looked at his older brother and laughed. "That in itself will not be too hard. But then he will have to win Clayton at a game of whist, and of course with Marcus, he will have to drink him under the table and then—"

The duchess gasped. "Marcus, do you drink to excess?"

Marcus gave his brother a curt glance and looked back at his mother. "Stephen jests, do you not, dear brother?"

Stephen covertly received another elbow to his gut and spoke through pained lips. "Jesting, Mother. Only jesting."

"This is not the place to jest, dear boy. Now, I need to speak to Emily."

"She's gone," Roderick said with a scowl.

"What?"

"She disappeared through the French doors."

"The cad," Clayton snapped. "I am going to break his confounded neck."

The duchess held Clayton back. "You will do no such thing."

"Then I will go," Roderick growled. "What does Bringston think he is doing? This was not in the plans."

"The same thing you were doing tonight, I suspect," Stephen added.

"What?" the duchess asked.

"We are wasting time," Marcus interrupted. "Our Emily is out there with that . . . that man!"

"Of course, he is a man," the duchess said. "*What*, pray tell, do you think Lord Bringston is? A monkey?"

Roderick heaved a frustrated sigh. "There is no time to argue about this. Our Emily is in jeopardy out there."

"What can happen?" the duchess asked with innocent eyes.

All four male mouths thinned.

"He is a man, Mother. That is all you need to know," Roderick snarled. "I am going to retrieve her."

His mother put a hand to his chest. "You are not."

He stiffened. "What?"

"You are not going to retrieve your sister. If you believe that Lord Bringston is the man for her, then you will leave well enough alone."

Stephen looked almost cross-eyed as he stared at the French doors, his arms flailing. "But he . . . the man . . ."

The duchess glared at her four sons. "He is a gentleman and will act accordingly."

All four men rolled their eyes.

"I forbid you to interfere with Emily and Lord Bringston," she commanded. "Do you boys understand?"

A tense silence filled the group. The music played on. The sound of voices drifted in and out of the family gathering. The duchess looked every one of her sons in the eye. Each acknowledged her command with a curt nod. Everyone except Roderick, whose jaw turned taut with fury. "Roderick?"

"I heard you."

"And?"

"I cannot in good conscience let Emily out there with *that man*."

"And pray tell, why not?"

"Because."

"Because you took Miss Jane Greenwell out there over an hour ago and you kissed her?"

Roderick looked up, momentarily speechless. "I—"

"What's good for the goose is good for the gander."

Roderick rubbed his hand against his jaw in confusion. "What the devil are you talking about, Mother?"

"Do not take that tone of voice with me, Roderick."

"Good evening again, Duchess." Wellington's baritone voice penetrated the family gathering.

"Ah, good evening," the duchess replied graciously. "You are familiar with my sons Clayton and Marcus?"

Wellington smiled. "They served me well at Waterloo. And I hear your youngest son served as well." The man was introduced to Stephen.

"And my eldest?" the duchess replied.

"We have met before." Wellington's eyes twinkled.

"Yes, before Waterloo," Roderick said as they shook hands.

"I hear Lord Stonebridge is about?" Wellington raised an inquiring brow at Roderick's two swollen eyes as if knowing the man in question had produced the damage to the young duke.

"Indeed," Roderick said, crinkling his brow. "At the moment, though, I cannot seem to place him."

Chapter Twelve

Miss Susan Wimble stood in the green room of Garrick Hall, her small white hands clenched at her sides. "You have no right to pay attention to that woman when I am your fiancée."

"No right?" Jared replied angrily. "How is it that I have no right when you have been paying attention to your so-called cousin in the country who is your third cousin once removed and very, very male."

Susan stiffened in response, then in a heartbeat she was as soft as silk. "Darling, we must not fight. I was just so jealous when I saw that girl."

Jared ground his teeth. "She is not a girl. She is a woman."

Susan flitted her hand in the air, then slid her palms up his chest. "Whatever you say, darling. Are we going to announce our engagement tonight?"

Jared wrapped his hands around her wrists, pushing her away. "There will be no announcement."

The lady forced out her lower lip like a ten-year-old child. "But you said after the Season was over."

"I said we would have this time as a grace period to work out the details. But it seems one little detail is yet to be worked out."

The lady wiggled her curvaceous body alongside him. "One little detail should not stop us."

"It might," he said, clenching his mouth tighter as he held her away.

"Well then, what detail are we talking about?"

Jared felt his patience waning as Susan plopped down on the chair that Emily had been sitting in only minutes ago. He watched in amazement as the lady began to fiddle with her nails.

"Oh, look at that." She looked up and held her hand in the air, showing off her ripped fingernail. "I believe I tore this one on the fireplace before I came to the ball. Father was in such a hurry, you know."

Jared barely listened to the lady's incessant chatter. His stomach twisted with guilt as he recalled Emily's pale face and lifeless eyes. He had hurt her deeply. Again.

"I have come to a decision," he said, staring down at Susan.

The woman looked up, smiling. "You will make the announcement tonight," she squealed and jumped up. "I knew it. Oh, I knew you would."

Jared was caught off guard when she pressed her lips to his. He immediately released her. "Stop it."

Her eyes began to glitter with tears. Jared would have cringed with guilt, but it was the best acting he had seen since Drury Lane.

"What is it, darling?" she asked pursing her cherry red lips. "Is it my perfume?"

Jared wanted to make this as easy as possible. In his heart he knew he had decided a long time ago not to marry this woman. Emily only solidified his choice.

"I cannot marry you, Susan."

Long thick lashes flew upward in shock. "You cannot marry me or you *will not* marry me?"

"Both."

"I see," she said with narrowed eyes. "And does this have anything to do with that silly halfwit who was in here moments ago?"

Amber eyes battled with blue, and Jared wondered what insanity had led him to ever consider marrying this

black-hearted witch. Her question did not even deserve
an answer.

"Then let me tell you one thing, my lord." The lady
sauntered toward the door and glanced over a creamy
white shoulder. "Had it not been for your sizable wealth,
I can guarantee I never would have looked at you twice.
And as for children," she laughed, "I would never have
had your heir. You can take my word for that. I would
never have taken the chance of having a child born to
me and lose my precious figure. So good riddance to
you. Mayhap I should work on the duke." With those
last words she was gone.

The chilly air nipped at Emily's neck as she sat on the
stone bench with Lord Bringston. His profile was strong,
yet boyish. His dark hair held a hint of gray at the tem-
ples, and she felt safe with him. But he was not Jared.

She stifled the sob that rose in her throat and looked
down the path. "My brothers have spoken to you?"

The marquess took off his black jacket, wrapping it
about her shoulders. "Yes, you are a beautiful woman,
Lady Emily. I would be a fool not to take them
seriously."

"I see, my lord."

"Call me William," he whispered, turning her cheek.

She gazed into warm brown eyes and felt a gentleness
in this man that touched her deeply. Though she would
never love him like Jared, she began to think that perhaps her brothers were right after all. Perhaps they had
chosen wisely.

"Why have you not married?" she asked boldly.

He looked up at the trees where the dappled moonlight played against his tender expression. A soft wind
ruffled his hair.

"I will be honest with you, Lady Emily," he sighed
and glanced toward the chandeliers that lighted the ballroom, "I fell in love once. The woman was four years
older than I, and her father forbid us to wed. A short
time afterward, she was married. By now she has all but
forgotten me."

"But you were a wealthy marquess? Who could deny you?"

"I was but seventeen."

"Seventeen . . . I see." Emily looked up at the moon and frowned. It was large and luminous—everything her heart was not. "I was seventeen when my father turned down one of my suitors as well. Believe what you will, but my brothers could never make me wed a man I had no wish to marry."

Lord Bringston took her hand in his. His grip was warm and gentle, like her father's. The more she thought about it, the more she began to realize her father probably thought her a mere child when Jared had called on him. Yet her father's rejection still hurt.

"I need an heir, Emily. Though my brother is next in line, he is not wed, and at this point, never plans to be. I cannot claim to love you because my heart has always belonged to someone else, but I can assure you, I will be faithful to you and provide for you always."

He knelt down before her, bringing her hand to his lips.

"I know our age difference may cause you to worry over an uncertain future, but I am in good health, and in time, I believe we will come to trust and respect one another. So, alas, dear lady, I am asking you to be my wife. If you wish, we can look upon it as a marriage of convenience. These things are done all the time."

Emily lowered her eyes. Two proposals in one night. One true. One false. "I do not know what to say."

"Pray, do not give me your response now. Take some time to think about it. I will give you two weeks and wait for your reply."

Emily was too dazed by his immediate proposal to decline his offer. She parted her lips to speak, but he stopped her by placing his finger lightly to her lips. "It is best that we return now. I am certain your brothers are scouring the grounds for you." His gray eyes sparkled with mischief.

Emily's lips slowly curved into a beguiling smile, followed by a bubbling laugh as they headed back toward the ballroom. "They are arrogant little devils, are they not, my lord?"

Lord Bringston patted her hand and chuckled. "Being four of them, my dear, and one of me, I believe they can be anything they want."

Emily smiled at him. He was not a bore as she had once thought he would be, but a true delight. Her slippers crunched slightly over the walkway as they approached the French doors to the ballroom. "But tell me, you are handsome enough, and wealthy enough, why have you chosen to marry me? You could have married anyone you wanted."

Lord Bringston looked beyond the crowd and sighed. "Do not take this as an insult, my dear, but I decided that it was time to marry and you are as close to my true love as I will ever come. I hope that does not offend you."

Emily paused, clasping his hand in a warm embrace. "I am honored. Thank you for telling me the truth." Emily knew that this man would treat her with all the respect and kindness she could ever ask for. He would give her everything but his heart, because his belonged to another, and so did hers.

Jared's black shoes slapped the Garrick hallway in an even, unhurried manner as he strode from the green room toward the ball. He had waited a good amount of time to take his leave until he knew Miss Susan Wimble was safely out of his immediate vicinity. The torment he had seen in Emily's eyes had severed his soul, but he intended to set everything straight soon enough. Perhaps a bouquet of golden daffodils would give him an edge. She had always loved those Wordsworth poems . . .

"Jared, or should I say, Lord Stonebridge."

The familiar voice reverberated in Jared's brain, and he turned, startled to see Wellington standing a few feet away. Beside the noted hero stood Roderick, half in the shadows of the white pillar just inside the ballroom.

"Evening, gentlemen," Jared replied calmly, wanting

to leave their presence and search the dance floor for any sign of Emily.

"Looking for someone?" Wellington asked with a laugh as he slapped Jared kindly on the back. "Or should I say some special lady from the looks of you?" He raised a discriminating brow in the direction of the dance floor. "Lost in the sea of eligible beaux I take it."

Jared smiled, feeling every dagger from Roderick's snapping eyes. "I am afraid you have caught me, sir. I am indeed looking for someone special."

After a few minutes of polite conversation, Jared made his excuses and strode toward Agatha and Jane.

"Have you seen Lady Emily?"

Agatha scowled. "I sent you into the hall to look for her. What happened?"

Jared watched the parasol twitch in the lady's hand, and he took a step back. "I do believe I lost track of her, and I did promise her one more dance."

"Three dances?" Jane clapped her fan closed. "Truly, Cousin Jared. Do not think me a simpleton."

"Simpleton?" Jared asked as he straightened his waistcoat. "Why the devil does everyone suppose I believe them simpletons?"

"That is beside the point, my boy," Agatha said, glowering at him as she nibbled on a small crumb cake.

Jared smothered a groan. "Have you seen her?"

"The question is," Jane said lowering her voice, "have we seen you?"

Jared tried to mask his irritation by putting on a calm face. "Me?"

Jane's eyebrows rose in disgust. "Yes, you."

"Come clear with me, Jane. What precisely do you mean?"

Agatha dabbed her lips with her napkin. "Our dear Jane is trying to tell you that we both eyed Miss Susan Wimble coming and going from the ballroom. One could only assume that with your absence during those times"—the older lady shrugged, looking beyond the bright chandeliers toward the entrance—"well, as you can see, dear boy, one thought evidently leads to another.''

Frustration took hold of Jared's mind. "Mere assumptions, I assure you. I am not engaged to Miss Susan Wimble. So if you would be so kind as to point me in the direction of Lady Emily, I would be ever so grateful."

Jane folded her hands across her chest. "Grateful? Hmphh."

Jared glared at his aunt, feeling a vein throbbing in his neck. "Agatha?"

The older lady's eyes flashed with pure annoyance as she lifted her parasol, pointing it in the direction of the French doors. "Keep looking and you may see your future going up in a puff of smoke."

A familiar laugh suddenly filtered over the music, drifting past the leaves of a large fig tree blocking part of the French doors. Jared ate up the floor toward the opening and stopped cold as a smiling couple emerged, stepping into the room—Emily and Lord Bringston. Except for the marquess's age, Jared knew the man was perfect for her.

"Lady Emily." Jared nodded curtly. "Bringston."

"Stonebridge," the marquess answered coolly.

Before Jared was allowed to say another word, Emily's voice broke into his thoughts. "Forgive me, Lord Stonebridge, but Lord Bringston was about to escort me home. I have suddenly developed a dreadful headache and need to take my leave. Would you be so kind as to excuse us?"

Jared's eyes clung to Emily's flushed face.

Emily bit her lip.

Bringston frowned, looking from Stonebridge to Emily, then back again. "Forgive us, Stonebridge. But we must take our leave; the lady did mention a headache." Bringston took hold of Emily's arm and escorted her across the room.

Jared paused, fighting the urge to take Bringston apart limb by limb. A flicker of apprehension took over his thoughts as he strode after them. Was Emily truly thinking about marrying the marquess?

"Ah, friend, so good to see you again," Clayton said, gripping Jared's shoulder in an iron hold.

Jared glared back into four pairs of reproachful eyes and took a quick step to the side.

"Sorry to detain you, old boy, but duty calls." Roderick blocked his path, moving the lot of them into a corner alcove and out of sight.

Jared bit out a curse when Marcus brushed up against his back. "Let her be, Jared. You do not love her. Any man is as good as the other if he can take care of her, and Bringston will do just that."

Jared felt every muscle in his body stiffen. He could not break through all four men. They fought like gladiators. He peered over the duke's shoulder and saw the last of Emily's white shoulders slipping down the hall. Curse the lot of them!

His eyes shimmered with a dangerous glint as he glared at Roderick. "I take this as all your doing, *Your Grace*."

The duke smiled. "All is fair in love and war. And we love Emily more than life itself. You will not be part of her life. Nothing personal, mind you. But she is too delicate for the likes of you."

"Delicate?" he ground out. "Where have you been this evening? You must be insane. You of all people should know—" He stopped, noting the set faces of the additional three brothers. Jared could not in good conscience blurt out the information about Emily's scars and her work in the war effort. An agent's work was top secret.

"You must see that this is nothing personal," Clayton replied with a frown. "From our point of view, our little Emily must have the best."

Jared sneered. The duke's rejection had taken another turn. "Evidently, I take it, the best is not me?"

Marcus slapped him on the back with a hearty chuckle. "Come now, you are quite like us. You know, drinking, gambling, women. Heaven above, we love you like a brother, Jared, but where Emily is concerned, the situation is not negotiable."

Jared noticed that Stephen had not said a word.

Jared angled an angry gaze toward the youngest brother. "And you. What say you of Emily's future?"

"I want her to be happy and hope that she will eventually come to love Bringston. He's an agreeable fellow." Then, as if suddenly he was hit by a lightning bolt, Stephen stared back with a frown. "Jupiter, do not tell me you love her?"

Jared stiffened. "What kind of question is that? I daresay, Bringston does not love your sister."

"See. He does not love her," Roderick answered, scowling.

Stephen's lips curled thoughtfully. "No, I believe that this time you are wrong, Roderick."

Clayton and Marcus laughed, letting their hold on Jared relax. "You are what we call an addlepated nincompoop, Stephen."

"Perhaps," Stephen said, stiffly. "And perhaps not. I feel that any man who will fight for our Emily is worth having his hat thrown into the ring."

Roderick scoffed. "You have always been the softhearted one. Especially when it came to Emily. Do not be fooled by Jared or any other man like him."

Jared carefully took in the sibling rivalry, watching with interest as Stephen's hands curled into two tight fists at the very suggestion of him being soft. Was the man going to go up against his three elder brothers?

Jared narrowed his gaze as Stephen edged himself between himself and Roderick. "I believe our friend here should choose, and that is why—"

With a quick jerk of his elbow, Stephen jutted Roderick in the stomach, then with two closed fists, bopped both Clayton and Marcus in the face. "I do believe this man should be given a chance.

"You best be good to her," Stephen said in a low voice.

Jared slipped from their grip and hurried to the exit, smiling to onlookers as they stared back at the Duke of Elbourne hunched over in an L-shape and his two brothers holding their noses.

*   *   *

"Are you and Lord Stonebridge *friends*?" Lord Bringston asked as he helped Emily into the carriage.

"We are acquainted." Emily took a place on the leather seat, feeling a dull ache beginning to grow in her chest.

"Acquainted? Sounds rather distant."

As the carriage rolled along the street, Emily avoided the man's discerning gaze and stared out the window while fresh tears began to dam on her lids. Lights from the lamps flew by in a hazy blur.

"Have you known the earl long?"

She gave a shrug, acting as if Jared meant nothing to her. Hopefully, Lord Bringston would believe her. "We have known each other for years. My mother is a good friend of his aunt."

Bringston reached over to cup her face with a gentle hand. "If a mere acquaintance can cause those tears, my dear, what will I do to you?"

She blinked. "I have a headache. That is all, my lord."

"Hmmm. A headache and a mere acquaintance. Not a good mix, I fear."

Emily let out a small, tremulous smile. "You are a wise man, Lord Bringston."

"William, my dear."

"William," she said softly, her throat aching with the memory of Jared and that woman.

"Is it that disagreeable?" he asked in concern, moving his hands to hers.

Emily nodded as the marquess wiped the tears from her cheek. She could not speak, the pain was so great.

"Sometimes, my dear, love is not meant to be." He pulled her beside him and threw a comforting arm about her shoulder. His scent was a mixture of almond soap and fine brandy.

"I would fight any man who would hurt you, Emily. You know that, do you not? But Stonebridge won't give up too easily."

She sniffed. "H-he has another woman."

"Another woman?" Bringston peeked out the window

where the sound of approaching hoofbeats thundered in the air. "A problem to be sure. But I can only believe there is some mistake, my dear."

Emily drew in a deep breath, wiping her eyes with his handkerchief. "Oh, no, there is no mistake." She sniffed. "I heard them talking about their engagement."

"Stonebridge engaged? That would be news. But there has been nothing in the papers."

She avoided his gaze. "They have yet to announce it."

"I see," he said taking quick glances out the carriage window. He turned and suddenly took Emily by the shoulders. "If you ever find it in your heart to marry an old man like me, I will be there for you. Will you remember that, my dear?"

Emily nodded.

"Stand and deliver!"

Emily bolted upright. "We are being robbed!"

Lord Bringston rested his head against the leather seat and smiled. "Do not be alarmed, my dear. I feel the gentleman caller has come to save you from my wicked hands."

Emily's eyes grew round when a masked man whipped open the door and shouted, "Your valuables, sir!"

Emily leaned over, shutting the door on the man's fingers. "Go away, you fiend!"

The highwayman man cursed. Bringston laughed. "Your game is up, Stonebridge. Take the girl and be good to her."

Jared lowered the mask, and Emily gasped in outrage. "Close that door, William. I have no wish to speak to him."

"William, now, is it?" Jared's eyes darkened as he took in the sight of Emily's body pressed up against the marquess. "Indeed, I may demand satisfaction after all."

"Best not push me, Stonebridge. I have already offered my hand, but it seems she wants another."

Jared lifted his brow. "Another?"

Emily felt a wave of heat fill her cheeks. "I want nothing to do with you."

Jared laughed, pushing his way inside. "Do you actually believe that would stop me, madam?"

Emily felt a ray of hope spark in her heart.

Suddenly her body slammed hard against Jared's as she was pulled to his side. "I will ask you politely, Emily. Will you please step down from the carriage?"

"N—" But her answer was stopped with a quick kiss.

Lord Bringston pushed his way between them. "Stonebridge! None of that! You will behave yourself. And by the by, what exactly have you done with my driver and footman?"

"Your footman has been given a bit of coin to visit the local tap where I dropped him off."

"Dropped him off?"

Jared shrugged, his eyes sparkling. "So to speak."

"And my driver?"

"Ah, now on that part, I was quite lucky. You see, the man once worked for my father, and I recognized him straight away. Jimmy Dewer. I conveyed to him it was all a jest you had devised for the lady."

Bringston narrowed his eyes in anger. "I do not take lightly to dropping my servants onto the streets. Neither do I care for you playing master to my driver. You have gone too far, Stonebridge, and have one minute to leave my carriage."

Emily watched in agitation as the air began to thicken with male pride. "Please, Jared. You must leave."

Jared took hold of her hand. "Not without you."

"Fifty seconds," Bringston said, taking out his pocket watch.

Emily was frantic. "Jared, I beg of you."

Jared ignored her plea, sitting back on the leather seat, making himself comfortable. "Convey to me when you are ready, my dear. Than I will leave . . . with you."

"Forty seconds."

Emily exchanged frenzied glances between the marquess and the earl. They were both maddening. "Very well. I will speak to you at the townhouse."

Jared crossed his hands over his chest as if he would

stay there forever. "Your brother has removed me from the premises."

"He what?"

"Has removed me."

"I know what you said!"

"Twenty seconds."

"You are engaged to another woman, and you proposed to me."

Lord Bringston looked up and scowled. "Fifteen seconds, and what have you to say about *that* Stonebridge."

Emily stared at the marquess, her jaw dropping.

"Who the devil asked you?" Jared snapped. "I am not engaged. Miss Wimble was never my fiancée and never will be."

Emily's lips parted. Could she believe him? He would not have retrieved her if he did not want her, would he?

Bringston's expression darkened. "Ten seconds."

"Insufferable man!" Emily grabbed Jared's arm. "I will go with you! But only to save your stupid hide!"

"Time's up." Bringston snapped his pocket watch closed.

Jared hopped out the door, sweeping Emily along after him. "What stopped you from saying that in the first place?" he said. "It would have saved us an entire sixty seconds."

"What would you have done if I refused to go with you?" she asked, trying to hold back her smile.

He wound his arms around her waist, lifted her into another carriage, and signaled for one of his footmen to take his horse. "What would I have done?" He ran a hand over her face, sending a tingling warmth through her veins. "I would have done this."

His mouth swooped down to meet hers in a possessive embrace. She gasped softly, and a dull ache moaned within her when he pulled away.

"And you are not engaged to that woman?" she asked.

He brought her hands to his lips. "I have told you the truth. What else can I do for the woman who saved my life?"

"Pray, do not feel obligated to marry me out of honor."

He closed his eyes and sighed. "I want you, Emily. You saving my life has nothing to do with it."

She choked on a blissful sob. "N-no more secrets, then?"

He opened his eyes and kissed the top of her nose. "No more secrets, sweetheart."

She buried her face in his neck, her heart singing with happiness. "I do love you, Jared, so much it hurts."

"I know, sweetheart. I know."

Chapter Thirteen

Emily leaned over the rosewood sideboard in the El-bourne breakfast room, filling her plate with eggs and toast. Beside her Roderick grunted, slamming a double helping of kippers onto his plate and taking a seat at the end of the table.

Emily plopped into a chair at the opposite end. "I don't believe a word of it," she said in a firm voice.

Roderick glanced up, his nostrils flaring, his right brow raised. "Truly, you are an obnoxious female. Since your stay with Agatha you have become intolerable, telling me no, disobeying my orders, and most especially, cavorting with the enemy." His hand hit the table, daring her to deny it.

"Cavorting with the enemy?" she snapped, pressing her hands to the sides of her plate. "I will have you know," she lowered her voice even though it was only the two of them in the room, "that the enemy was France, not the Black Wolf. In fact, your mighty dukeness"—at the sound of Stephen's familiar nickname, Roderick growled—"if my sources are correct, the Black Wolf saved your stubborn hide more than a few times over the past few years."

Roderick turned red. Over embarrassment or anger, Emily was not quite certain, but this was the first time she had truly opposed her eldest brother without thoughts of leaving the room, and something wonderful inside her began to grow.

"The war was one thing, Emily Anne. You are another. I know *him*, and he is not for you."

Her eyes narrowed dangerously. "Why, Roderick? Is he *too* much like you?"

This time Roderick's face could not turn any redder. "We are not speaking about me," he hurled back. "You are becoming quite insolent with your nineteen years, young lady."

In the hall the grandfather clock struck nine, and Emily smiled. "Oh, and another thing, I am not nineteen, Roderick." She sipped her juice and glanced over the rim. "You forget once again that I am twenty."

"Do not jest with me, Em. You know you cannot marry without our consent until you turn twenty-one."

"Ha. One more year and then your life will be so much simpler, should it not?"

Roderick shot from his chair, his hands fisting at his sides. "I forbid you to marry that man!"

Emily flitted her hand in the air. "Forbid away. I won't listen."

"Have you forgotten what I told you?"

"How can I not? You mentioned it last night and then again while I was sampling Cook's eggs."

"And?"

Emily dabbed at her food, afraid to show her brother her true feelings. For in reality, she was afraid that his facts were indeed true. "I do not believe that he has a child that he cast away like a piece of broken porcelain."

"He was married. You cannot defend that."

Emily swallowed. "Yes, he was married. His wife is dead. Pray tell, how does that change my position?"

Roderick shook his head in exasperation. "He will not love you, Em. He has discarded his only child. Shipped the poor thing off to some remote cottage outside London. Some old hag takes care of her now."

Emily shoved a helping of eggs past her lips and almost gagged. Roderick did tend to exaggerate. But could it be true? Could Jared truly have a child that he had abandoned?

"I don't believe he would do such a thing. An old hag? Sounds like a fairy tale. And besides, Lord Bringston does not love me, so love does not strengthen your argument here, Roderick."

"No, but Bringston will not abandon you."

"I assure you, Roderick, I know what I am about."

But Emily's stomach began to sour at the thought of Jared lying to her. If he had a daughter, why would he keep the truth from her?

Later that afternoon her doubts about their relationship increased to monumental proportions when she met Jared in Hyde Park. Stephen had assisted her with the rendezvous by giving her a ride in a new phaeton, away from Roderick's prying eyes. But the youngest brother had also let Emily know his feelings about Roderick's recent findings concerning the earl's child, feelings that were no longer favorable toward Lord Stonebridge.

Tooling the phaeton beside the earl's awaiting carriage, Stephen gave the man a cool, assessing glare, then returned his gaze back to his sister as he handed her down. "I will meet you here in one hour, Em. Pray, do not make me come after you."

Emily nodded and took Jared's hand as she entered his carriage.

"I thought Stephen to be with us," Jared asked, frowning. "His cool glare told me he was not happy about you being in a closed carriage with me."

"He wants only what is best for me," she said curtly.

"And am I best for you?"

Emily turned a confused gaze toward the park.

"Emily?"

She gazed over her shoulder. "What about your wife?"

"She's dead. What else must I say?"

"Tell me about her?"

Jared knew it was within Emily's right to know his

past, at least where his wife was concerned. Later, he would tell her about Gabrielle. When things were safe.

"I believe I loved Felicia, in a protective sort of way. But for a while, I was not even certain of my own feelings on the matter. You see, Felicia had always been a frail thing, and the trip to India almost killed her." He paused. "Eventually it did. She died of typhus."

Emily drew in a sharp breath. "How dreadful."

Jared scolded himself for holding back the fact that his wife had died three weeks after giving birth to Gabrielle, who was now two. But he had no reason to tell anyone about his daughter or her whereabouts until he was quite certain Monsieur Devereaux was no longer a problem. And now that Jared knew the role Emily had played in the war effort, it was all the more reason to keep her distanced from any conflicts that might arise. Devereaux would surely kill her if he discovered her identity.

Ignoring his thoughts, Jared clasped his hands around Emily's face and dropped a finger to where her locket rested in the hollow of her neck. "A past love?" he asked, smiling.

Emily blushed. "A gift from my father. It holds one of the daffodils he gave me that spring you left for India."

Jared dropped her hands, his jaw stiffening at the mention of the old duke.

Emily seemed not to notice his tense disposition, and she continued, "But what I cannot understand is why my father would not give you my hand in marriage? He would have given me anything. If only you would have told me, I could have spoken to him. Perhaps he thought I was too young."

"No, there was another reason. It seems our respective grandfather's were in a duel a long time ago, and my grandfather lost his finger. Card game gone awry, I believe."

Emily's brows gathered into a confused frown. "And that is why my father refused you, because of his father's silly duel? How preposterous. Neither of them died from it."

Jared made a brief comment about a couple in the park, and their conversation took a turn to other things. At this point, their relationship was too fragile, and he was not able to convey to Emily the remainder of the story. How could he tell her that the silly duel had been passed on from generation to generation? How could he tell her that her father, someone she adored, had wanted the hand of Jared's own mother and was refused, all because of a lost finger and a man's pride? But most of all, how could he tell Emily that her father, bitter and vengeful, had refused Jared's suit and forced Jared into marriage with another woman so Emily would never have him?

No, Jared would tell Emily the whole of it another time, when their union was secure.

Later that evening Jared raised his head from the Elbourne dining table and tightened his grip on his wineglass as soon as the duke entered the room.

"What is *he* doing here?" Roderick's mouth twisted dangerously.

The duchess knitted her brows, patting her snow-white feline, which to Jared's bewilderment had taken a seat on the corner of the lace tablecloth. "Why, Roderick, I asked him to stay for dinner. Those meals at White's are not the same quality that Cook makes for us. A young man such as Lord Stonebridge needs a healthy meal. I simply cannot understand why he must reside at some wayward club or hotel when we have plenty of bedchambers to fill."

She glanced at Jared and he flashed her a stunning white smile, knowing that it unnerved Roderick to no end. "Indeed, the meals here are truly the best I have ever had, Your Grace. Besides yours, dear Aunt."

Seated at the other end of the table, Agatha raised a discriminating brow.

The duchess laughed. "See there, Roderick, he is ever the gentleman. Come and take your seat."

Roderick emitted a low growl, sinking into his chair at the head of the table.

"And where are your brothers, pray tell?" the duchess asked. "I thought they would be joining us tonight."

"Marcus and Clayton will be coming straightaway. However, I fear they may miss the meal. But as to your youngest son, madam, I have no notion of his whereabouts."

The duchess waved her hand as the footman marched in with two platters of beef and ham. "Yes, yes, I do remember now. Stephen has gone off with your sister to visit with some lady by the name of Mrs. Allison. Business, he said."

Roderick raised his brow toward Jared. "Ah, Stonebridge, you are acquainted with a Mrs. Allison, are you not?"

Jared's hand faltered on his wineglass. Mrs. Allison was his child's nurse and nanny. He was to tell Emily about his daughter tonight. Minutes before he had left for the Elbourne House, he had received a special missive directly from Whitehall declaring that all was safe. There was no longer a reason to keep Gabrielle in seclusion because Monsieur Devereaux was indeed dead. However, Jared's suspicions had also been confirmed that the man had not died when Roderick had shot him. A bleeding Devereaux had made his way to a small village outside Paris and died months later, vowing revenge with his last breath.

Jane looked from one man to another and frowned. "Who is this Mrs. Allison?"

Jared ignored Jane's question and glared at the duke. "Am I to presume that you were the very person to bestow your sister with the information about the lady in question."

Roderick smiled as he begun to cut his beef. "Suffice to say, a good brother does his best by telling his sister all the facts about a particular state of affairs."

Jane picked up her fork, her expression thoughtful. "But it was Stephen who was meeting the lady for *business*, was he not?"

Jared ignored the looks coming his way and chewed his beef slowly, his reproachful eyes still on the duke. "And you told her all the facts, I take it?"

"My, my, my," Agatha interrupted with a sigh. "I daresay, Anne, this is by far the best beef I have ever tasted. What is that sauce your Cook uses?"

While the duchess went into a long monologue on Cook's famous French sauces, Jared glared at Roderick. Roderick glared back at Jared, the tension in the room sparking like the front lines on a battlefield.

After dinner the women departed for the drawing room while Roderick insisted the two men drink their port in the dining room.

When the door snapped closed, Jared turned on the duke. "You have nerve subjecting your sister to the facts without letting me speak to her first."

Roderick let out a coarse laugh. "Ha! You speak to her first? And when would that be? After you have carried her off to Gretna Green and married her?" His dark eyes glinted with rage. "Or after you have had your first child?"

Jared shot him a cold look. "If you were not her brother, I would call you out right here."

Roderick glared back in contempt. "Well, confound it, do not let my sibling blood stop you."

Jared ground his teeth. "I vow, Elbourne, you are the most infuriating man I have ever come across. I had reasons for my silence."

Ignoring him, Roderick went on. "Tell me, Jared, if you wed Emily, and when your first child comes, will you abandon him or her as well?"

The blow to Roderick's jaw was swift and brutal. "Say another word about my child, Your Grace, and I will kill you."

Roderick rubbed his jaw, not appearing the least bit remorseful. "I daresay, then, you tell me from your own lips, why you have abandoned your own daughter. I would never have thought it of you, but times do change a man."

Anger flashed dangerously in Jared's eyes. "You know the reason. It was because of Devereaux. I could not take the chance of him discovering Gabrielle."

The duke paused, his eyes narrowing. "But the man's dead."

"Not when you shot him. He died later in a village outside Paris."

"You should have told me."

"I only discovered the truth earlier today."

"And what about Emily? Does she know?"

"No, I was going to inform her tonight."

"It matters not, Jared. I still forbid you to marry my sister. You carry too much baggage. There are things I know about you, things you've done, things that Emily should never have to live with."

"The devil, Elbourne! It was war. You did the same things as I."

"But Emily did not. Her missions were different." Roderick grabbed Jared by the cravat and pushed him back. "Stay away from her. She deserves better."

Jared lunged forward and took another swing. Roderick struck back. After a few minutes of scuffling, both men lay on the floor panting for breath.

Jared breathed heavily. "Whether you like it or not, I will marry your sister."

"No, you will not!"

Both heads whipped around as Emily's voice filled the room. She stepped past the dining room doors, her face an angry shade of red. Turning, she slammed the doors shut, then faced the two disheveled men.

"How dare you two decide my life." She pointed a shaking finger at Roderick. "You! I will no longer have you deciding what I can and cannot do, whom I can see and whom I cannot!"

Jared smiled.

"And as for you," she snapped, turning toward Jared. "You are an insufferable lout."

Jared's brows lifted. This time it was Roderick's turn to smile.

"Now," she said almost too calmly. "Roderick, you will leave this room and let me speak to Lord Stonebridge alone." She glared at her immobile sibling.

Finally, Roderick unfolded his tall body from the floor and walked toward his sister. "I will not leave. You may speak to this man, but by heaven, I won't leave you alone with him."

Emily's eyes narrowed. "So help me, Roderick, if you deny my request, I will give Jane a detailed history of your past female acquaintances the last three years of your life."

Roderick's expression became one of disgusted horror. "Why, you little vixen. How would you know anything about my . . . my past?"

"You forget, dear brother, Silver Fox is capable of many covert activities."

Roderick's face was as taut as a violin bow. He looked at Jared, then back to Emily. "We will speak of this later."

Emily managed a stiff smile. "I thought you would see it my way."

"Yes, well, whether you like it or not, I am still your guardian, and you have exactly five minutes."

"More than I should ever need."

A wide smile spread across Jared's face as he watched the Duke of Elbourne leave the room.

However, Jared knew he was walking a fine line, for it was most likely the lady had discovered his secret. He stepped toward her with open arms. "Emily, sweetheart."

The bottle of port flew by him in an angry crash, spraying the red liquid over the front of his white linen shirt.

"Perhaps you should have told me the truth," she said, her fists balled at her sides.

"The truth?" His mouth tightened as he grabbed a napkin off the table to wipe his face.

"Yes, the truth. Do you even know the word, my lord?"

His head snapped up, his expression cold with fury. "The truth that your father was in love with my mother all those years? The truth that my grandfather denied his offer of marriage? The truth that my mother loved another and not your father? Is that what you wanted to hear? The truth that your father denied my suit because of revenge?" His hand fisted about the napkin. "The truth that he planned for Felicia to fall into my arms that night, thereby compromising me . . . and her?"

"No!" Emily took a faltering step back. Her father had planned Jared's marriage to Felicia?

"It's all true, Emily. Every word of it."

No, this could not be true. Her father had loved Jared's mother and took revenge on the woman's son, keeping Emily from the man she loved? No!

But a tiny voice whispered in her head that her father's love for another woman made too much sense not to be true. Her mother and father fighting. Her mother's sobs at night. The late duke's abandonment of any type of romantic notion and passing the same sentiments on to his sons.

"N-no," she said on a more somber note, "I wanted to know about your daughter."

"Yes, I have a daughter," he voiced in irritation as he slapped the napkin back over the seat of the chair. "Her name is Gabrielle. And your brother has quite a mouth."

His annoyance at her was unbelievable. He was the one who lied, not her. "At least *he* has a heart!"

Dark amber eyes flashed a firm warning. "And what do you mean by that, madam?"

"You left your child in the country as if she had never been born. How could you do such a wretched thing?"

"My child is not your business," he ripped out angrily. "You, madam, are not the child's mother."

Emily flinched as if he had slapped her. No, she was not the girl's mother, and he would never let her forget that fact. Her anguish peaked, destroying the last shreds of hope for their future. "A fact I am certain you will not forget."

Jared's face changed and he took a step forward, his voice softening. "You don't understand, Emily. I had to keep Gabrielle safe."

Emily fought hard against the tears clogging her throat. "Did you have any idea that Mrs. Allison spent your money on a lavish lifestyle, almost ignoring your daughter completely?"

His expression grew hard again. "Impossible. I obtained glowing reports of Mrs. Allison from Whitehall."

Before Emily could respond, the door opened and a child's gentle laughter floated into the room.

Jared turned. "What the devil?"

Emily's skirts brushed past him as she stalked toward the door. "Not the devil, my lord. Your daughter."

Shocked, Jared flung his gaze to the squirming blond bundle held in Agatha's arms. "Gabrielle?"

"This. This." The little girl's high-pitched voice was like a tinkling bell on Christmas morning. How long had he been gone from her? He watched in awe as her small, delicate hand groped for Agatha's parasol. His heart ached to hold her.

"How could you not have told me?" Agatha's sharp whisper pierced the air like a thousand well-aimed arrows.

"I had my reasons," he said coolly, pulling back his port-stained shoulders, knowing he had never visited Gabrielle for reasons of safety, but now he felt the fool ten times over.

Gray eyes burned into his face as Agatha lowered the girl to her feet. "I could have taken care of her, Jared. You should never have left her in that woman's hands."

Jared cringed. How could he have been so wrong? Mrs. Allison's recommendations must have been forged. But he should have known. The lieutenant who sent him the report about the lady had been caught embezzling government funds only last week. Yet the man's previous record had been impeccable. Jared had never thought there would be a problem with Mrs. Allison.

He stared at Gabrielle as she toddled toward him. Adorable yellow curls framed a pair of pale cheeks. He felt as if someone had taken hold of his heart and squeezed. He would personally see to it that Mrs. Allison never cared for anyone else's children. Ever. Yet he knew he had failed again.

He peered up at Agatha. "I could not disclose her whereabouts. At least, not until today."

He knelt on the floor when his daughter tried to grab his pocket watch, yanking it from his coat. "This. This," she said, her amber eyes sparkling with glee.

He managed a smile and gave her the watch. At least her spirit was not broken. "Gabrielle," he said, wrapping his arms around her delicate frame. "Baby . . . I missed you."

"I pray you will search your heart, my lord," Emily said in a hoarse whisper, "and do your duty with your little girl. I dearly hope that as you do, your wife can finally rest in peace."

Jared was stunned by Emily's comment. "I don't think you understand. I had to leave my daughter in the country."

Emily bit her lip. "What kind of father are you?"

Agatha lifted her chin and thumped her parasol against a chair. "Really, Jared. How could you?" With those scorning words, she marched from the room, closing the door behind her.

Jared felt his collar grow warm as Emily glared at him. Perhaps he should have done things differently, but it was too late now. "Maybe I should have told you about my daughter and asked for help. But it was because of my work, Emily. You have heard of Monsieur Devereaux?"

A muscle twitched in Emily's cheek. "Of course."

"He swore to kill me."

"But he died in Paris."

"No, he died in a village outside Paris months after he was shot. His death was not truly confirmed until earlier today. I could not take the chance of letting the man go after my family. You must see that. I had to keep Gabrielle safe until I was certain of his death."

"Papa!" Squealing with glee, Gabrielle rolled on the floor, playing with Jared's pocket watch.

Emily glanced at the little girl, then shifted her teary gaze back to Jared. "You knew you could trust me,

Jared. You, of all people, knew who I was. Yet you kept this from me, deliberately, just as you kept the truth from me about my father. He may have been wrong about what he had done, but you were wrong keeping the truth from me. We cannot have a relationship based on half-truths."

Jared knelt down and brushed Gabrielle's soft curls. "I did what I thought was right."

"And so will I," Emily said, retreating.

Jared lifted his head. "Where are you going?"

Emily reached for the door and glanced over her shoulder, her violet eyes brimming with tears. "You should have told me."

Jared opened his mouth to speak, but before he could say another word, she slipped from the room.

"Papa," Gabrielle whispered as she stroked his cheek.

Jared turned to his daughter and buried his face in her hair. "Gabrielle," he said, his throat closing with emotion.

How had Emily known his child had been in trouble when he, the Black Wolf, had no idea? Emily had brought his little girl back to him, and for that, he would be forever grateful.

He would take Gabrielle back to his townhouse tonight. The refurbishing of his home had been finished two days ago. Agatha and Jane could return with him as well.

Tomorrow, after apologizing to Emily, Jared would formally ask for her hand in marriage. She would forgive him. She loved him, did she not? He assured himself that all she needed was a day to cool her temper, and although futile, he would request Roderick's permission to wed his sister. As for Emily, she would demand her brother's cooperation.

Jared smiled, kissing his daughter's cheek. He and Emily would be married by special license as soon as possible.

"I have no more patience, Agatha. I have only one heart and he has broken it time and time again. I am a human being. I want stability. I want trust. I want love, unconditionally, and if he cannot give both to his daughter and me, I cannot marry him. I would rather marry Lord Bringston. At least I know where I stand with him." Emily's voice broke miserably as she fled up the steps to her room.

Agatha stood planted at the foot of the stairs, two fat tears trickling down her plump cheeks. "Oh, Jared, what have you done?"

Chapter Fourteen

A cluster of gray clouds hung in the sky, giving way to a brisk, chilling wind wailing outside the Elbourne townhouse. Emily sat in the family carriage as her trunks were being packed. She was returning to the country where she would sort out her emotions, finalize her engagement with Lord Bringston, and move on with her life.

With a tired sigh, she rested her head on the back of the seat and closed her eyes. She felt empty, drained, numb to everything around her. One of her footmen called out, but his words were muffled in the wind. She had no reason to look up when Stephen climbed in beside her, the leather creaking against his weight as the carriage door clicked closed behind him.

"Dreaming, sweetheart?"

Emily's eyes jerked open at the sound of Jared's amused voice. Deep amber eyes stared back in amusement. "Where's my brother?"

"Which one?"

Emily felt the full force of his smile, and her stomach knotted. "What do you want?"

"I want to thank you for returning my daughter to me."

"Then, I am happy for you. Is that all?"

"Is that all?" He looked stunned. "I mean to go forward and ask Roderick for your hand. I was hoping you would be there. But it seems you are leaving."

Her eyes widened and she looked away, the pain of his lies clawing at her heart. "No need to avail yourself to such a displeasing confrontation with my brother. I see no future for us. You deliberately lied to me about your daughter . . . and my father."

"Your father?" he said incredulously.

"Yes." She swung back to him. "You should have told me everything sooner, including the fact that you had a child."

There was a distinct coolness in his eyes when he spoke. "I beg to differ. I already told you that I revealed my information when I deemed it necessary."

"When you deemed?" Her temper flared. "First you thank me for reuniting you with your daughter, and now you contradict yourself, sir."

The bronzed skin against his cheekbones pulled taut. "And you, madam, are a spoiled daughter of a duke."

Her face burned with humiliation. "I may be the daughter of a duke," she sputtered, "but you . . . you are a liar."

"Is that how you see me, then? As a liar?"

Emily became increasingly uneasy under his scrutiny and waved her gloved hand at him, dismissing him as if he were another one of her misguided suitors. "My brother may be here any minute, you best leave."

"And hide beneath the bed, madam?" His laugh held no humor. "You think me a coward as well as a liar, then?"

A sudden chill hung onto the end of his words, and Emily knew without doubt that her future rested on her reply. She bit her bottom lip, feeling an acute sense of loss. He had misled her. Strung her along like a puppet for the last time. She owed it to herself to cut the string forever.

"Yes." Her one-word reply was like a harsh echo.

In one fluid motion, he leaned forward, his fingers clamping hold of her chin. "By Jove, if you were a man, I would call you out for that."

Emily measured him with an icy glare and jerked away. "How indelicate of me to be born a female, my lord. But pray, do not let that stop you."

"Then *adieu*, madam. I won't embarrass you by my presence any longer. I wish you a safe and healthy journey." He flipped open the carriage door and jumped to the ground.

She hesitated, then called out to him. "Jared!"

He glanced over his shoulder and raised a mocking brow. "Setting the time and the place, madam?"

Emily's nails bit into the leather seat. She would not let him know how much he had hurt her. "No."

"No?" he answered harshly. "Forget something, then? My heart on a silver platter perhaps?"

The icy reserve between them grew.

Her silence caused a thin smile to appear on his lips, and he bowed. "Your servant, madam." The carriage door clicked closed with a push of his hand, and she was alone.

Emily tilted her head toward the window, listening to his heels clapping hard against the walk. He seemed to be distancing himself from her as swiftly as possible, as if a rifle were pointed at his back.

She noted it had started to rain again and closed the curtains, leaning her head against the leather seat, helpless to stop the stinging tears that collected in her eyes.

"Hell's bells, Em," Stephen said, flipping open the door of the carriage and wiping his wet face. "What on earth vexed Roderick this morning. His tyranny act at breakfast did nothing for my digestion, I can tell you that."

"I believe it had something to do with Miss Greenwell," Emily said, dropping her watery gaze to her gloved hands.

Stephen shook his head. "No future there. Stonebridge would never allow it."

Emily nodded. No, Jared would never allow any type of attachment to her family now. The man despised her.

"Would you mind asking the driver to stop at Lord Bringston's on the way?" she asked.

Stephen's expression clouded. "You jest?"

She avoided his unwavering gaze by watching the angry raindrops slapping against the cobblestone street—much like the tears beating against the ragged chambers of her heart. She swallowed a sad laugh. Wordsworth would have been proud.

"I have made my decision, Stephen. In fact, I made my choice known to Roderick this morning."

Stephen plowed a hand through his already disheveled hair. "By Jove, do you realize the implications here?"

"I know precisely what I am doing, Stephen." *I'm marrying a man who will never lie to me. I'm marrying a man who will care for me. I'm marrying a man who does not love me.*

Sitting in the drawing room of his townhouse, Jared lifted his gaze from the *London Gazette* as Jane's blue eyes burned a hole through his paper.

"Would you mind very much if I took the carriage?" she asked him, sitting on the sofa beside Agatha, the two ladies keeping Gabrielle busy with a ball.

"Take Agatha with you," he said, glancing back at a piece about Parliament. "And I still forbid you to speak to the duke."

Jane stomped her slipper. "But it has been two weeks."

Agatha frowned, handing Gabrielle to the nanny stepping into the room. "See to it that she gets her snack, Mrs. Nelle, and then I believe a nap would be in order."

"Very good, Miss Appleby. Come along, precious. Nellie will give you some biscuits."

At that exact moment Nigel thumped into the room, jumping at Gabrielle and barking unceasingly. Gabrielle giggled. "Doggie mine. Mine. Mine."

Smiling, Jared stood and kissed his daughter on the forehead. "Yes, he's yours, poppet. Now, go along with Mrs. Nelle and eat your biscuits."

"Bipkit, mine. Mine."

Nigel barked, hanging onto every word Gabrielle uttered.

Jared's eyes crinkled with laughter as he watched the trio retreat from the room. At least something in his life was going right. He jumped back when Agatha rapped her parasol on his boot. Almost everything, he thought with a scowl.

"What?" he asked, clearly irritated.

"Insufferable," she snapped.

"Insufferable? What are you talking about?"

"The duke," she ground out.

Jared groaned and took his seat, shifting his gaze back to the paper, ignoring Jane's glare as well. "I may be at fault for many things, Aunt, but I will not take the blame for that odious windbag."

Jane gasped.

"Insufferable, insufferable, insufferable," Agatha fumed.

Jared pursed his lips, looking up. "Insufferable? I daresay, I am swiftly tiring of that confounded word."

"You must allow Jane to see the duke. His Grace has been here three times the past two weeks, and you have refused him entrance. I cannot believe you would dare to slight a man of such consequence. Emily has nothing to do with this."

"Consequence indeed." He tried to disguise his annoyance at his aunt's reference to Emily by turning back to the paper once again. "The answer is still no."

Jane let out a sob and rushed out of the room.

Agatha shook a chubby hand his way. "How could you hurt her so? I will have you know that I can see to having you removed from London in a matter of days."

Jared almost laughed at Agatha's threat. "Do tell? And how, pray, would you go about doing that?"

Agatha rang for tea, sinking back into the sofa. "La, you of all people should have discovered the true facts by now."

Jared put down his paper, deciding to let his aunt have her say. "What facts?"

"Emily for one."

His hand stiffened on the arm of his chair. "That is not a fact, that is history."

Agatha's gray eyes glinted with understanding. "Ah, so that is how the wind blows. You are still in love with her."

Jared rested against the cushions of his chair, picked up his paper, and sighed. "I won't match your wit today, Aunt. Tell me what you wish, then let me be."

"Let His Grace see Jane. She will be seen in the park with a man of consequence. You need not worry about a permanent attachment. It's not as if the duke is offering marriage."

Jared snapped the newspaper taut. "To use your words, you know which way the wind blows on that. The subject is closed."

Her shoulders stiffened. "Very well, you force my hand."

Jared lifted an amused brow. "What will you do, send me to my bedchamber without supper?"

"No." With parasol in hand, she stalked across the room and shut the drawing room doors with a resounding thud. Her parasol slapped angrily back across the Aubusson rug as she folded her plump body onto the sofa. "I believe I will send you and the duke to St. Helena to spy on that Little Corsican."

Jared's spine straightened and his concern grew. Something in Agatha's manner told him the lady meant every word she said. The nape of his neck began to prickle. The assignment concerning Napoleon had been canceled, and no one had news of the missive except Roderick and Emily. "What did you say?"

Her gray eyes gleamed with determination. "Are you deaf?"

He considered her challenge with a scrupulous stare. "I am not deaf, and I would appreciate it if you never asked me that again. The phrase has become quite tedious, but I believe you owe me an explanation as to the source of your information, madam, as we have been down this road before."

Agatha lifted her double chin. "You will be taking the trip as soon as I can see to the arrangements."

"And how will you perform this grand feat?"

Both heads turned when the maid knocked on the door and proceeded to stroll into the room, tea tray in hand. Jared rose from his seat and paced the room in uncertainty as the tea was poured and the maid retreated, closing the doors behind her.

Agatha raised her cup to her mouth. "Now, as I was saying, a little call to Headquarters and you will be shipped off as soon as I say the word."

"You think they will listen to you?" Jared laughed. He had been to Headquarters. They seemed to know nothing about Agatha.

Agatha snorted. "How do you think I obtained knowledge of Emily's misfortune?"

The thought of Emily's dangerous assignment that saved his life made his stomach turn. He looked up, acutely aware of Agatha's scrutiny and managed an amused expression. "For the love of King George, you are picking at straws, Aunt."

She clanked her china cup onto the saucer, her lips thinning in irritation. "How do you think Emily made contact with Headquarters? Through the local milkmaid?"

A vein throbbed in Jared's temple. "Not you?" The thought of Agatha formulating any directives during the war sent his emotions swirling out of control.

"'Course, it was me. Among other things."

Jared felt his heart stop. "You arranged for the meeting that evening at the ball?" he said in a choked voice.

His garbled response seemed to amuse Agatha. "La, my boy, I have been involved behind the lines more years than you ever need to know. My desire to be part of the war effort led to an opportune position that would undoubtedly surprise anybody."

Surprise was too lame a word for the feelings Jared harbored just now. "But I cannot fathom . . ." He shook his head and stumbled for the precise words that explained his feelings.

"Fustian." Agatha picked up the paper and slapped it hard against Jared's shoulder. "Take a good look at that, *my lord.*"

Confused, Jared glanced at the paper, noting only that she had opened to the announcement section. "Roderick is engaged?"

"No, you *addlepated nincompoop*!"

Those two words were making the rounds. Jared would have smiled if his aunt had not wrapped him hard against his thigh with that confounded parasol.

"See here." Agatha's finger jabbed at the paper.

"What? Mr. Cletus B—elopes with Lady R—"

"No." Agatha sat back on the sofa and huffed. "Read on."

Jared hesitated, then dropped his eyes to scan the doings of the Town. "Ah, here it is, the Duchess of G—'s gown catches fire while she is engaged in faro at H—'s gaming hell."

"Jared! You would do best to heed my warning."

"Ha. So this is a warning now, is it?"

"If you do not want Lady Emily to marry Lord Bringston, I daresay, this is more than a mere warning."

Jared's fingers tightened around the paper. "What?"

"Do not strangle it, my boy." Agatha placed her teacup on her saucer. "The wedding is to take place next week by special license. The location is not mentioned. Of course, Roderick would know. So, if perchance His Grace did happen to stop by and you let him visit with Jane"—she shrugged—"your ward might possibly discover the place of this monumental wedding."

Jared stiffened. "Pray, why should I care?"

Agatha slowly made her way to the door, her gray brows arching in irritation. "Oh, pray forgive me for my intrusion, dear boy. Why should you care, indeed?"

Chapter Fifteen

A tremor rippled across Emily's lips as she peered into the looking glass of the dressmaker's shop and pressed her hands lightly to her pale cheeks. There were dark circles under her violet eyes, making her more aware of the restless nights she had spent in the country after accepting Lord Bringston's offer of marriage.

She had returned to Town yesterday and was being fitted in a beige-colored silk wedding gown decorated with yards of delicate lace. Strings of shiny pearls and rows of tiny porcelain buttons were sewn up and down the back. Madame Claire and her assistant had said nothing about her scar, but at this point, Emily really did not care, because what they had not seen were the scars embedded deep within her heart. Scars, that unlike her back, she would feel every day of her life.

Madame Claire clapped her hands in glee. "My lady, your gentleman will not be able to take his eyes off of you."

Emily forced her lips into a smile. "You have done a wonderful job with the dress, Madame Claire."

But the elder lady was not deceived, and she frowned. "He is a kind man, no?"

"Yes, very kind."

Two brown eyes narrowed like a mother hen's. "The

gentleman does not make your heart go thump, thump, no?"

Hiding her frown, Emily dropped her gaze to the pearls adorning her gown and shook her head. "No thump, thump."

"Oh, *ma petite*," Madame Claire sighed, clasping Emily's hands. "You must not marry him, then."

Emily looked up, confused. "If I do not marry the gentleman, you will not make the sale of this beautiful gown."

The small, dark-haired woman peered back and smiled when she spoke. "You will wear this beautiful gown on your wedding day, *ma petite*. But it will not be with the marquess." With those jolting words, the woman bent down and stuck the end of a needle in her mouth, turning the hem.

"Not Lord Bringston?" Emily asked, clearly surprised at the lady's outburst.

"No," was the murmured reply. "The other gentleman your heart desires."

For some maddening reason, Emily felt she could confide in this woman. "But the other gentleman does not love me, Madame."

The French dressmaker rattled on in her native tongue, a language of which Emily was very familiar. *Marry the one you love or you will be miserable the rest of your life*, she said.

One of Madame Claire's assistants stepped into the small room, peeking around the door. "*Excusez-moi*, Madame, but a gentleman and lady are in the shop in need of your expertise. The ones you were expecting."

Madame Claire offered her apologies to Emily. "Sabrine will help you with your gown. It will be finished in two days, no?"

Emily nodded, her throat tight. "The wedding is in three days."

"All will be well, *ma petite*. But *pleaze*, whatever commotion you hear outside, do not concern yourself. These customers are not so calm as you." The lady laughed.

"They have been known to scream when zings are not perfect. But stay in here with Sabrine, and she will make the adjustments. We will have your dress finished in no time, never fear."

Madame Claire rushed out of the dressing room, making her way toward the front of her shop. "Ah, Miss Appleby, what may I help you with today?"

"Good afternoon, Madame Claire, this is my nephew Lord Stonebridge. We are in need of some clothing for his daughter."

The introductions were made, and Madame Claire led them toward the back of the shop. Agatha pointed her parasol to some white muslin and dyed blue lace. "There, Jared. That would look fine on Gabrielle."

Jared smothered a groan and turned to his aunt, lowering his voice. "I see no reason why I have to attend to such matters. The devil, Agatha. This is woman's work. I feel like a silly popinjay in this fluff and nonsense. Last time I was in here, I was accosted by a host of simpering mamas looking at me as if I were some prize to be auctioned at Tattersall's."

"But no," the dressmaker interrupted, giving a covert wink to Agatha. "This is man's work, too. You have an eye for color, yes?" She touched Jared's crimson waistcoat and smiled.

Jared cleared his throat. "I will stand by the door if you are in need of me, Aunt. You may choose any colors or fabrics you wish for Gabrielle, but I beg you, make your decisions as swiftly as possible."

Agatha gave a grudging nod and moved her plump body purposely past the bolts of fabric. She stopped abruptly when her gaze set upon a familiar violet reticule and matching bonnet resting on a settee near the dressing room door.

At that moment Madame's assistant walked out of the room and nodded to the dressmaker.

"The gown is ready to be stitched, no?" Madame asked.

"*Oui, Madame.*"

Agatha shifted her gaze back to her nephew, then back to the dressing room door, nodded to Madame Claire . . . and then she screamed.

Jared leapt over a table of buttons, knocked down a row of bolts, and grabbed hold of his aunt's shoulders. "What is it?"

Agatha stared at him, trembling, her expression as pale as the bolts of muslin behind her. Jared noted with confusion that Madame Claire was quivering as much as his aunt.

"There," Agatha cried, pointing her black parasol in the direction of the dressing room. "There was a gigantic rat."

"A rat," Madame Claire said in horror. Then to Jared's astonishment, she fainted at his feet.

Agatha went to the lady's side. "Mercy. I saw that rat scurry into the dressing room. It was dreadful, Jared. You must save that woman in there."

"Woman?" Jared looked horrified, reading his aunt's mind. "You think me mad?" He shook a firm finger toward the door. "I am not going into that dressing room with an undressed female. Regardless, the door is closed. How could a rat close a door?"

"Jared, I beg you," Agatha said, her lids blinking, "I distinctly heard her scream."

Jared cleared his throat and lightly patted Madame's cheeks. "The rat will not harm her. Calm down and fetch some smelling salts."

Agatha frowned, digging into her reticule. "What if the child hit her head when she swooned."

His head snapped up. "Who said she swooned? And who said she was a child?"

"Oh, Jared," Agatha wailed. "Have you no heart?"

That hit a nerve. "As a matter of fact, madam, it has been said that I have no heart at all. So tell me why should that come as any surprise to you?"

"Jared, please."

Jared stared at his aunt as if she had gone mad, then

clenched his hands in disgust. "Blast! If this little escapade puts me in a compromising position, I will blame you entirely."

Agatha waved the salts beneath Madame Claire's nose, trying to revive her. The dressmaker groaned. "Blame away, Jared, but I fear for the woman's life. The rat was dreadfully large, with sharp fangs."

"Fangs?" Jared grabbed a chair resting outside the door and started into the room as if he were preparing to stave off a man-eating lion. Behind him he missed Madame Claire opening her eyes for a peek. Agatha gave the lady a wink, and they both smiled.

"Sharp fangs, mind you," Agatha whispered from behind. "A huge, ferocious rat, Jared. Do be careful, my boy."

Jared's mouth tightened in disgust. Blast it all. He hated rats.

"Duchess, you are looking more beautiful than I remember."

The deep masculine voice drew the Duchess of Elbourne's gaze toward the open door of her carriage. Her heart sped at the sight of the handsome man that she had loved so many years ago. He would make her daughter a good husband. "Good afternoon, Lord Bringston. La, you were always the flatterer."

The marquess smiled. "I was a little scoundrel, was I not?"

The duchess let out a nervous laugh as she leaned out the carriage and nodded to the footman to allow the man his stay. "I am so very glad that my Emily is marrying you, William. She needs a firm, but loving hand."

Lord Bringston poked his head into the carriage. "I will take care of her, Anne. You must never be concerned about her safety."

The duchess swallowed. "I never doubted it, William."

"But what about our past, Anne? Should we tell her? She deserves to know the truth."

His eyes searched hers and she looked away.

"No. I don't want Emily to know a thing. You are to marry my daughter in a few days. What we had in the past cannot matter now."

Without being invited, Bringston slipped inside the carriage and sat across from her, pulling the door halfway closed. She gasped, but did not send him away.

Bringston leaned forward, his hands on his knees. "Anne, what we had in the past was stopped by both of our fathers, not us. We were young and in love. It was nothing to be ashamed of." He drew in an unsteady breath. "I was angry for a time, but seeing you now with your family, I realize that it was best we never wed. You have wonderful children, Anne. I envy you."

"I loved my husband, William," the duchess said, her lips quivering. "I loved him until the day he died." She wiped a gloved finger beneath her eye and sniffed. "Of course, I knew he never truly loved me the same way. He loved someone else, and you see, I believe he always knew about my first love and never let me forget."

Bringston took hold of her hand. "Dear, sweet Anne. I had no idea."

The duchess slipped her hand from his grasp and looked down at her lap. "Emily is fitting for her gown at this very moment. We must be friends, for her sake, William. Let us not bring up the past. We are mature adults now. Our past should not matter."

Bringston frowned and pushed a hand through his hair. "Still, I was hoping I could speak to her. Tell her the truth of the matter. It does not seem right."

The duchess's dark lashes swept upward in dismay. "Goodness no. You must not tell her, William. Promise me you will not. She does not deserve that. Please, William. She means too much to me. I know it is not a love match, but she needs you. Her life has been hard after her father died."

Light brown eyes clashed with violet blue. Bringston's hands clenched at his sides. "Very well, I promise you, Anne," he said stiffly. "If that is what you wish."

*　　　*　　　*

Roderick leaned against the outside wall of Madame Claire's establishment as he waited for Emily to finish her last fitting. The duchess had insisted on the duke acting as their escort, since Emily had been looking a bit under the weather. Roderick easily complied, but now he was rethinking his plans.

At present he could use a good, stiff drink at White's. There were only so many boot, cravat, and snuffbox shops he could handle. Boring as it may be, after his lone tour of the nearby shops, he situated himself back in the shadow of Madame Claire's, deliberately trying to avoid overzealous mothers hoping to pluck a duke for a son-in-law. If he did not make a departure soon, word would spread, and he was bound to be swallowed up by a convergence of mother hens.

The very idea made him scowl.

He looked up and caught sight of Lord Bringston making his way across the street. Relief swept through him. He was grateful for a man with whom to pass the time and was about to hail the marquess when the gentleman hopped inside the duke's own carriage and started conversing with the duchess.

Roderick started toward them, but stopped in midstride when the carriage door began to close and bits of Bringston's voice leaked to his ears. *"Anne, what we had in the past was stopped by both of our fathers, not us."*

Roderick's feet would not move. He felt the world tilt when his mother's voice floated just above a whisper. *"Emily is fitting for her gown at this very moment. We must be friends, for her sake, William. Let us not bring up the past."*

It could not be true. Roderick's mind went a thousand different directions. Was his mother in love with the man that was to marry Emily? Had Bringston loved his mother all these years? What the blazes was he to do? All his senses went temporarily numb. He even became blinded to the Stonebridge crest on the awaiting carriage only twenty feet away.

*   *   *

Jared treaded valiantly into the dressing room, holding the chair in front of him. The devil, he hated rats.

"Sabrine, are those vexing customers of Madame's at it again?" The female voice broke into his thoughts like a blow to his midsection.

There, behind the flimsy white dressing screen, the silhouette of an extremely well-shaped woman, pressing her hands against the sides of her gown, took his breath away.

"Sabrine?"

Jared halted. Emily?

He jerked his head to the door slipping closed behind him. Rats indeed! Two conniving rats if he knew his aunt. The silhouette turned and Jared stood immobile, entranced by Emily's beauty. He was going to strangle Agatha when this day was done!

"Never mind, Sabrine. It sounds as if Madame has taken care of the situation. However, I find myself in an awkward situation. It seems the two top buttons have become undone, and I cannot reach them to see how my bodice holds up to this silk."

Jared almost choked on his own saliva as he edged himself toward the screen. He watched Emily's shadow pivot again, and he nervously pulled at his cravat. Sweat formed along his brow.

"Sabrine?"

Jared stretched his neck in discomfort, then pulled at his waistcoat, moving around the screen.

Still oblivious to her awestruck onlooker, Emily bent down to touch her slipper. "There," she said as she wiggled, trying to fix something, then stood up, her back to the mirror.

Without saying a word, Jared stood wide-eyed, reached toward the gown, and gently slipped the delicate buttons into their perspective places.

"Will that do, sweetheart?" he said in a husky whisper.

Emily spun around, her violet eyes widening in disbelief. "This is most improper, my lord."

Jared picked at the lace attached to her dress, his fingers trailing along the edge of her sleeve. The last bit of his fierce determination to stay angry with her was instantly squelched. He could not let her marry another.

"Improper is what you are doing," he said curtly, dropping a stiff hand to his side.

She looked away, her slim fingers tracing the edge of the screen. "I'm to marry Lord Bringston in three days, so if you have anything to say about it, please . . . wish me a happy life."

Jared stared at the black tresses piled above her slender white neck and waited for a sign that she still wanted him, still loved him. Pride kept him from begging her to come back to him. With more control than he knew he had, he kept his hands stilled at his sides.

"You cannot marry him. You do not love him."

Her shoulders slumped and she pressed her hands to her face. "I have made my choice and you have made yours."

"I was afraid for my daughter because of my work, is that so hard to understand?"

Without warning, she pushed past him and fled from the room. He opened his mouth to call her back, tell her he loved her, but the words would not come.

Agatha suddenly popped into the room and rapped her parasol against his Hessians. "What kind of Englishman are you?"

"One with a broken toe if you do not desist your insistent thumping of that blasted weapon, madam."

Indifferent to his warning, Agatha rapped her parasol harder against his leg. "Go after her, you fool!"

Jared's patience was slipping. "I will meet you outside, madam, because if I do not, I will surely be tried for murder."

But Agatha was not about to be slighted. "Kidnapping, bribery, anything will work. I thought you learned something the last three years!"

He grabbed the handle of the door and stared over his shoulder. "Fool? Kidnapping? What a wholesome mixture, Aunt. Just swipe Emily from the bosom of her family, and she will be mine. Why ever did I not think of that before?"

"La, you think me mad, do you?" Agatha snapped, lowering her voice. "So you are telling me that you are just going to sit around while sweet Emily has some other man's babe?"

At the thought of another man giving Emily children, Jared pounded his fist against the wall in rage. "The devil she will!"

Agatha's eyes twinkled with triumph as she drew in a deep sigh. "I daresay, *kidnapping* sounds lovely, does it not?"

Jared regarded his aunt with a detached inevitability. "Lovely."

Chapter Sixteen

Emily dabbed a drop of rose water on her neck, staring at Jane through the looking glass of her bedchambers at Elbourne Hall. "Happy? How could I not be? Lord Bringston is gentle and kind, everything I should want in an agreeable husband."

Jane frowned, setting a curled tendril of Emily's ebony hair over her ear. "Kind and agreeable? But is that enough?"

Emily took in the soft silk wedding gown she was wearing and forced a smile. "I will have my freedom, Jane."

"Oh, Emily. But is freedom worth your heart?"

Emily brushed an imaginary piece of lint off the lace of her dress, weary of arguing. "Lord Bringston will take care of me. I will want for nothing."

She gazed back into the looking glass, giving her pale cheeks a pinch for color. "My brothers seem to agree."

Jane curled her fists in anger. "Your insufferable brothers! I will never forgive *him*, the mastermind of it all."

Emily's brows drew together in concern. "Jane, please, you must not blame Roderick. It was my choice."

"Did you know Cousin Jared sent me a letter yesterday?"

Emily shrugged, not wanting to show her interest. "And?"

"And he has given me his blessings concerning Roderick."

Emily turned around and gave her friend a hug. "Oh, how wonderful. Now I will have a sister."

Jane pulled back and held Emily's hand. "You must see that Cousin Jared is not an ogre, dearest. He has a heart. It's not too late to cancel the wedding."

Emily sighed. "I don't want to speak of it. Please. But back to you, I am assuming Roderick has asked for your hand."

"Yes, but he never said he loved me, you know."

Emily's eyes widened. "Gracious, did you refuse him?"

"No."

"He loves you, Jane. He is just a bit proud." She wondered if Jared had the same pride.

"And arrogant. And stubborn." Jane's eyes flashed with mischief. "And handsome."

Emily smiled. "And that is why you love him?"

"Oh, Emily, that is not what I wanted to talk with you about. You would not have felt forced to choose Bringston if those fool brothers had not interfered in your life, including Roderick. You and Cousin Jared would have had a chance."

"Your guardian made his choice the day he kept his secrets from me, Jane. It was not Roderick who did that. Please, let us not bicker on my wedding day, I beg you."

"But, Emily—"

Emily shook her head. "I will be a married woman soon. Be happy for me, Jane. I am happy for you."

"Very well. I won't try to stop you, and I do so want you to be happy." Jane giggled. "But I must tell you that one of the maids mentioned she thought she saw Mr. Fennington wandering about the village yesterday."

Emily smiled. "I doubt the man is within twenty miles of here." But her memory of Jared booting Fennington out of the conservatory brought her thoughts full circle.

Jared. The undeniable fact was she still loved him, and Lord Bringston knew it. Yet the marquess was still going through with the wedding.

"Nevertheless, I believe he wants you very badly," Jane said, her eyes dancing. "But seriously, dearest, anyone could fall in love with you. I believe Mr. Fennington is not such a fool after all. You do make the most perfect bride."

Perfect, Emily thought sadly. With pearls, lace, silk, and her friends and family at her side, everything was perfect.

Everything but her heart.

Stephen paced the floor of the Elbourne library, his expression grim. "By Jove, you have certainly botched this affair with all the glory bestowed on your dukedom, Roderick."

Roderick's penetrating gaze turned black as midnight. "Correct me if I am wrong, but was it not you who voted on Lord Bringston being the best choice for Emily?"

Clayton snorted, raising one black pump shoe toward the hearth. "We are not fools, Roderick. Give us some credit. You were the one that instigated this entire affair."

Marcus narrowed his gaze on his eldest brother. "Yes, indeed, *Your Grace*. You have unquestionably bungled this entire affair into cataclysmic proportions."

Roderick downed his third glass of brandy and slapped the snifter onto the sideboard. "How the hell was I supposed to know Bringston was mother's childhood sweetheart?"

"Childhood sweetheart?" Stephen snapped, halting by the duke's desk. "I would say it was a bit more than that."

Roderick scowled. "He was a mere child at seventeen. Mother was what? Twenty-one? None of it makes sense."

Stephen snorted. "Ha, and what pray tell were you thinking at seventeen, Roderick? Or doing? I am quite certain your life was not mere child's play."

Marcus gave a sarcastic laugh, his fingers slowly drumming the sideboard near Roderick. "Bringston is no longer a mere child. He is in love with our mother and not his wife to be. The situation is intolerable, and you, Roderick, are the cause."

All at once Marcus raised his hand and cuffed Roderick on the shoulder, splashing brandy on the duke's white linen shirt.

A tense hush fell over the room.

Roderick shot Marcus a scorching glare. "I will forget that happened only because it is Emily's wedding day."

Marcus's gray eyes flashed with contempt. "Your shirt has a bit of a spot on it, does it now? And you wish to pass on boxing my ears? Thunderation, I am overwhelmed at your benevolent indulgence, Duke. Thank you kindly."

Stephen's smile turned into a full-fledged grin. "Looks as though you have been shot, Roderick. Right through your sordid, dukie heart."

"Very good, gentlemen," Roderick said in a stern voice, "make your jests, but if we fail to derive a plan in the next thirty minutes, Mother's future as well as Emily's will be forever *our* fault."

"Our fault?" Clayton scowled. "Ho! Do not include us in this little scheme of yours. 'Tis your fault, Roderick! Your arrogant, egotistical fault!"

Roderick's first blow made contact with Clayton's chin, sending the man flying against Marcus's chest with a thud.

"So that's the way of it, is it?" Stephen countered, a challenging smile crossing his face as he immediately tore off his jacket, watching Clayton staggering to a standing position.

"You keep out of this," Marcus said indignantly, as if Stephen had no right to question their authority.

Stephen's first blow swung wide, knocking both Clayton and Marcus to the floor. "That, you conceited oafs, is for Emily." He shrugged. "And me."

"Well done," Roderick said, smiling. "Well done, indeed."

Stephen's eyes twinkled, his only warning before he granted the duke a facer, sending the gentleman to the floor.

Stephen pulled his shoulders back in triumph. "Gentleman Jackson has been giving me a few pointers, boys. Now," he said, clearing his throat, "enough of your harebrained schemes involving Emily. This is the plan that we will follow . . ."

Emily nervously fingered her book of Wordsworth poems and choked back a sob. "Oh, Jared. What am I going to do?" *If only you had told me you loved me, I would have had some hope.*

She pressed the book to her chest, knowing in five minutes that she was to exit her chambers and make her wedding vows. Yet she knew she could not follow through with it. Lord Bringston deserved a woman who loved him, and no matter what Jared had done to her in the past, Emily would always love him.

It was useless. She dropped the book onto the bed and buried her face in one of her pillows, smothering a sob.

Oh, Jared.

A light scratch at her window brought her head about. Wiping the evidence from her face, she groaned at the thought of Mr. Fennington bothering her today of all days. It could not be him. The maid had been wrong. It had to be the wind.

Another scratch.

She stiffened. "Dear heaven, not again."

Another scratch.

She would have laughed at the situation if she did not find herself in such wretched circumstances. Blinking back tears, she marched across the floor and tore back the curtain. A pair of scuffed Hessian boots hung onto the sill. She could not see the rest of the man, but she had no doubt of the identity of her caller and her lips thinned.

"Mr. Fennington, my brothers will surely kill you if they discover you. This is not the time to play the knight in shining armor. I have made my choice. I should think—"

She was interrupted when the man began to wobble. With a groan, she reached out to grab hold of Fennington's leg. "Sir, I declare you are vexing me to no end. To no end!"

With one hand wrapped around his calf, she froze. Mr. Fennington's powerful limb surprised her, sending a shiver of recognition throughout her body. Mercy, she was truly mad if Mr. Fennington made her heart thump.

"Hold on to me and climb inside." You fool!

Suddenly she felt herself falling backward with a resounding oomph. Mr. Fennington slammed on top of her, knocking the breath out of her. She pushed at his chest, clasping a more massive body than she had ever remembered. Not that she had ever touched Mr. Fennington so intimately before, perhaps that time in her bedchamber and then in the conservatory. But . . . oh! This was the end! The wretched man was not making a single move to leave her person.

"Mr. Fennington! Remove yourself! This is most improper."

"Improper? I thought it rather cozy myself."

Emily froze at the sound of the silky, baritone voice caressing her right ear. "Jared?"

"Mr. Fennington? I am most offended." There was a trace of laughter in his voice, and he rolled off her and stood.

Emily raised a disbelieving gaze. He took her breath away. "What are you doing here? I am to be married within minutes!"

Deep set amber eyes locked onto hers in a gentle but firm warning. "Is it so surprising that I have come for my wedding?"

"Y-your wedding?"

He let out a deep, rumbling laugh, bent down and scooped her into his arms, embracing her like a babe to his breast. The shock of him holding her ran through her body like liquid fire. He smelled of fine soap and very, very male. She wanted to cling to him forever, but she was no longer the girl he remembered from three years ago and her heart ached with regret.

She pushed her hands against his chest. "Put me down."

"No," came the husky reply.

"No?" she swallowed and felt his chest rumble. Why, the man was laughing at her. "I said put me down."

Paying no heed to her plea, Jared carried her to the window and peered over the ledge. "Put you down?" He repeated her words in a mocking, but amused tone.

Emily closed her eyes and tightened her hold on his arms. "What are you doing?" she screeched. "Not out there!"

The gentle kiss to her forehead caught her by surprise. "I won't drop you out there. I'm going to carry you out instead."

She stared back at him, the blood pounding in her veins. "Carry me out?" There was a devilish gleam in his eyes that told her he was not lying.

"You don't believe me?" he said dryly. "You, of all people, must know the means Black Wolf used to disappear from an enemy's home."

Emily found herself speechless when he lifted her closer toward the opening. She tightened her grip. "Jared!"

"Take a look into the courtyard, sweetheart."

"You are not going to throw me out?" she asked, enjoying the sound of his heart beating against her ear.

"Well, perhaps . . ." He sounded amused as he tipped her toward the courtyard below.

Emily squeezed her eyes tight, her body melting at his touch. But she had to remember Lord Bringston. She was pledged to him, not Jared.

"Now, what do you see?" he whispered close to her ear.

"Nothing, now put me down. You . . . we . . . well, you must see this is most improper."

"You see nothing?"

Had the man heard a word she'd said? "Nothing but black."

His laughter wrapped around her heart like a fur-lined cloak on a winter day. "Then open your eyes, sweetheart, or I *will* drop you out that window."

Emily opened her eyes. "You would not, would you?"

"Look down," he commanded.

"Very well, but on one condition."

"What?"

"That after I do, you will leave."

His eyes studied her with an intensity that burned through her very soul. "There is only one way I am going to leave here, Emily." Her heart gave a sudden lurch. "And that's with you."

Before she could reply, he tipped her farther toward the courtyard where a sea of yellow flowers fluttered about the grounds like golden butterflies flitting in the wind.

She gasped. "Daffodils. There must be hundreds of them." Her throat tightened with emotion. "They're beautiful."

He pressed his lips against hers, then pulled away. "As your man Wordsworth would say, *my heart with pleasure fills, and dances with the daffodils.* I love you, Emily. Marry me, sweetheart. I was wrong to have kept the truth from you."

"Oh, Jared."

"Ah, sweetheart. I have been such a fool keeping my life from you. My pride almost killed our love. Marry me and my daughter. Take us all. I need you." There was a strangled sound to his voice when he spoke. "Desperately."

Tears pricked her eyes. "But what of Lord Bringston?"

His face went taut. "The man will survive. I heard his brother is to marry soon. His obligation for an heir should ease. But never mind Bringston, I must warn you that if you do not accept my proposal, your good friend Agatha suggested kidnapping as an alternative."

A smile pulled at her mouth. "Kidnapping?"

His brows raised in a challenging stare. "You think I

jest? I will have you know there is a post chaise and four near the stables awaiting my command at this very moment."

He let her feet slip to the floor, keeping her body pressed close to his, and his gaze softened. "So I ask you, my love, will you go with me on a journey that will last you a lifetime?"

A wave of happiness flowed through her. "I do love you, Jared. With all my heart."

"And I love you, my dear, sweet Emily." He slid his hand behind the windowsill and smiled. "I have something for you."

When he placed a bright yellow daffodil in her hand and closed his strong, tapered fingers over hers, Emily swallowed, too emotional to speak. Tears flooded her eyes.

He brought their binding grip against her breast and gazed into her eyes. "Let your heart no longer hold the shadows of yesterday, love, but only the promise of tomorrow."

She leaned toward him and, standing on tiptoe, kissed him, reclaiming his lips, his heart, his love. All that she had hoped to ever hold was now hers. She lifted her mouth the exact moment the door whipped open, sounding like cannon fire. Her jaw dropped in shock at the sight of her four brothers and Lord Bringston walking stiffly into the room.

"Morning, gentlemen." Jared's voice was loud and clear as he possessively slipped his hand around her waist.

Emily never loved him more than at that moment. And to think she had called him a coward.

"What the devil is going on here?" Roderick asked, his eyes snapping at Jared's possessive hold on his sister.

Without hesitation, Jared stepped toward the five gentlemen, allowing his hold on Emily to ease. Not to be left behind, she followed, sliding her hand in Jared's. Strong fingers engulfed hers in a feeling so wonderful she felt the world spinning out of control, and she loved every minute of it.

Roderick raised his right brow in accusation. "What do you have to say for yourself, Stonebridge?"

"Say for myself?" Jared's sardonic expression worried Emily. This was not the way to go about appeasing her brothers.

"Jared," she said nervously.

"Hush, love." He smiled at the gentlemen. "Does this answer your question?" He swiftly swung Emily into his arms and kissed her soundly.

Her body molded to his. She became lost in his touch, oblivious to the horrified expressions of her onlookers.

The kiss was so thorough that even Stephen had turned around in embarrassment. "By Jove, have you no decency?"

Jared pulled back at the remark, his eyes twinkling with delight. "Not where your sister is concerned."

Roderick's hands clenched, but before he could move, a soft wind blew through the bedchamber windows bringing in a stream of bright yellow petals floating like a whisper from heaven.

"What the devil is that?" Roderick glared at the petals surrounding his feet.

Emily raised her head to the sweet smells that surrounded her and lifted a hand to the locket resting on her neck. "Papa loved daffodils, too, you know," she said to Jared.

Jared's smile reached deep into her heart. "I know."

Emily's throat ached with love for this man, for she knew without a doubt that Jared had finally forgiven her father for his part in their separation.

"Emily, pay attention here." Roderick slapped the palm of his hand to his hip. "Because of this compromising position we find you in, you have no choice but to marry Lord Stonebridge."

Emily stiffened at the command. She would no longer have Roderick or any man demand her to do anything ever again. "How dare you tell me what to do. I will not m—"

Jared stopped her tirade by placing his lips against hers in another demanding kiss. After what seemed too short by Emily's standards, Jared pulled away and turned toward her brothers. "I agree. We should marry immediately."

Emily stared, tongue-tied. In fact, she almost completely forgot about Lord Bringston until he stepped forward and gently took hold of her hand, his eyes smiling. "Lady Emily, I feel our future is not to be, is it? But I believe this is best."

Emily kissed the marquess on the cheek. "I am certain you will find someone else, William."

Scowling, Jared pulled the two apart. "William? Now, that is improper."

Stephen snorted. "Hell's Bells. William, Bringston, stepfather, whatever we call him, it will be all in the family."

"Stepfather?" Emily looked at Stephen and frowned. "What are you babbling about now?"

Stephen put a hand to his mouth and yawned. "This plan of yours, Roderick, is going extremely slow. Should have done things my way. Let us get on with it, shall we?"

"What plan?" Emily asked, but no one seemed to be listening to her, least of all Stephen, who kept talking about plans and Gentleman Jackson's and special licenses.

"I daresay," Stephen said, "if everything is set, we can all venture out of this room and see to the double wedding in no time." He eyed Roderick. "We can fill Emily in downstairs."

Emily caught the wink Stephen sent Jared, and a disturbing suspicion took hold of her. "For some reason I feel I have been had." She glared at the five men retreating from her room.

Jared laughed, wrapping a strong arm around her waist, jerking her toward him. "Not had, just overpowered. I have a special license in my pocket. We can be married today."

Emily's heart skipped a beat. "Today?" She stared into twinkling amber eyes and could barely speak from the happy tears that clogged her throat.

Chuckling, Jared fingered the flower in her hand and swept her like a feather into his arms. "I will love you longer than forever. I believe from the first day I saw you, I loved you."

Overcome with emotion, Emily buried her face against his cravat. "Oh, Jared, you say the sweetest things." And then she started to giggle.

He stared back, confused. "Are you laughing at me?"

She looked up, horrified. "Oh, no."

He frowned. "What? Tell me?" He stretched his neck. "Is my cravat soaked from your tears?"

Emily's eyes danced with amusement. "No, but I do believe Mr. Fennington may need a hand at the window."

Jared spun around, dropping Emily to her feet. "The devil, I will kill that man!"

Emily bent over and laughed. Jared stopped in mid-stride and spun back around. "Why, you little vixen. There is no Mr. Fennington, is there?"

Emily staggered back. "Now, Jared, 'twas only a jest. We are even now. You with the license, me with Mr. Fennington."

He marched toward her, seeming to enjoy her struggle. "You call that even? There is no even here, madam."

Laughing, she backed up toward the open door and ran into the hall, her wedding dress rustling against her legs. Before she could go three steps, a strong arm lifted her high into the air, spinning her around to face him.

"You, my Silver Fox, will never be boring."

She fell against him, his lips recapturing hers, sending her pulse pounding.

At the foot of the stairs, Stephen glanced up at the kissing couple and smiled. He turned to Roderick and jabbed the duke in the ribs. "You planning to leave old Fennington tied up in the pantry the entire day?"

Roderick narrowed his eyes at the struggling man being dragged down the hall, his mouth stuffed with a wedding napkin and his hands and feet tied like a cooked pig, a trail of daffodils lingering in his wake. "If

I let the stupid chap out, Jared might shoot him this time. Stroke of luck he missed seeing the fool only minutes ago."

Stephen dropped his gaze, flipping Fennington's opulent quizzing glass from palm to palm. "Monstrous piece of glass. The man is more of a nuisance than Beau Brummell."

"Who? Stonebridge or Fennington?"

Stephen laughed. "I daresay, we will find out soon enough." Cupping his hands around his mouth, Stephen shouted up the stairs at the kissing couple. "Vicar is waiting! As is my bet at White's. Hurry up you two, so I may collect! You are to marry in the courtyard, orders from Mother!"

Roderick stood back, horrified. "Your bet at White's?"

A pair of twinkling brown eyes laughed back at Roderick. "Quite so. If those two marry by tomorrow, I will be twenty thousand pounds richer. All the merrier for me, I daresay."

Roderick looked ready to spit fire. "You traitor. You had this all planned out from the very start."

Stephen backed up against the wall, his gaze alight with amusement. "Now, now, your mighty dukeness, you might want to consider marrying Miss Greenwell in the next two weeks, for if you do, I could make another ten thousand pounds. Think of it as helping out your younger brother. What say you to that?"

Roderick grabbed Stephen by the cravat. "I'll have your hide when this is over."

"Ah, here come the lovebirds now." Stephen rolled his eyes toward the stairs and lowered his voice. "Better drop the dukie act."

Eyes burning with rage, Roderick released him as Jane came into the hall. "We are not done with this, little brother."

"Good gracious, he's only jesting, Roderick," Emily said with a laugh as she hurried down the stairs with Jared by her side. "Don't be so dukie."

"Yes, Roderick," Jared said sternly, "Don't be so dukie."

"Thunder and turf! I am not dukie!"

Laughing, Jared swept Emily into his arms and strode into the courtyard of Elbourne Hall, where a trail of soft, yellow petals led the way to the rest of their lives.

A dog barked. A little girl squealed. And Fennington was gagged in the pantry. Jared felt his heart swell. All was right with the world.

REGENCY ROMANCE
Now Available from Signet

The Scandalous Widow
by Evelyn Richardson

Beautiful young widow Lady Catherine longs to live
her new life in freedom, so she opens a school for
girls. But when a dashing man enrolls his niece,
Catherine finds herself fearing more for her heart than
for her independence.

0-451-21008-5

The Rules of Love
by Amanda McCabe

As the author of a book on etiquette, Rosalind Chase
can count every rule that handsome Lord Morley
breaks. But when she can't get him out of her mind,
Rosie begins to wonder if she's ready to break all the
rules of love.

0-451-21176-6